THE BEAT IS YOURS
FOREVER

To Liz

THE BEAT IS YOURS FOREVER

by

PETER YIRRELL

Peter Yirrell

Published in Great Britain by Twenty First Century Publishers Ltd.

A catalogue record of this book is available from the British Library.

Paperback edition - ISBN: 978-1-904433-71-2.
E-book edition - ISBN: 978-1-904433-72-9.

To order further copies of this work or other books published by Twenty First Century Publishers visit our website:
www.twentyfirstcenturypublishers.com

To Lesley, Jonathan and Charlotte
with my love

Acknowledgements

With thanks to Andy for his regular support and suggestions, to Darin for having the confidence to run with it, to Charlotte for proof reading, but particularly to Brian, who believes that dreams really can come true.

The beat is yours forever
And the beat is always true,
And when you really really need it the most
That's when rock and roll dreams come through.

Jim Steinman

Chapter 1

Luke Marshall sat staring out of the window at the pigeons browsing under the beech trees in Grosvenor Gardens. Slowly he spread his hands across the top of his desk as if groping for a phantom keyboard.

"For Christ's sake, Luke, when will you learn?" Si was peering at him over the partition.

Luke started, but after a moment resumed his position, fingers gently caressing imaginary ivories. "Just trying to find the missing chord," he said. "Works like that sometimes you know. Relax," he half closed his eyes emphasizing the point, "and you can form a link between the ears and the hands, no need for the brain. Pretend to play the piece and the hands find the way on their own. I've done it before."

"Sure you have." Si came around and leant on Luke's computer. "I remember Mrs Madigan's class, year five. She didn't half give you what for when you were practicing, instead of copying out the maths questions."

"That was a long time ago. This is different. I've been working on a new song, but there's one chord that won't fit. It's been niggling me all day."

Si shrugged. "No point in asking me. You know I'm tone deaf. Why don't you wait until you get home, then you can try it out on a real piano?"

Luke clenched his hands in his lap, keeping them under control. "Suppose that's what I'll have to do," he said. "So long as Metal Mickey doesn't keep us working late."

Si rolled his eyes. "If you'd been paying attention instead of playing at Liberace you'd have seen the Metal One getting in the lift. Reckon he's got a meeting with God, won't be back for at least an hour."

Luke checked the clock and right on cue it ticked over to five. It was as if the all clear had been sounded; desks were emptied, computers shut down and jackets collected. Apparently Si wasn't the only one to have noted Metal Mickey's absence. The entire office staff stood as one and headed for the lifts. In a matter of minutes, Luke and Si were scurrying along platform three searching for a couple of empty seats.

"Got any plans for tonight?" Luke asked as the train moved off.

"Jeanette's cooking spag boll, then there's a play on the telly she wants to watch. What about you?"

"Thursday," said Luke, and Si nodded.

"Don't tell me, *The Souls of Discretion* are playing a gig."

"Got it in one. And tonight they're at *The Billy*, just down the road. Why don't you join us?"

"I'd love to, but I have to stay in. Jeanette's due in the next couple of days. I can't risk it."

As they pulled out of Brixton the train gave a lurch and shuddered to a halt. It sat stationary for half an hour before an announcement informed passengers of a signal failure at Herne Hill.

"Well isn't that just typical," Luke groaned, amid general mutterings of annoyance. "The one night we get out of the bloody bank on time and the train does for us. It's fate I tell you. I'll never be famous at this rate."

"You won't ever be famous full stop," said Si, placidly, folding his newspaper at the crossword. "Writing songs for a tuppeny ha'penny outfit like *The Souls* isn't likely to get you noticed. If you want to be a successful songwriter then you need to be out there, knocking on doors, finding an agent, that sort of thing."

Luke sighed. "*The Souls* are all right, in fact they're very good, almost professional."

"Pull the other one it's got a gold disc on it."

The train gave another lurch and travelled all of twenty feet before coming to a stop again.

"Well, Vic was a professional once."

"Vic was a one hit wonder back in the sixties. What was it he wrote, *Pretty in Pink?*"

"He wrote the lyrics and he played bass. The record went double platinum on both sides of the Atlantic. Vic still gets a regular royalty cheque. They used it in that deodorant ad last year; must have been worth a few quid."

"Good luck to him. I can't imagine that record shop he runs pays a living, not by a long chalk."

Luke sighed. "Yes, well that's as maybe. These days I write the music for Vic's lyrics; we're a partnership. You wait, someone will discover us soon, then you'll eat your words."

"Dream on, Luke, dream on."

The twenty minute journey from Victoria to Penge East took an extra couple of hours that night, so that by the time he got home, Luke only had ten minutes to change before heading for the pub. The rogue chord would have to wait for the weekend.

Luke strolled into *The Billy* and forced his way through the crush at the bar. Part of the floor space was cordoned off with metal framed chairs so that the larger-than-normal crowd was compressed into a smaller than normal space. It took Luke a couple of minutes to catch Christine's eye, but as soon as she had finished serving she bustled over.

"What's it to be, love," she said, taking a glass from the overhead shelf, "lager?"

"Please." Luke took the small change from his pocket and sorted out three pound coins.

"Don't bother, dear," she said, as he offered the money, "this one's on the house. Vic was telling me only the other day about your contributions to the band. If I had my way, they'd be playing here every night of the week instead of just a couple of times a year; look at the business they generate. Can't you have a word?"

"I think your customers might get a bit bored after a while," Luke tested his pint, "and anyway the guys are all part-timers. We only play once or twice a week you know, and there's lots of other pubs crying out for us. But thanks for the beer. If I knew it was free I'd certainly come here more often."

Christine threw her head back and laughed. "You're welcome whenever you like, darling. Think of this place as your second home; there's plenty who do that I could do without. Yes, my love, what's it to be?" and she was off.

Luke found a seat at an empty table. He watched Vic fiddling with the mixer, fussing over guitars and amplifiers, making sure everything was ready, the true professional. Eventually the lights dimmed and the band came onto what passed for a stage, to raucous applause from the assembled locals; someone even switched off the fruit machine. A few of the regulars waved or stopped for a chat between numbers, but by and large Luke was left alone to enjoy the music. As ever the boys were tight and polished, and it was no surprise when they were called back for a second encore.

After the set, Vic winked at Luke and nodded towards a quiet corner of the bar. He bought them both a pint and took a sip.

"Good gig," Luke said and settled down beside him.

"The band's coming on," smiled Vic, "thanks in no small part to you, Luke."

Luke shuffled uncomfortably. "It's you and the others up there doing the business," he offered. "I just write a few tunes."

"Not just a few tunes, lots of tunes and good ones." Vic took another mouthful of beer. "I can't imagine how we'd get on if you hadn't wandered into my shop that day. Without your music we'd just be another amateur band looking for somewhere to perform. All we could do before you came along was play covers, and bands like that are ten a penny. You've given us another dimension. With your music we can be original, something different to offer, that's why we get regular work. Look, maybe I'm not putting this very well, but the truth is you are good, very good."

Luke took a swig, hiding his embarrassment.

Vic continued, "You ever thought of turning pro?"

Luke snorted, beer shooting over the top of the glass. "Are you having a laugh," he said, wiping slashes from his jeans. "Come off it, Vic, I work in a bank. Music is what I do in my spare time, my hobby. You and the lads have all got day jobs too, careers to go home to. That's what makes it fun; we don't need to make a living out of it. You really can't be serious."

Luke stopped as if paralysed by Vic's steady stare.

"Now be honest, Luke," he said slowly, "it's what you dream of isn't it? Ever hear of Kenny English?"

Luke said nothing, quickly closing his mouth. Vic sniggered, taking another measured sip.

"I can see you have," he said.

"Now you're taking the piss." Luke found his voice. "Kenny English, the most successful lyricist of the last thirty years. Have I heard of him? Do me a favour."

Vic continued. "Ken is an old mate of mine, we go back to the early days with *The Shakers*. Lost touch for years, of course, as you do, what with him being such a success and all. Any road, who should turn up in the shop the other day but old Kenny?"

Luke nodded, frowning slightly.

"Don't ask me what he was doing in Penge. All I know is there he was, large as life and twice as wealthy, browsing through my collection of compilations as if he had just popped in out of the rain. Nearly did for me, I can tell you, after all these years. He hasn't changed much, not as you'd notice. Few inches on the waistline, grey around the temples that sort of thing, but not bad for his age. Guess three marriages and three divorces must be good for you or something."

"Must have been a bit of a heart stopper," Luke interrupted, "but what has all of this got to do with me?"

"I'm getting there, I'm getting there." Vic paused for a sip. "As you are no doubt aware, you being an aficionado and all that, Kenny only writes the words. He collaborates with different composers depending on what sort of song he has written and who he's writing for. Over the years Kenny must have worked with a dozen or more musicians, but he tends to go back to ones that did well. He's not written that much recently of course, but he's still got the name and working with him would be a great way to break into the business."

One of the regulars leant over Vic to shake his hand, slurring a few complimentary comments about the gig. Vic was after all the closest thing that *The Billy* could boast to a celebrity, and Mr-Vic-Fan had a young girlfriend in tow, trying to impress, reflected glory. Vic the master of diplomacy after years of practice sent the punter packing with a big smile and a pat on the back.

"Where was I? Oh yeah, turns out our Kenny has a commission to provide the songs for a West End musical, sort of rock opera. You know all those retro pop musicals, Abba, Rod Stewart, Queen and what have you. Seems some impresario wants to go a step further and produce a performance about a fictional rock group and he's hired Kenny to write the lyrics. What's more, seems it's been left up to him who he chooses as a composer, and that's where you come in."

Vic sat back on his stool with a done deal look. Luke's face wrinkled in confusion.

"What, I'm supposed to apply for this job am I? Me a complete amateur, an unknown?"

"Would your uncle Vic do that to you? Course not. I already got you an interview."

Smug was the only word to describe Vic's expression. He sat there beaming like a Cheshire Cat who's just come into two free pints of gold top.

"How do you mean?" was all that Luke could manage.

"I told you, Kenny is an old mate. We had a cup of tea and a bit of a chat, and I said that I knew an undiscovered talent. If he was looking for a composer, I had just the bloke. I told him all about you, and he was interested."

"How interested?" For the first time Luke seemed willing to believe.

"Interested enough to want to meet you. Interested enough to offer to buy you dinner. You're to be at *The Ivy* at eight o'clock tomorrow evening for what you might call a preliminary chat. If the two of you get on, then he might ask you to write something for him, see how you pan out. What have you got to lose?"

Luke sat mulling things over for a few moments. When he spoke it was in a quiet voice, slowly as if his mind was allowing the thoughts to develop at their own pace. "You really think I could make it as a professional?" He didn't bother to look up at Vic for confirmation but went on as if talking to himself. "Do it for a job? No more office, no more 8:17 to Victoria? No more impossible targets, no more performance reviews? Just spending my days writing music?" This time he chanced a look, and was rewarded with an avuncular smile. "Christ, I could be rich. We could move out to the country, me and Erica, somewhere with a bit of land, fresh air. Big house, smart car, plasma screen TV."

Vic was nodding. "You could have all those things, mate," he said kindly. "You're good enough, don't doubt it. All it takes is a break, a word in the right ear. This is your break. The rest is up to you."

Luke stared at him. "I don't know how to thank you, Vic, I really don't. You are an absolute bloody diamond."

"The best way to thank me is to make it happen, sunshine. Be a success, write beautiful music. But don't let it go to your head. Believe me, I know how easy that can be. Just remember where you came from, remember who your mates are. Remember who you are and you'll be fine."

A tear hovered on Luke's eyelid, and once more he sought refuge in his pint. Vic chose the perfect moment to defuse the situation.

"This time next year, Rodney," he said in his best Peckham, "we'll all be millionaires." And they laughed.

Chapter 2

It was just after eleven when Kenny English stepped out of the black cab in Berkeley Square.

"That'll be seven forty, chief," said the cabbie, pulling down the window and resting an elbow on the sill.

Kenny took the wallet from his jacket pocket and pulled out a crisp twenty. "There you go," he said, "keep the change."

"Cheers, squire," said the driver, slipping the cab into gear and pulling away from the kerb with just a little more haste than was probably necessary. Kenny looked into the wallet which was now nearly empty. He grimaced for a moment, then shrugged and, skipping up the steps of the apparently innocuous town house, entered *Clarrisa's*.

"Good evening, Mr English". The receptionist's smile was immediate and flawless, the perfect teeth an impossible white, matching the crisp blouse beneath her dark grey business suit. The hair tied back in a small bun completed the image of tactful professionalism. She led Kenny through to a table in a discreet booth.

A waiter came over with a menu. "And what can I get you this evening, Mr English?" he asked.

"The usual," said Kenny without pausing for thought.

"Bollinger," said the waiter with an approving smile, "the '82?"

This time Kenny hesitated slightly before nodding. "Why not, let's go for it, and put a couple more bottles on ice; may as well enjoy it while I can."

The waiter disappeared but was back in seconds with the bottle already opened in a silver bucket. "Would sir like one glass or two?"

Kenny sighed. "Two I'm afraid. To be honest I could use a bit of time on my own, but as you have rightly concluded, I am expecting company this evening."

"Might one presume of the female persuasion sir?" The waiter poured champagne into one crystal flute, leaving the other on the tray.

"Not on your life. Women and I are through, at least for the foreseeable future. No, tonight it's my accountant." Kenny spat out the words before taking a hefty slug from the flute.

"Not one of sir's favourite people then?"

"You can say that again. You know there are three types of vermin in this world." Kenny drank again and the waiter refilled the glass. "There's lawyers of course, particularly those working for one's soon to be ex wife, and journalists, except when they are hired to celebrate one's latest triumph, and then only on the strict understanding that they stick to the script. But first and foremost, there are accountants." Kenny drained the second glass and sank further into the banquette as it was again replenished. "They only exist to look after your money, and the longer they hang around, the less you're likely to have."

The waiter sniffed. "Well at least we can try and ensure that sir's meeting takes place in comfort. Is there anything else I can get you? Scrambled eggs and smoked salmon maybe. Chef knows just how you like it."

Kenny waved a hand. "Not just now thank you, maybe later." And the waiter was gone.

Kenny sipped champagne alone for a few minutes, thumb and forefinger pressed to his eyes, lost in thought until his reverie was finally broken.

"Evening, guv. You're not looking too happy with life." Andrew Prentice FCA dropped a calf leather portfolio on the table as he eased himself into the booth next to Kenny. He helped himself to a glass of champagne, sipped and smacked his lips in appreciation.

"You of all people should know why," Kenny responded. "Let me know the worst, don't spare my blushes, how bad is it?"

"Well, to put it bluntly, you're skint," replied Andrew, taking a sheet of paper out of his case.

"Very professional, I don't think," said Kenny catching the waiter's eye and signalling for another bottle. "Can you try and be a little more specific?"

"Certainly." Andrew scanned the figures in front of him. "Depending on how you look at it you're either skint, very skint, or not so skint."

Kenny opened his mouth to say something, but Andrew was too quick for him.

"Let me explain. In court we showed that you had assets of around £12 million. No doubt about it, no quibbles from either side. Your ex-wife…"

"Whose name we are not going to mention."

"Whose name we are not going to mention, your ex-wife argued that she should have half of your estate in settlement and you declined to defend her petition. The judge was left with no alternative but to find in her favour."

"Bastard," muttered Kenny, as he filled his glass from the new bottle without offering Andrew a top up.

"Acting on your explicit instructions, I have arranged your affairs so that the court's wishes have been effected in the shortest time possible. Consequently, you are now worth approximately £6 million."

"Not exactly what most people would consider the breadline then, hardly qualifies as skint." Kenny was starting to sound sulky.

"Your problem is not one of net worth, rather it is a question of your cash position. As we say in the business, you are asset long and cash short."

"Meaning?"

"Meaning that whilst you have possessions, you have nothing to spend. Worse still you have negative cash: you are seriously in debt."

Andrew took a sip of his champagne and continued, guiding Kenny's attention to the piece of paper.

"Here I have a list of your assets, which as you can see primarily consist of property. There are three houses, the one in Hamilton Terrace…"

"That's my home you're talking about."

"Exactly, your primary residence. Then there is the mansion in Farnham"

"That's just my country retreat and it's hardly a mansion. A mansion, I seem to recall, has at least 12 bedrooms and my little country home has a mere eight. It doesn't even have a swimming pool, so I will thank you not to make out it's some sort of palace. No wonder the ex-wives get so much when you talk it up like that."

"I think you will find that the ex-wives get what the ex-wives get because you can't keep your hands off other women. The house in Farnham was valued at £1.8 million, so I reckon it qualifies as a mansion."

Kenny slumped on the banquette arms folded, a petulant frown on his face.

"Add in your holiday home in Antigua, a couple of cars and the contents of your various properties and you are still the proud owner of total assets worth £12 million."

"You said £6 million just now. How am I supposed to follow what you're up to when you keep moving the goalposts?"

"I said that your net worth was £6 million. From your asset position you need to deduct the outstanding debt, this little sum at the bottom."

"Six million quid in loans!" said Kenny, reading the figures next to Andrew's finger. "Where did that lot come from?"

"You specifically requested that we put the court's judgement into effect as quickly as possible." Andrew spoke very slowly, as if instructing a particularly imperceptive child, "so we had to borrow the money in order to pay whatsername off." He paused and looked at Kenny, clearly waiting for the obvious question. Kenny was left with no choice but to oblige.

"And precisely when did I agree to this little deal, eh? Show me where I signed on the dotted line, I think I should remember."

"It's all here, Kenny," Andrew removed a sheaf of papers. "Signed, sealed and delivered by your fair hand. If you recall we met at *Giselle's*, in Hanover Square, about three weeks ago."

Kenny rocked back and closed his eyes. "Now you come to mention, it I do recall the meeting. Non-vintage champagne that night, wasn't it? Probably accounts for the temporary memory loss. Lots of papers to sign, you telling me all would be well. Yes, it's coming back to me now, £6 million bridging loan." Suddenly Kenny sat up straight, alert. "Hold on a sec, that's it. You told me it was a bridging loan, you said it was only for six months. Surely that means that if we wait a little while it will just go away." Kenny picked up his glass and beamed optimistically at his accountant.

Andrew immediately dashed his hopes. "I am afraid that is your biggest problem. Because of the urgency, as you insisted if you recall, we were unable to shop around for the best deal. Further, you refused point blank to provide an income statement..."

"Because of the Inland Revenue I think," objected Kenny indignantly.

"Because of whatever." Andrew shifted his position so that he looked Kenny square in the face, his body language screaming that he was the one in control of this conversation.

"Without an income statement we couldn't negotiate a long term loan because we couldn't prove your ability to repay from cash flow. Not that it would have made much difference. You barely have any residual income after one takes into account your regular outgoings." Andrew looked pointedly at the second bottle of vintage Bollinger as Kenny emptied it's contents into his glass.

Kenny ignored the look and nodded for another. "How can you possibly say that? Over the last thirty years I've written hundreds of songs that still sell by the million, well, the hundred thousand at least."

Andrew sighed. "When did you buy the house in Hamilton Terrace?" The irony in his voice was hard to ignore.

"1995, when I married her whose name we are not going to mention. I do remember that."

"And how did you pay for it?"

"How am I supposed to know? You made all the arrangements. Something to do with royalties and copyright, I think."

"Very good." Andrew's tone was now openly sarcastic. "You sold the copyright to everything that you wrote prior to 1992. You gave up any call on royalties in perpetuity in order to raise the five and a half million quid that you paid for your primary residence so that you could impress her ladyship. In a nutshell, Kenny, your only source of income is from what you have written in the last twelve years or so, and I am sure that you will agree that your output in that time has been some way short of prolific. As far as income is concerned, you have just about enough to keep body and soul together, in a luxurious sort of way."

"So I'm not exactly on the breadline then?" Kenny's voice had taken on a slight whine. He was grasping at straws.

"Not just yet awhile, but I'm afraid you will be in six months, or more precisely five months and one week. The loan is due with interest in one lump sum at the end of the second week in October. Unless you can refinance it before then, I am afraid that your creditors are going to take possession of your various properties with a view to sale for the purpose of recovering their outstanding indebtedness." Andrew paused and Kenny blinked a couple of times. "Whilst the mortgagee in possession owes a duty of care to the legal owner to maximise his interest and indeed to account for any equity…"

"What?" Kenny raised a hand, admitting defeat. The combination of champagne and legalese clearly left him feeling anxious and bewildered, and it was obvious that Andrew was enjoying his discomfort.

The accountant's tone was becoming openly contemptuous. "The bank can't just sell the assets for any price. They have to be seen to be doing their best, and you will still get any leftovers. But if you don't repay the loan and interest when due, they will sell your houses to the first person who comes up with a reasonable offer and in reality there is unlikely to be anything left."

"What am I going to do?" Kenny's voice was now a whimper.

Andrew drew a deep sigh as if the effort to keep it simple was too great a burden to him. "Your best bet is to get shot of Hamilton Terrace. If you sell it on the open market, you should get upwards of nine mill. That will repay the loan, leave you plenty to buy another house and leave your other assets intact. Otherwise it's forced sale time, and that as I say could mean losing the lot."

"But it's my home."

"Face facts, Kenny. Annual interest on a loan of £6 million is around three hundred thou. There's no way on this earth that you can afford that with your current income. Paying the fees and interest due in October won't leave you much change out of two hundred thousand, and the only way that you can come up with that sort of dough is to sell assets. Farnham and Antigua together won't be enough, so I'm afraid it's got to be St John's Wood."

"I'm not selling the house," said Kenny flatly.

"Then your only alternative is to start earning some serious money. Write a few new songs, that's what you are supposed to be good at, though with this sort of money you'd need an opera. And you'd better be quick, I reckon you've got maybe two months to prove that you could service £6 million of debt in order to get the paperwork done in time to meet the October deadline. If you can't we need to start looking for a buyer pronto."

"And that's your final word on the subject?"

"Nothing more to say."

"Then you had better bugger off and leave me to sort it out in my own way." Kenny lifted his glass, trying to look insouciant. Andrew picked up his briefcase, nodded goodnight and left the club.

Chapter 3

The old Vauxhall was parked in Eaton Row. The street was quiet, a nearby lamppost providing a sulphurous glow. He leant over to the passenger seat and booted up the laptop. It took less than a minute to load the settings and pick up the network.

```
Please enter user name..............
```

He paused for a moment, his eyes scanning the street as if concerned that he might be observed. He typed.

```
MDALTON
He pressed Enter.
```

```
Please enter password..............
```

Looking down at a sheet of paper in his hand, he typed again.

```
GARY
He pressed Enter
```

```
Please enter password..............
```

He cursed under his breath and typed again.

```
gary
He pressed Enter
```

```
Please enter password..............
```

He wiped a stray bead of sweat from his forehead, muttering incoherently. He tried again.

```
Gary
```
He pressed Enter

```
You have entered an incorrect password, this
session will now terminate.
```

"Bastard!" there was no mistaking the expletive this time. He looked up at the bare brick of the building, sheer hatred in his eyes. "I'll be back," he whispered, turning the key in the ignition.

He closed the laptop lid and pulled away from the kerb.

Chapter 4

Friday morning found Luke sitting on the eight forty-seven. As the train entered the Penge tunnel, he studied his face reflected in the window, picking gingerly at the scraps of toilet paper specked with dried blood. "You bloody idiot," he muttered to himself. He tightened his tie and checked to see that his shirt was tucked into his trousers before leaning back on the seat and closing his eyes. About ten past nine the train pulled into Victoria and he woke with a start, looked around in embarrassment to find the carriage otherwise empty, and wiped the inevitable snail trail of drool from his chin.

It only took a couple of minutes to negotiate the station, and then it was no more than a hop, step and a jump across Buckingham Palace Road and into Grosvenor Gardens. As if on autopilot, he walked, head bowed until he came to the steps of the Georgian townhouse that was the London office of *Rousseau Frères*. The front door stood open and he entered the high ceilinged banking hall, lit by an oversized chandelier and dominated by a reception desk. To the left of the door, two matching Chesterfields flanked a large walnut coffee table, beyond which a pair of doors led to the euphemistically named courtesy rooms. To the right, the little turnstile affair set up beside the reception desk, and behind that, the lifts set in the end wall.

Luke used his swipe to activate the turnstile before pinning the card to his pocket where it doubled as an ID. Charlie, the security guard watched with thinly veiled indolence, looking pointedly at his wristwatch, but finally smiling and giving Luke an encouraging wink. Luke hurried on into the lift.

By the fourth floor his jacket was off, folded over his arm, and he assumed the jaunty step of the busy young executive as he crossed the office floor before collapsing into his chair. He switched on his computer, slung the jacket over the back of the chair and moved a few papers around his desk

15

"You're late!" The voice was stern and strident, and Luke turned slowly to face his aggressor.

"Don't do that," he said, heaving a sigh of relief. "You scared the life out of me."

Si laughed. "Should have seen your face. Wish I had a camera." He held his belly as if in pain and continued to chortle.

"When you've quite finished," said Luke at length. "Where's Metal Mickey?"

Si folded his arms on the partition. "Not in."

Luke looked shocked. "What, he's late as well?"

Si shook his head. "Not coming in apparently, working from home. Rumour has it he's come down with a cold."

"That's not like our leader. He hasn't had a day off since he started here; must be at least six months."

"Seven, actually. I've been counting. And you're right, he hasn't had so much as a sniffle, nor a day's holiday, come to think of it. Perhaps it's because it's a bank holiday weekend, you know, wants to get an early start."

Luke shrugged. "Doesn't sound exactly in character. Here, watch my phone. I need a coffee."

At the coffee station Luke set the machine for strong black and poured himself a plastic cup of water. He downed the cupful in one and managed to fill a second before the machine stopped brewing. Si hadn't moved by the time he got back to his desk.

"Did we have a good time last night?" he asked, as Luke opened his emails.

"Yes thanks," he said noncommittally, browsing through the spam as if looking for something important.

"Couple of drinks maybe?" Si persisted.

Luke looked up. "Why do you ask?"

"Because you look like shit warmed over, that's why. Never could hold your drink, Luke Marshall. What were you doing, partying?"

Luke groaned. "Is it that obvious? I had a couple with the boys in the band. We were celebrating. Last thing I remember was going back to someone's flat, bottle of Tequila, I think. Then it's all a sort of blur. Erica wasn't any too pleased when I got home, I can tell you. I remember that much. I forgot my key."

Si sniggered. "Can't imagine your sister taking kindly to having her beauty sleep disturbed."

Luke rolled his eyes. "Even when I told her my news, she was none too impressed. Perhaps I didn't explain it very well."

"What news? What were you celebrating anyway?"

At that moment Luke's phone rang. He answered the call, made a few notes on a scrap of paper and put the receiver down. "Tell you later," he said heading for the lift. "Urgent call for some metal warrants. I'll only be minute."

He took the lift down to the third basement and stepped out into a small area dominated by an old desk with a computer terminal on it. To his right, a thick steel door stood open, revealing a Plexiglas panel. He swiped his card through the reader beside the glass and after a heartbeat's delay the panel slid open with a hiss. As he stepped over the threshold fluorescent lights flickered on, showing a long room filled with rows of metal cabinets. Checking the note in his hand Luke wandered down the aisles, reading the numbers on the doors of the safety deposit boxes. He stopped, consulted the note again and tapped a four-digit code into the relevant keypad. The door to the box swung open. It took him a matter of seconds to rifle through the documents inside and extract the three LME zinc warrants that he wanted, and soon he had closed the box, swiped his way out again, and taken the lift back to the office. About the same time as Luke returned to the fourth floor, the lights in the vault went out.

Si was talking on the phone, so Luke made a second trip to the coffee station, replenishing his mug and helping himself to further cups of water. He settled back in his seat and made arrangements for the warrants to be couriered round to the customer, then sat back and closed his eyes.

"Suffering, eh?" Si was back at his appointed position. "Serves you right. You should know better than to lay it on thick on a weekday. Don't come to me looking for sympathy."

Luke groaned. "I told you, it was a special occasion. You know I can't take spirits. Tell you the truth, I feel bloody awful."

"That's often the way with a hangover. At least you can look forward to feeling better in the fullness of time."

"Really, when?"

"Oh, say about August."

Luke's head slumped onto his desk. "Thanks, mate."

Si just chuckled. "So what's this bit of news you wanted to tell me anyway?"

Luke lifted his head and rubbed his eyes as if to dispel the pain. "Well," he started, "you know how I like to write music?"

"Yes."

"And you know how I've always had this sort of dream that maybe I could do it for a living?"

"Yes."

"And you know how Vic used to be in the business, made lots of money, knows lots of people and all that?"

"For pity's sake get on with it."

"Well he's only arranged for me to get together with Kenny English, hasn't he?"

Si looked bemused. "Kenny who?"

Now Luke rolled his eyes. "Sorry, I forgot what a Philistine you are. Kenny English, as everybody knows, has written songs for just about every major band in the history of pop music. He's a superstar, a household name."

"Never heard of him."

"Well, maybe not in your household, but he's a legend in the business."

"So what's he to you? Surely you're the competition?"

Luke sighed. "I can see I'll have to spell this out to you. Kenny English is a lyricist: he writes the words. I write music. Put us together and you've got a song."

Si frowned. "Still can't see why he needs you. Surely there are composers beating a path to his door."

"Possibly," Luke shrugged. "But according to Vic he wants someone new to work with, someone different. Apparently he's got to write a rock opera. I suppose he wants some new ideas or something. Whatever, as Vic said, what have I got to lose? Worst comes to the worst, I get a free meal and a chance to see how the other half lives. If things go well I might write a song or two, you never know. Even if I worked on one song in a musical it would be a start."

Si thought for a while, as if weighing up the pros and cons. Finally he seemed to make his mind up. "Well good luck to you, mate. Just remember though, when you're rich and famous, who your friends are." And he wandered back to the other side of the partition.

It was after one when Si appeared back at the partition. "You want a sandwich or something? I'm just popping out."

Luke lifted his head wearily from where it had been resting on his arms, which in turn were folded on the desk. "Don't think I can eat anything, thanks."

18

"Bloody hell, mate, you look even worse. Are you sure you're not coming down with something?"

"Dunno, but if this is a hangover, it's a real cracker. My head's thrumming and my bones ache. Can't seem to stay awake."

"Why don't you go home? I'll cover for you. The Metal One would never know, so you've got no cause for concern in that department."

"I would, but I've got this meeting to think of. If I go home now I've got to come back to town this evening. What if there's a problem with the trains like last night? I'd never get back in time. All I need is some kip."

Si looked over his shoulder as if checking that the coast was clear. "Why not pop down to the vault, where it's quiet? There's that old sofa in the office, nice and comfy, you can stretch out. Stand on me. It's safe as houses. You won't get caught."

"You think so?"

"I know so. Everybody does it from time to time, and what with Metal Mickey out of the way, who's to complain? Half the office is down the pub anyway." Luke looked about to see that he was right; the office seemed all but deserted. Si turned away and ferreted about in one of his drawers. Finally he came out with two pills covered in silver foil. "Here take these, they'll set you straight."

"What are they?"

"Don't remember exactly. Jeanette had them for period pains, so they've been surplus to requirements for the last few months, as you can imagine. They always helped her when she was feeling under the weather. Can't see as they can do any harm."

"Don't you ever throw anything away?" asked Luke, looking dubiously at the tablets.

"Waste not want not is what my mum always said. Now come on, down the hatch, and then I'll tuck you up for the afternoon. Can't have you turning up for the big meeting looking like something out of *Night of the Killer Zombies,* can we?"

Luke swallowed both tablets, and then turned for the lifts. "I can tuck myself in, thank you," he said. "Just remember to wake me up before six or I'll be stuck in there for the duration."

"Have I ever let you down?"

Luke made his way drowsily to the vault. Inside the Plexiglas door he turned right to a small office equipped with desk, computer and phone. Without bothering to switch on the light he collapsed onto the three-seater sofa which ran along one wall, pulling his jacket up to his chin. Within seconds he was asleep.

It was about four thirty when Si's phone rang.

"Simon Martindale."

"Mr Martindale, glad I found you. My name's Sophie and I'm calling from Farnborough hospital. Your wife arrived about ten minutes ago. She's in labour. If you want to be at the birth I think you'd better get over here as soon as possible."

In one movement Si switched off the computer, picked up his jacket and checked for his keys. "I'm on my way," he said.

Erica Marshall stripped off the marigolds and dropped them into the bucket with the dishcloth and detergent. Brushing a stray lock from her forehead she surveyed her handy work and gave a curt nod of approval. Mrs Armstrong peeped into the bathroom and smiled. "All done then, love?" she said.

Erica turned and picked up the bucket. "I reckon so, I'll just put this back under the stairs and then I'm on my way."

"Don't worry, dear. I'll see to that. I know you're in a hurry to get off." Mrs Armstrong looked about her at the shining porcelain and sighed. "You do such a lovely job. I can't think how I'm going to manage when you graduate. How long is it now?"

"About six weeks till I hand in my dissertation, then it's a case of waiting for the marks to come through."

"I do love that word, dissertation. Makes you sound so intelligent. What was it you were writing about again?"

Erica took the opportunity to head for the bathroom door, leading her employer downstairs. "*The Impact of the Maastricht Treaty on the UK Balance of Payments,*" she said, wearily. "It's not what you would call a page turner, I have to admit. If it wasn't part of the course I'd happily burn it, I can tell you."

"Right over my head, I'm afraid, but I'm sure you'll do well. Then I suppose you plan to become some big shot in the City, just like your brother."

Erica took her coat from the peg and allowed herself a small laugh. "I don't think Luke would call himself a big shot; he's not really that interested in his career."

"No? Well I'm sure he does his best."

"Oh, don't get me wrong. Luke has his talents, but not when it comes to business. He's more your artistic type if you remember, music."

"Of course, you've mentioned it before, silly of me to forget. Writes songs, doesn't he? Yes, I do recall you saying. Well, each to their own. I've no doubt you'll be the bread winner before long."

Erica pulled on her coat. "Don't know about that. There don't seem to be that many jobs going at the moment. Could be I'll be cleaning houses for some time to come, so unless you have any objections, I'll be back same time next week."

"My pleasure, dear," said Mrs Armstrong, taking an envelope from the hall table and handing it over. "You'll find it's all there, same as usual, and I'll see you next Thursday."

While Mrs Armstrong held the front door open, Erica pocketed the envelope and left. She picked up her bike from the side alley and pedalled off down the road. The sky was slate grey and it looked likely to rain. Already some of the houses had lights on inside, and Erica could see clearly into the sitting rooms as she passed. She made her way along the suburban roads, taking a short cut through the recreation ground, heading for Penge. By the time Erica dismounted and leant her bike up against the front fence it was nearly five o'clock. Half an hour later, bathed and changed, Erica headed for Clock House Station.

She had less than ten minutes to wait for a train, but as it arrived she paused at the open door and looked along the platform towards the exit. "Come on, girl," she said to herself through gritted teeth, "don't be a baby," and she stepped aboard finding a quiet seat in a far corner well away from other passengers.

The journey into central London took less than half an hour so that shortly after six she was negotiating the traffic on the Charing Cross road, heading for Covent Garden. *TGI's* was heaving, a press of bodies thanking God that this particular week it was not only Friday but a long weekend to boot. The music was loud and the videos projected onto outsized screens even louder. Erica peered through the smoke laced atmosphere but couldn't see anyone she recognised, so she bought a beer at the bar and found a table near the door. Sipping her drink she took out her mobile and checked for messages. Nothing. She frowned slightly and then clicked to send. *Best of luck for 2nite,* she tapped, using both thumbs in unison, *hope all goes well. tb.* She sent the message to Luke's mobile, and as she did so, Joanne appeared at the other side of the table, a bottle of white wine in one hand and two glasses in the other.

"I didn't notice you when I came in," Joanne said, as she hugged Erica and air kissed both cheeks. "You look like you're hiding from someone."

"Just trying to find somewhere quiet," said Erica, a little defensively.

"You always were the shrinking violet," said Joanne kindly.

"And you the glamour puss." Erica smiled.

"Probably why we get on so well, you know, opposites attracting and all that. Who were you texting?"

"Luke. I haven't seen him since last night. He's got an appointment in town this evening, so he hasn't been home."

"And how is your sexy brother then?" Joanne pouted provocatively as she poured a glass of wine, and Erica glared at her.

"He's fine thank you, and you can take that filthy idea off your face. For the umpteenth time he's not going to be one of your conquests. He's at least ten years too old for a start."

Joanne grinned, emphasising her high cheekbones, as she pressed a hand against her sleek black hair. "Suppose you're right," she said, sipping. "It's a nice idea but it would be a bit like incest. I've known him so long he seems just as much my big brother as yours. Mind you, I reckon it won't be long before someone snaps him up, soon as you're off his hands, that is."

Erica nodded. "I was thinking the same thing myself the other day. He seems to have made so many sacrifices for me one way and another. Maybe when I'm independent he'll get his own life back on track."

"So who's he meeting tonight, some femme fatale?"

"No, silly. Actually he's having dinner with Kenny English." Erica looked away and busied herself with her beer. Joanne brought her glass down on the table in mid sip and stared at her. "Not **the** Kenny English?"

Erica's face was a mask of innocence. "Is there more than one?" she said, ingenuously.

"You mean the songwriter, the one with all the wives? That Kenny English?"

Erica couldn't suppress the grin. "That one exactly," she said. "He's a friend of a friend as it happens. You know Luke writes music…"

"For that pub band, what do they call them, *The Indiscretions?*"

"*The Souls of Discretion,*" Erica corrected. "He writes the music for their songs, and apparently this Kenny English wants to see if he's good enough to do it for a living, you know, to work together."

"Blimey!" Joanne drained her glass and refilled it, as if in a daze.

"Least ways, I think that's the story. He was a bit incoherent when he came in last night and I'm afraid I gave him short shrift for waking me up, but I think I got the general idea."

"Blimey!" Joanne repeated, and then seemed to come to her senses. "Here, you could have a famous brother, you'd be like a mini celeb. Imagine my old mate, little Erica, hobnobbing with the rich and famous. Who'd ever have thought!"

"Yes, well it's all a long way off. All Luke's got is dinner at some posh place with some rich bloke. We'll just have to see how it goes. So how's life in the world of Corporate Finance?"

Joanne rolled her eyes. "I'm a legal secretary, not a management consultant, not yet anyway."

"It all sounds very exciting when you're an impoverished student."

"Yeah, well, it's not all it's cracked up to be, believe me. Hang on, here's the other two now. No doubt they'll tell you all about it."

Two girls, each carrying a well stocked tumbler, sashayed over from the bar area. Like Joanne they were dressed in smart business suits and had clearly spent time over hair and make up. Erica looked down at her faded denims and Timberlands, the perennial t-shirt, self-consciously running a hand through her unruly locks.

"This is Louise, and this is Faye. We work together."

The two both raised a glass in ritual welcome and Erica nodded, lifting her chin and her glass to return the salute.

"Erica was just asking how things were at work," said Joanne as they all settled at the table.

"Oh, you know, the usual. Overworked and underpaid," returned Louise. "No, to be honest, things have been pretty quiet for the last few weeks. Since the last take-over fell through there really hasn't been that much around, has there Faye?"

Faye appeared to be only half listening, as she tried to catch the conversation of a group of young men at the next table. "No," she slurred, "it's been dullsville, bloody dullsville. Can't wait until things hot up again, but I guess that's just the way things are in the world of M & A"

Joanne grinned. "Ignore them," she said to Erica. "We're nothing but glamorised gophers, believe me. Take her out of the office, away from all those clever legal types, and Faye here wouldn't know the difference between M&A and M&S." She paused, draining her glass again and refilling in one movement. "Or S&M for that matter," and the three of them collapsed into fits of giggles while Erica tried to smile.

Gradually she slipped into silence as the conversation moved on to office politics, mostly of the who fancies whom, who's shagging whom, who's a bitch and who's on the way out variety. Surreptitiously, she checked her phone and then pondered the menu.

"Were you planning to eat here or to go on somewhere else?" she asked Joanne, during a rare hiatus.

Joanne looked at her workmates, who both drained their glasses. "How about another round?" asked Faye and Louise nodded.

"I'll have a vodka and Red Bull," she said. "We can eat later. What's yours?"

Erica thought for a moment and then caved in. "A beer," she said, "thank you."

Faye's expression could only be described as patronising, and Louise looked away.

The next round of drinks came with extra shots, but this time Erica declined.

By eight thirty the other three were, if not rolling, certainly swaying drunk. Faye's interest in the guys at the next table was now an open secret and a cause of much merriment. Erica drained her glass and picked up her handbag.

"Not off are you?" said Joanne, in what could almost pass as sincere dismay. Faye and Louise looked positively eager to be shot of this wet blanket.

"Got an early start tomorrow," Erica lied. "You lot have a good time. I'll give you a call over the weekend, eh?"

"Do that. We can have a proper chinwag, somewhere you can hear yourself think." Joanne really did look slightly shamefaced. "Maybe mixing friends and workmates wasn't such a good idea."

Erica waved the apology away. "Maybe I'm just not in the mood. See you later."

On the walk back to Charing Cross Erica checked her phone again, frowning when there were no messages or missed calls. On the train she tried Luke's number, but only got voicemail. She shrugged, trying to dispel the feeling of creeping concern.

Less than a quarter of a mile from *TGI's*, Kenny English sat in *The Ivy* nursing a very large gin and tonic, admiring the fine selection of postmodern paintings and the art deco stained glass windows. At this hour on a late April evening the windows were not at their best, the colours muted by the lack of light from outside, but even so, the casual observer could not help but be impressed by the overall atmosphere of opulence.

Kenny took another sip from the heavy crystal tumbler and rattled the ice cubes as he swallowed.

A white-coated waiter arrived at his elbow. "Are you ready to order sir?" he asked.

Kenny considered for a moment. "No thanks, I'm waiting for someone. Should have been here half an hour ago. Could you check that no one's here to meet me?"

The waiter raised an eyebrow. "If anyone had asked for you, we would have brought them straight over, Mr English. Now, can I get you another drink while you wait?"

Kenny scowled and looked at the half empty glass. "No thank you," he said at length. "I'll make this last." The waiter disappeared and left Kenny to his thoughts. Reaching into his jacket pocket he took out the letter that had arrived earlier in the week.

The paper was heavy, not the average eighty grams, rather a quality notepaper, sort of cream velour, like parchment. The letterhead was familiar and showed that this particular communication came from Sir John Charles. For the umpteenth time Kenny read the words, the commission to write a rock opera, concentrating on the figures, the up front fees, the sums due on completion, the share of royalties. Finally he looked at the deadlines and blinked as if to shut out the problem.

"Hello, Ken my son." Kenny was brought back to the present by a hefty slap on the back.

"Assistant Deputy Commissioner Blaney," he said formally and half rose from his chair to shake the other man's hand.

"Francis, please call me Francis. No need to stand on ceremony, not when we're old mates." ADC Blaney made himself comfortable in one of the spare chairs and held another out for his partner.

"This is Sergeant, I mean Tracey McEntyre," he said, and the police officer smiled unsurely at Kenny. "This is Kenny English, Tracey. You remember me telling you about him. You know, the famous songwriter. We're sort of neighbours, aren't we Ken?"

Kenny nodded and looked slightly worried. Francis Blaney was dressed in black tie, and his consort was wearing an evening dress whose plunging neckline showed off her impressive décolletage. She sat wobbling slightly in her chair as Blaney continued.

"Yes, old mates. When was it we went to Lord's together, Ken. Last summer, year before?"

"Two years ago," said Kenny, in a voice that made it clear the memory was not a happy one, clear to any one but Francis Blaney.

"You wouldn't believe it, Tracey," he persisted. "Old Ken here knows them all. Got us seats in the pavilion he did, introduced me to my friends.

You know, Jagger, Clapton, even Tim Rice. Could quite have gone to a bloke's head, I can tell you."

Kenny smiled tightly. "So where are you two off to tonight?" he asked politely.

Tracey opened her mouth to speak but Blaney was too quick. "Opera," he said. "Had to use a bit of pull to get a table here at short notice. Who knows where we'll end up later, eh Tracey love?" and he gave her a nudge that threatened to send both the police sergeant and her chair flying. "Still, we mustn't keep you from your dinner, must we. See you soon, Ken." And with that they were both gone.

Kenny sighed and called the waiter over. "I'll order now," he said.

The waiter took out a pad and pen. "And your guest sir?"

"Doesn't look like he's going to show does it? If he does turn up, we can sort it out then. In the meantime, I don't see why I should go hungry."

The waiter pursed his lips. "As you please."

Without consulting the menu, Kenny ordered potted shrimps and calves liver.

"And the wine, sir?"

Kenny thought for a moment, looking at the still half full tumbler of gin and tonic. "Chablis," he said at last, "and make sure it's well chilled."

"Certainly, sir. And would that be with one glass or two."

"One," said Kenny firmly. "Anyone who keeps me waiting for nearly an hour drinks water."

By the time Kenny had finished his meal he had all but memorised the letter from Sir John Charles. He folded it as the waiter arrived with coffee and put it back in his pocket. "Would you like me to call a cab?"

"Yes please."

"And shall I say where to?"

Kenny thought for a moment, swilling the last of the Chablis in his glass.

"Oh sod it," he said. "May as well go home. Tell him to take me to St John's Wood."

Chapter 5

The glow from the laptop lent a light blue tinge to his face. He looked up as a couple, arm in arm, passed along the street. They turned the corner without giving him so much as a second glance, and he breathed a sigh of relief. He looked back at the laptop, the wireless card flashing green, and turned his attention to the words on the screen.

`Please enter password..............`

He looked at the list in his hand and typed.

`MICHAEL`

Before he pressed the Enter key he took another look at the screen.

Frowning he pressed the L key several times but to no avail. He sat back for a moment, glaring at the letters in front of him, and then rolled his eyes upwards as the truth dawned. Carefully he took the paper and crossed through all the potential passwords with more than six characters.

He tried the next three combinations in order, before the system locked him out again. Biting his lip in frustration, he sat for several minutes, deep in thought before driving off.

Chapter 6

Luke woke slowly from a deep sleep, tossing and turning on the narrow sofa as he gradually surfaced. The room was in complete darkness, and for a few moments he lay blinking, trying to remember where he was. He lifted his head from the cushion that had doubled as a pillow and felt his jacket fall to the floor. Slowly, painfully slowly, he brought himself up to a sitting position, at the same time running his tongue around his mouth. He stood stiffly and groped for the light switch, bringing both hands up to his face as the room was suddenly drenched in a harsh brightness.

Gradually, he let his hands drop, allowing his eyes to become accustomed. He looked balefully down at his crumpled shirt and suit, and finally checked his watch. The dial showed just after five thirty and for the first time Luke allowed himself a brief smile. He took a couple of deep breaths, clearing his head and made his way out of the small office.

As he went into the safety deposit box area the lights came on automatically and he made his way towards the water cooler that stood along the wall from the Plexiglas panel. The cooler was nearly full and Luke helped himself, slugging down two cupfuls before sipping more gently at the third. He stretched and shook himself, rolling his neck around to remove the kinks. Next to the office was a washroom, where Luke splashed cold water on his face and took the opportunity to check his reflection. He cringed at the image before him; pale, with loose skin hanging under bloodshot eyes. He repeated the cold water treatment, this time massaging his features in an effort to inspire the blood to flow back to the surface and at least make him look alive if not exactly healthy. The result was an improvement, albeit minor, but enough to encourage the suspicion that in a short while he could look quite presentable. Tucking his shirt into his trousers and making a few futile attempts to remove the various creases from his clothes, he went back to the office to collect his jacket. As he walked towards the Plexiglas he unclipped his ID.

It was only as he was about to swipe his card that Luke stopped short. For several seconds he stared at the transparent surface in front of him as if trying to make sense of what he saw. The Plexiglas panel was there, complete with the reader to the right hand side, but beyond it was nothing but a dark grey wall of metal. As if in a trance Luke took his card and ran it through the reader. He waited for the usual pause, the fraction of a second that the machine took to identify the card as properly authorised, the slight beep when the light changed from red to green, but nothing happened.

Stupidly he swiped again, but the panel failed to budge or even to register that it had been activated. Luke placed both hands on the surface of the panel, trying to move it sideways, the way it would normally open, but it resisted his efforts, totally motionless. Luke stopped and wiped a smear of sweat from his forehead. He stood back, resting against the nearest stack of deposit boxes and just stared at the inside of the vault door. Slowly the truth began to dawn, no matter how much his mind tried to fight it.

"Holy shit," he said quietly. "Holy fucking shit!"

He glanced quickly from side to side as though looking for an escape route, but his feet remained rooted to the floor. He looked again at his watch, and his shoulders slumped. He closed his eyes, willing the vision before him to go away, but when he opened them again it was unchanged. As if for nothing better to do, he retraced his steps to the water cooler and poured another cupful. Then he slowly made his way back to the office.

Luke sat on the swivel chair by the desk and looked about. There were no windows at third basement level, and lighting came from a series of powerful bulbs recessed into the dropped ceiling. His eye fell on the telephone next to the computer, and immediately he perked up. Lifting the receiver, he listened for the tone before dialling nine for an outside line. Immediately the tone stopped, to be replaced by a constant whining sound. Luke frowned, rattled the cradle and tried again: same result. It wasn't until he was rattling for the third time that he noticed the typed message glued to the body of the device: Internal Calls Only.

Luke stared at the ceiling in frustration for a moment before turning his attention to the computer. He switched on and it booted to the bank's standard sign on screen. Luke rushed his user name and password to such an extent that he had to type it four times before it would allow him access to the network. Once it had loaded his profile he clicked on the Date/ Time icon in the tray. He let out a low sigh as the calendar confirmed his worst fears: just after 5.30 am, Saturday 30th April. Luke leant forward, steepling his fingers in front of his nose. For several minutes he didn't move, and then in a flurry he clicked on the email icon. Running his hands through his hair he paused before typing a short message:-

I am stuck in the bloody vault. Get me out for God's sake.

He clicked on the address book and after another pause for thought he selected Si's name, before clicking *Send*. Putting his hands behind his head, Luke sat back staring anxiously at his only link to the outside world.

Erica awoke with a start, looking about her as if she had forgotten something. Taking a deep breath, she slipped out of bed and tiptoed out of her room and onto the landing. She stopped, and her face fell. Her last conscious action the previous night was to make sure that the hall light was lit. If Luke came in late, it would provide a welcome, and anyway it would stop him from disturbing her by crashing around in the dark as he normally did after a late night. Now she could see that the light was still on.

With little enthusiasm, Erica cracked the door to Luke's room. Everything was exactly as she had left it last night: he clearly had not been home. Erica screwed up her fists in anger, picking up a discarded shirt and throwing it on the bed, but her rage quickly evaporated and she folded her arms in frustration. She wandered down to the kitchen and set the kettle to boil. That's when she noticed her phone sitting on the worktop, attached to the charger.

Eagerly she grabbed it, but as soon as the display lit up, she could see that there were no messages or missed calls. Even so, she checked her inbox and voicemail but without success. Luke had made no effort to get in touch. The kettle boiled, and Erica made a mug of tea. She put some stale bread in the toaster and sat at the kitchen table, deep in thought. When her mobile rang she didn't bother to look at the display before snapping the green button.

"Luke, where are you?" she said breathlessly.

"Hi Erica, it's me."

"Oh, Joanne." Erica's shoulders slumped

"There's no need to sound so disappointed. You're not still angry with me about last night are you?"

"No, not at all. Sorry, I thought you might be Luke."

"Isn't he home then?"

"No, his bed hasn't been slept in and the landing light was still on. Even if he'd been home and gone out again he'd have switched the light off. You know what a stickler he is about the bills."

"Yeah, I remember you saying. So where do you think he's got to?"

"Probably gone to some all night party with his new showbiz mates, no doubt," said Erica, trying to sound upbeat.

"You'd think he might have sent you a text or something, let you know."

"Possibly, but then Luke has a long and dishonourable record of forgetting to charge his phone. The battery's probably dead. I tried ringing him last night but the message said he was switched off. To tell you the truth if he walked through the door now I could strangle him. Anyway, enough of my problems, what can I do for you?"

"Oh, nothing really. I was just wondering if we could get together, you know, have a proper chat. Last night was a bit of a disaster one way and another, wasn't it? Maybe we could have a quiet drink locally, you know, catch up. We haven't talked properly for ages. You have to let me know what you're thinking of doing after you graduate. Perhaps I could put in a word for you at work, see if they've got anything that might suit."

Erica wandered out of the kitchen into the sitting room. There were books strewn on the floor in the corner by the computer, papers littered the desk. She ran a finger along the mantelpiece, making a trail in the dust.

"That's a kind thought, but I'm not sure I'm cut out for a career in town," she said. "I don't think I'd get on with your workmates."

"You mean that pair last night? Don't worry, they're not all like that. You wait till I tell you about what they got up to after you left. They were outrageous. But believe me, some of the people I work with are almost human."

Erica smiled. "Yes, I'm sure. Problem is, if I don't get this dissertation finished, there won't be a graduation, and I'll be looking for a full time job as a skivvy."

"So that's what you've got to do right now. Tell you what, you finish your college work and I'll buy you a drink tonight. How's that for an offer?"

Erica thought for a moment. "I don't think I could manage the required level of concentration," she said, "not till Luke gets home. I need something practical to do, but a drink sounds a good idea."

"So what are you going to do instead?"

Erica looked about her again. "When the going gets tough, the tough go cleaning," she said firmly. "I'm going to give this house a good seeing to, it's well overdue. Then you can buy me a drink at, say eight o'clock tonight?"

"It's a deal. Where do you want to go?"

"Like you said, let's make it local. How about *The Billy*?"

"*The Admiral Bligh*, bloody hell, I haven't been in there for years! I think the last drink I bought at *The Billy* was an illicit cider when we were at school. It'll seem a bit odd being legal. OK, I'll see you at eight. And keep your pecker up, Luke'll be fine, you mark my words."

Erica put the phone in her pocket, checking first that she hadn't missed a call or a message. Upstairs she threw on an old pair of jeans and one of Luke's sweatshirts that was several sizes too big. She made another mug of tea, ate the cold toast and then with a look of resolution, she took out the hoover.

Gordon sat at the long pine table, polishing silver. He stopped his tuneless whistling for a moment to breathe heavily on the prongs of a dinner fork before buffing it to a perfect shine. He held it up to the light from the tall kitchen windows, admiring his handiwork, before placing it carefully in the canteen and selecting a knife from the pile of cutlery in front of him. He was so wrapped up in his work that he failed to notice the footsteps on the stairs and jumped when a figure appeared in the doorway.

"My sir, you gave me quite a turn. I wasn't expecting you for another couple of hours."

Kenny English wandered over to the double sink, tightening the belt of his thick white bathrobe and scratching his head. "I got home rather earlier than expected last night," he said pouring a glass of tap water. He yawned and turned towards his butler.

"Not a successful evening then, am I to assume?" Gordon left his polishing and busied about the kitchen making coffee.

"Complete waste of time: the boy didn't show."

Gordon raised an eyebrow. "How strange. Weren't you were doing a favour for a friend?"

"I was. Seems there's no gratitude in this world anymore. Left me feeling a right prune, I can tell you."

Gordon poured boiling water on the coffee grounds, inhaling the aroma. "I thought you liked being on you own, sir, thought you were happy with your own company. That's what you normally say."

"I am, but only when I want to be. Stop splitting hairs." Kenny sat at the table.

"Well it must have done you some good. I can't recall the last time you were out of bed before twelve. And unless I'm much mistaken, there's no hangover this morning."

Kenny scratched his head again. "No, you're right," he said, a little surprised. "I feel quite good, as it happens. Suppose my liver must have got to the point where a large gin and tonic and a bottle of wine is tantamount to sobriety. Perhaps I should cut down on a regular basis."

"You know I'm not one to nag, sir, but I think that might be a good idea."

Kenny looked at him quizzically. "Well, good idea or not, we'll just have to see. I'm not making any promises."

"Perhaps if you were working, that might be some incentive?"

Kenny scowled. "No point in writing lyrics without the music. That young lad was my best hope." He took the letter from his dressing gown pocket and looked it over again. Gordon put the coffee pot on the table and walked around so that he could see over his employer's shoulder.

"You know, Gordon," said Kenny, without malice, "for a gentleman's gentleman you're not much of a gentleman are you."

Gordon snorted but didn't stop reading. "I find it pays to keep an eye on what's happening. I don't like to think of you getting up to anything without my knowledge."

"You're worse than a wife sometimes, and that's about as far away from a compliment as I can get."

Gordon smiled and poured coffee. "What I can't understand," he said, "is why this young man is so important to you. Why can't you just write the songs and then get one of your other contacts to put them to music."

"If only it were that simple. The fact is Gordon that I can't get anyone to work with me."

"But surely you're a big name, you're a success. I'd have thought they'd be queuing round the block."

Kenny shook his head. "As far as the general public is concerned maybe I am still a big name, but in the business word has it that I'm washed up. Let's face it, I haven't written anything in months, and the last time I had a hit must be at least three years ago. It's a tough world out there, Gordon. Once you start to slither down the slippery slope to obscurity there's no coming back, not unless you get very lucky."

Gordon sat down at the table and carried on polishing, deep in thought. "Surely Sir John has faith in you," he said at length, "otherwise he wouldn't have asked you to write the songs for his new musical."

"Sir John is throwing me a scrap," said Kenny, frankly, sipping coffee. "Look at the deadlines: he wants the first draft by the end of May. That's only four weeks off. If I don't come up with anything, he'll cancel the deal and move on to someone else. He's testing me, and the way it looks right now I'm going to fail."

"Don't you think you can come up with some songs in four weeks? It's not as if you have anything else pressing."

"Writing lyrics isn't the problem, never has been. Shit, I've got songs coming out of my ears. I've written whole albums inside a week in the past, and I can do it again. It's not even as if I have to start from scratch: the plot for the musical has already been agreed, so I know what to write about and when. There's only fifteen numbers in total, it's a breeze."

"But you still need someone to write the music."

"Precisely. And then there's the question of money."

"I'm sure you get very well recompensed for your efforts."

"That's not the point. Sir John is paying me for the songs. How much the composer gets is down to me. The total deal is worth upwards of half a million if the show's a success, at least two fifty even if it flops. Anyone who's anyone would want half, possibly more, but if I work with a newcomer I keep the lion's share."

"So what are you going to do?"

"That's what I've been trying to decide. I hate to say it, but I suppose I'll just have to give this bloke another chance."

"Do you think it's worth it?"

Kenny shrugged. "What have I got to lose? As I've said, it's not as if I've got a lot of alternatives is, it? Anyway, Vic said he's good."

"But surely Vic's past it. Talk about washed up, he's been out of the business for nearly forty years! What does he know?"

Kenny nodded. "Vic may not be a professional these days, but take my word he knows what he's talking about. He didn't leave the business because of lack of talent believe me."

"Then why did he give it up?"

"The old story: drink and drugs. When *The Shakers* had their big success it rather went to Vic's head. He did every kind of noxious substance you can think of and then a couple more. Ended up in rehab. That's where he met Maureen."

"His wife."

"The very same. She dried him out, and they set up the music shop together. Rumour has it that he's allowed the occasional pint or two, but otherwise she keeps him on a tight rein. If it wasn't for her, he'd have been dead years ago, and she made sure that he kept well clear of the music business. But all the same, in his day Vic was a true pro, and he could write lyrics. More than that he knows a good tune, and if he thinks this Luke whatshisname is worth talking to, then that's enough of a testimonial for me."

"So phone Vic, see if he knows where this young man has got to."

"That's the problem. I haven't got his number. I only stopped at his shop by accident, been visiting the parental grave in Beckenham. Can't remember the name of the shop either."

"So you're stuck." Gordon finished the cutlery and rose to put the canteen away in one of the kitchen cupboards.

"Not exactly. I know where the shop is. Thought I might take a trip down to Penge and see if he can tell me where the guy hangs out. Who knows, he might have the flu or something, maybe he just got cold feet. If I go and see him perhaps we could find out there and then if he's good enough."

Gordon stood, hand on hip, a dubious look on his face. "Well," he said slowly, "I suppose it's your time."

"It's a bank holiday weekend. What else have I got to do?"

"There is that. Talking of bank holidays I was thinking of popping over to see my mother in Southend. You don't object do you?"

"Not at all, you've got plenty of holiday owing. Take one of the cars."

"That's very kind. Which one will you be using?"

Kenny finished his coffee and stood, heading for the door. "I'll take the Aston," he said. "You can choose whichever you want from the others. I'll see you sometime Monday."

Traffic was predictably light in central London in recognition of the holiday weekend. It was not until he hit the queue for road works at the north end of Westminster Bridge that Kenny had to stop for so much as a traffic light. He adjusted the Aston's air conditioning and waited patiently. The lights changed and Kenny slipped the car into drive, zipped past the road works and crossed the river. On a whim he ignored the direct route south through Elephant and Castle and instead took a sharp right, following the main traffic flow as it edged along beside the river. At Vauxhall he turned left making for Kennington.

As he came abreast of the Oval Kenny stopped the car, parking two wheels on the pavement. He got out and wandered around the perimeter of the ground, peering at the deserted buildings. At the main gate he stood for a few minutes, looking at the entrance to the stands, the doors to the pavilion, deep in thought, before making his way back to the car and driving off. Thirty minutes later he was in Penge.

A steady drizzle began to fall, as Kenny found a parking space in a side street. He locked the car and plunged his hands into the pockets of his leather coat, as he looked around, trying get his bearings. He started north along the High Street, looking for some kind of landmark, but the rain made it difficult, and it took a full fifteen minutes of trial and error before he saw the shop on the other side of the road. Finding a break in the traffic, he crossed over and entered.

Inside the shop was well lit, warm and welcoming. There was a smattering of customers, most of whom seemed to be browsing or chatting rather than actively engaged in buying anything. Once his eyes had become accustomed to the light, Kenny made his way over to the cash desk which was guarded by a busty teenage brunette.

"Hi," he started, "is the boss in?"

"You mean Vic, mate?" responded the young lady, the south London accent so thick you could cut it with a knife.

"That'll be the one," Kenny confirmed, in his friendliest voice. He noticed that the girl had a small stud through one nostril, the skin around the piercing red and sore. Kenny stifled a wince.

"He's in the back, who shall I say wants him?"

"Just tell him it's Kenny. He'll know what it's about."

"Vic," yelled the young lady, barely turning her head in the direction of the doorway immediately behind her, "bloke calls himself Kenny here for you."

Kenny looked over his shoulder at the other customers, none of whom seemed to have paid the slightest attention to the exchange.

"Send him through," Vic's voice echoed from the confines of the back room. The girl looked straight at Kenny and gave an almost imperceptible jerk of her head over her left shoulder

The walls of the back room were lined with a variety of musical instruments, but mostly guitars: electric, acoustic, classical, toy even. Vic was bent over a workbench patiently restringing a Telecaster. Neither man spoke and time seemed to stand still as Vic tightened a string, selected a fret and played two strings together, his face a mixture of concentration and contentment.

"You look happy in your work," said Kenny breaking the spell.

"There's something very satisfying in doing a job well, I always think," said Vic, putting the guitar down to shake Kenny's outstretched hand. "And yes, I do enjoy my work. Life's been good to me all in all."

Kenny looked around the room. "I can see that," he said. "This place even smells happy."

"So what do I owe this pleasure to then? You're like a London bus; nothing for ages then twice in succession. How was it last night, how did you get on with young Luke?"

"It wasn't, and we didn't," replied Kenny.

Vic looked bemused. "What do you mean?"

"He didn't show did he?" Kenny's voice had a hard edge. He stopped for a moment, then continued more gently as if trying to make a joke of it. "Left me sitting there all on my own. I felt a right prat, I can tell you. Can't say it hasn't happened before of course, but with a bloke, well that has to be a first."

"Luke didn't turn up? That does surprise me, not like him at all, usually so reliable." Vic looked and sounded really concerned. "Something must have happened," he trailed off.

"Well that's what I was thinking, sort of why I'm here. Thought if he wasn't up to it for some reason, I could come and meet him on his patch. Give the bloke a second chance."

"Nice of you to think like that. Hang on, I'll give him a bell."

Vic took out his mobile and pressed a couple of buttons. He held it to his ear. "Sounds like he's switched off," he said. "Maybe he's still in bed."

"You got his home number?" asked Kenny, eager to get on with it.

"Hasn't got one. You know what these youngsters are, live life on the mobile. Don't think he's had a phone at home for the last five years."

"So how do we get in touch?"

"He only lives round the corner. You could pop over and introduce yourself. Here's the address."

Vic scribbled something on an old till receipt and handed it to Kenny. "It's just along the High Street and turn left at the *Pawleyne Arms*. Number 27, a couple of doors past *The Admiral Bligh*. Tell you what, I'll be finished here in ten minutes or so. You get on down there and I'll follow. You may need a bit of help persuading Erica you're kosher."

"Erica? That the wife?"

"No, sister. Little sister, by some way, but she protects him like a lioness with a cub. Can be a bit abrasive if you don't know how to handle her, so go careful."

"No worry. You know me and women. I'm an old hand. Left at the *Pawleyne* you say?" And with that he was out of the door and gone.

The drizzle had turned to steady rain as Kenny returned to the High Street. The pavements were greasy from the wet, and Kenny's Docksiders barely afforded him sufficient traction as he negotiated the plastic boxes on sale outside *Supersavers*. He saw the pub through the rain and broke into a run, hands in pockets, collar raised. Within minutes he was outside number 27. He pressed the doorbell and stood back from the front step in the growing deluge.

The sound of the bell echoed through the house, but Erica missed it as she hoovered the back room. By chance, she switched off the vacuum cleaner at the same moment as Kenny pressed the bell for a second time. She stuck her head out into the passage. Through the pebbled round of glass at the top of the door she could make out the unmistakeable shadow of a man's head. A tall man, with dark hair, not unlike Luke. Erica ran to the front door.

At the same moment, Kenny decided to ring the bell for a third time. As he stepped towards the door, it opened and he stood teetering, framed in the doorway. For a second Erica stared at the great bear of a man wavering on the threshold until he regained his balance and quickly stepped back down to ground level. Erica hardly gave him a moment to recover his balance.

"What do you want?" she demanded in a peremptory manner.

The bear looked up at her, rainwater dripping from his eyebrows. "Hi, I'm looking for Luke Marshall. Vic told me he lived here."

Erica studied Kenny carefully, taking in the expensive looking leather coat, the greying hair matted to his head by the rain. She hesitated, holding on to the door like a security blanket, momentarily nonplussed.

"Who are you?" Again her tone was terse, but now with a suggestion of interest.

"Sorry, I should have introduced myself," Kenny made an involuntary move towards her, but quickly stepped back as Erica made as if to slam the door in his face. "I'm Kenny English. Luke was supposed to meet me up in town last night but he didn't show. I just wanted to make sure that he was all right."

Erica tilted her head back as she took in the news. "What have you done with my brother?" she asked slowly. "Where is he?" she added, standing on tiptoes to peer over Kenny's shoulder.

"I'm afraid I haven't met your brother. He didn't turn up for dinner last night as we'd arranged," said Kenny. He seemed about to add something else, but Erica interrupted him.

"You'd better come in out of the rain then," she said, holding the door open, her whole attitude softening.

Kenny complied, towering over her and seeming to fill the small hall with his leathery wetness. She made him take off his coat and his rather soggy shoes, before he was allowed off the doormat, and took the wet things from him, as she led the way into the kitchen.

Kenny followed like an obedient puppy, padding down the hall carpet in his socks, the wet bottoms of his trouser legs flapping. In the kitchen Erica turned away to hang up his coat and placed his shoes by the boiler to dry. She spun back to see Kenny looking around inquisitively.

"You'll have to take us as you find us," she said spikily. "I suppose you're used to rather grander surroundings,"

"Not at all," Kenny held up a hand in defence. "I was just thinking how this house was exactly the same as my parents'. I grew up down the road in Beckenham you know." Erica still looked unimpressed, so Kenny continued as if to prove his credentials. "Don't tell me. There's two downstairs rooms, that's if they haven't been knocked through, and upstairs there's three bedrooms, two at the front and then one at the back next to the bathroom. Am I right?"

Erica nodded, but still said nothing. "My room was the small one at the front. Mum and dad had the master bedroom of course, and they kept the second one as a guest room, though I can't for the life of me remember us having any guests." Kenny sat down on the nearest kitchen chair "I can see my room now, bed along one wall, desk in the corner for doing my homework, big poster of Ken Barrington."

"Tea?" Erica interrupted Kenny's babbling.

He nodded. "No sugar and just a splash of milk please."

While Erica made tea, Kenny took the opportunity to give her the once over. Late teens, early twenties, short and petite, not exactly a classically pretty face, more what people called interesting, interesting and intelligent.

"So you're the famous song writer then?" Erica handed Kenny a steaming mug and sat at the far side of the table.

"That'll be me," Kenny responded, trying to keep the mood light. He sipped his tea. "Though I'm not so sure about famous, or even a songwriter for that matter. You'd have to be a bit of an anorak to be able to name anything I've written in the last few years."

"Sorry, can't help you there, music's not really my subject. You need Luke for that one. I bet he could spout a list of your songs if you asked him." Erica smiled momentarily. If you blinked you would miss it, but Kenny was paying close attention. He saw the smile and just for a split second it seemed to warm the room. Then it was gone.

"So where is Luke, then. Not well or something?"

"I was rather hoping that you could help me out on that one. I thought he was with you. I haven't seen him since yesterday morning, no idea where he is." There was just the slightest quaver in Erica's voice as she finished the sentence.

"Like I said, he didn't show last night. I've never so much as met the guy."

"Then it looks like he's disappeared," said Erica slowly, looking down into her mug.

"Has he done this before?" asked Kenny, trying to sound positive.

Erica's startlingly blue eyes grew, for a moment threatening to pop out of her head. "Never," she said firmly as if controlling a rising temper. "Luke is the most reliable person you could meet. He's never let me down in his life, and to be honest I don't know what to do next." Once again the quaver, giving away her worry and fear. At that moment the doorbell rang.

Erica stood up as if scalded. She stood by the table and waited as if torn between hope and the fear of disappointment

"That's probably Vic," said Kenny gently. "He said he'd be over. He'll know what to do next."

Crestfallen, Erica tramped down the hall and let Vic in. He'd had the foresight to bring an umbrella which he shook outside before propping it against the hall wall. "Hi, Erica," he said. "Is Kenny here?"

"He's in the kitchen." Erica's tone was cold. "You'd better come on through."

Vic nodded to Kenny and looked around the room. "So where is he?" he asked.

"Seems he's disappeared." Kenny was the first to respond. "Hasn't been home since yesterday morning apparently."

"What?" Vic looked from Kenny to Erica, who nodded in confirmation. He sat in the only available chair. "That's not like our Luke, not like him at all."

Again Erica nodded. "I don't know where he could have got to, and I don't know how to find him. We were rather hoping you might have a suggestion."

Vic looked down at his feet, seeking inspiration. "Let's not start to panic now, shall we," he began slowly, gradually gaining confidence. "There's probably a logical explanation. Let's look at the facts and see if we can't retrace his steps. That way maybe we'll bump into him on the way, if you catch my meaning."

Kenny and Erica both nodded and Vic continued. "When exactly did you last see him?"

"Yesterday morning, about eight thirty, he left for work." Erica spoke calmly as though checking for accuracy.

"Luke works up at Victoria," Vic turned to Kenny for a moment then back to Erica, "so he'd have taken the train as usual, yes?"

"I assume so," Erica replied. "As far as I know he was headed for the station when he left here, just like any other day. He normally meets up with Si, that's his best friend, but yesterday he was late. After work he was supposed to be going out to dinner, or at least that's what he said."

"So we don't know if he ever got to the office then."

"No, we don't. He doesn't usually call me during the day, and I was out working anyway. I sort of thought he might come home to get changed, or text me if he wasn't going to, but really there was no reason for him to be in touch until he came home."

"Right. Well if there had been an accident on the train or something we'd have heard about it by now. I've had Capital Radio on in the shop all morning and they haven't mentioned anything, so I think we can rule out a rail accident." Erica flinched, her hands opening and closing, but Vic didn't seem to notice. "If he was taken ill in the street" he went on, "or got knocked down crossing the road, I think you would have been contacted by now. He would have had some ID with him, wouldn't he?"

Erica nodded. "He must have had his season ticket and photo card, not to mention his driving licence. He always carries that. He'd have his swipe card from work too, so even if he was unconscious they'd have been able to track him down, find out where he lived. I've been going over this in my mind all morning; if anything had happened on the way to work, I'm sure I'd have heard something. It's almost as if he's disappeared on purpose."

Vic sucked on his finger. "What we need to do is find out when he went AWOL. Did he get to work and, if so, where did he go after that? What about this mate of his, Si?"

"They work in the same office. Simon lives in the next road, but I can't for the life of me remember which house. I tried phoning earlier but there was no answer."

Kenny listened quietly, sitting on his hands in worried frustration.

"Simon, that'll be Simon Martindale eh?" Vic went on. "I remember Luke mentioning him more than once. He came to a *Souls* gig a couple of years back. Nice guy, bit quiet, but all right. Can't say he left a lasting impression though. No idea where we might find him."

Vic and Erica lapsed into an uneasy silence and sat looking at each other as if for inspiration. Both totally ignored Kenny until after a few moments he spoke.

"What about the phone book?" he asked.

Vic looked at Kenny as though surprised that he was still there, and then back at Erica.

"I told you I already tried ringing. There was no answer," Erica said, dismissively.

"But if his number's in the book, it will have his address as well. If it's just round the corner, we could at least pay him a visit."

Erica looked doubtful for a moment, but finally she turned in her chair and reached for a drawer in the kitchen unit behind her. She took out a rather moth eaten telephone directory and began leafing through. "M" she said, running her index finger down the page, "Ma...Martin... Martindale... Martindale S. Here it is. There's only one." She compared the number with the display on her mobile. "It's the same number," she said, sounding slightly disappointed.

"What's the address?" asked Kenny quickly before Erica put the phone book down.

"Sorry, not thinking straight," said Erica. "Let me see, here it is, 72 Latimer Close. Like I said, it's the next road along."

"Let's get round there then," Vic said, standing and starting to button his coat. You never know, he might come back any time."

"And if he doesn't," Kenny followed Vic's lead, looking about for his belongings, "we can leave a message for him to get in touch."

"Seems like the best alternative," said Erica, handing Kenny his shoes and reaching for his coat.

The rain had stopped by the time they set out, and the pavements steamed gently as a thin sun found its way through the occasional gaps in the clouds. 72 Latimer Gardens was a clone of Erica's house. The paintwork could have done with a bit of attention, and the front garden was a rather muddy mess where once it had been a lawn, but otherwise it looked well cared for and welcoming. Vic rang the doorbell. The sound echoed through the house, but there was no response

"Probably gone shopping," said Vic, and Erica nodded. Vic looked through the letterbox and into the hall, searching for signs of life. Kenny, who was still standing in the street, looked up at the first floor windows. "Didn't bother to draw the curtains before they went out," he remarked, "maybe they're still in bed."

"It's after one, who would be in bed at this time of day?" Erica snapped.

"I can remember plenty of occasions…" Kenny began, but then seemed to think better of it.

Vic shrugged. "It is a holiday weekend after all. Let's try again." So saying, he leaned heavily on the doorbell and allowed the ringing to resonate for several seconds. He pulled his finger away and resumed his position at the letterbox. After a pause there was the sound of feet stumbling down the stairs inside the house. Vic allowed the letterbox to close and turned to the others.

"Sounds like you were right," he said to Kenny, and before he could add anything they could all hear the sound of a bolt being drawn, a chain being removed. The door opened.

Simon Martindale stood on the doorstep and peered rather timidly at the group of people on his front path. It seemed to take a while for his eyes to become accustomed to the light, but his gaze fell on Erica and his face lit up in recognition.

"Hello there." The voice was firm and confident, belying the owner's rather weedy physical state. "It's Erica isn't it? Didn't expect to see you today. Come in." Simon turned and led them into the front room of the house. Kenny brought up the rear and carefully shut the front door.

Erica was introducing Vic by the time Kenny arrived, and Simon was making noises about recognising him from an earlier meeting. Erica introduced Kenny as simply "Kenny a friend of Vic's", and Simon indicated that they should all sit down. It wasn't that easy to find a vacant spot, as the two rather threadbare sofas were covered in an assortment of clothes, books and old newspapers. Simon made largely ineffectual efforts to tidy things away, and eventually they were all settled. "I'd offer you a cup of tea, but I haven't any milk, I'm afraid," Simon said apologetically. "Things have been a bit hectic this last day or so." They all nodded sympathetically, but without conviction.

"It's the baby, you see." Simon was still surrounded by blank looks. "Jeanette, my wife, had a baby last night. Girl, seven pounds five ounces. We're calling her Emily. She was pretty much on time, so I suppose we should have been better prepared, but you know how it is. She arrived in the early hours of this morning, that's why I was in bed. Simon indicated the towelling dressing gown that was wrapped around his scrawny form, and which apparently was all that he was wearing. "I'd still be asleep if you hadn't come round." He looked at his watch. "Bloody hell, I'm supposed to be in Farnborough by three, just as well you woke me up. I'd better get dressed."

Before the others could say anything, Simon got up and headed out of the door. They could hear his footsteps climbing the stairs and he must have very nearly reached the top when he stopped, paused for a moment, and returned. He came back, rather sheepishly, into the front room to find that the others had not moved.

"What are you all doing here anyway?" he asked. "I mean it's nice to see you and all that, but if you didn't know about the baby, why the visit?"

Kenny looked at Vic, Vic looked at Erica, Erica spoke. "It's lovely to hear your news," she began, "hope Jeanette and the baby are both well, wouldn't normally bother you at this time, don't like to intrude when you've got more important things on your mind and that." She paused, seemingly unsure as to whether she could impose at a time like this. Simon sat back down and made the decision for her.

"What can I do for you?" he said, in his calm controlled manner.

Erica took a breath. "It's Luke" she said, "he's disappeared."

Simon stared at her, his mouth half open, as if he was tempted to laugh, but he scanned the sombre expressions around him and realised that they were for real.

"But he was fine last time I saw him. Bit hungover, thought he might have a touch of flu, but otherwise fit as a flea. Looking forward to a big meeting last night, least I think it was last night. It is Saturday today isn't it? Afraid I'm a bit disorientated."

Kenny was the first to respond.

"It is Saturday, and it was last night that Luke was supposed to be meeting me. Trouble is he didn't show up, and he hasn't been home since. That's why we came round. We guessed that you would have seen him yesterday, and thought you might have some idea as to where he's gone."

"Right, so you're the famous songwriter. Sorry, Luke did tell me your name but it didn't register. He was well up for your meeting I can tell you; can't imagine what could have stopped him from showing up. Now I see your problem." The look on Simon's face told them all that he had finally grasped the situation. "Well, I can tell you that last time I saw Luke was about half past two yesterday afternoon, nearly twenty four hours ago, and that he was as well as can be expected for someone who had been overdoing the sauce the night before, if you get my drift. Had a bit of a headache, so I gave him some pills." Simon stopped and looked into the half distance frowning.

"That's right, yesterday afternoon, had a headache, wanted to recover for his big meeting, gave him a couple of tablets, he went for a lie down. That's the last time I saw him, when he got into the lift."

They all sat in silence, no one knowing what to say, as they digested the new information.

This time Vic spoke first. "When you say got into the lift, where was he going for this lie down?"

"Where we always go, down to the vault." Simon said it as if it was the most obvious thing in the world but immediately seemed to realise that his audience was in need of further explanation. "If you want a bit of time to yourself you go to the vault, you see." He paused, looking at the sea of blank expressions. "The vault is in the third basement. It's where we keep the valuables, you know, title documents and that sort of stuff for customers. We all have to go there from time to time when a customer needs something. We have a swipe card that lets us in and out. Like I said, if we want to take a bit of time out, you know skive off, there's an office down there with a big sofa. If Metal Mickey, that's the boss, if Metal Mickey comes looking for you there is a built in excuse; so and so had to go to the vault for a customer. Quick phone call and you can be back at your desk in minutes, no questions asked. Luke seemed in serious need of a rest and I was going to call him about four so he'd have time to get ready for his meeting, oh shit!"

Simon broke off and stared at the other three suddenly very serious.

"I was going to call him at four, but I got the message from the hospital just after three. I forgot all about him, had to get a move on. They said it was due there and then; how was I to know it would take another twelve hours?"

Simon seemed close to panic, as Erica reached forward and put her hand on his arm. "No one's blaming you for anything Simon, I'm sure we understand that you had other priorities. Are you saying that Luke is still in the office?"

"Not just the office," Simon paused, allowing the full impact to hit home. "I reckon he's still in the vault."

Chapter 7

In the vault Luke was playing *Solitaire* on the computer. Every so often, he checked his in box for messages, frowning more with each failed attempt. He sipped water from the cooler and gradually his headache cleared. Finishing the game, he got up and wandered into the vault. Slowly he walked down the rows of boxes, allowing his fingers to trail over the metal casings, as if wondering what riches they held, riches that were totally useless to him in his current predicament.

He looked over at the Plexiglas panel, which stayed stubbornly shut, showing the inside of the metal door closed beyond it. At the far end of the office was another door of reinforced steel that led to the inner vault. Beside the door was a small cupboard. Luke stopped, looking at the door as if he hadn't seen it before. He walked over and turned the handle. The door opened towards him, and he looked inside.

Arranged on several shelves were bits and pieces of electrical equipment, parts for computers mostly, some stacked in their original cardboard wrappings, others which must once have been used left lying around, redundant. Luke pulled out a couple of boxes and browsed through the odds and ends, dusty mice, sound cards, memory chips. As he opened the third box he gave a little whoop of delight that echoed around the empty room. Pulling out a pair of speakers he admired his bounty, carefully checking that the wring was complete with power plug and mini jack. He took his prize back to the office and plugged it into the computer. Browsing his user area, he opened the *My Music* folder, clicked on a song at random and watched while the machine opened the media player program.

Luke adjusted the volume and sat back in the chair. For the first time that day he allowed himself a small smile.

They all stared at Simon. It was Vic who spoke first. "Are you saying that Luke is trapped in a safe?"

"No, no, not a safe exactly," Simon held up his hands in defence, "more like an office with lots of safes in it."

The others looked at each other, all of them registering their own confused expression. Erica found her voice. "I'm sorry Simon, but you are going to have to be a bit clearer on this one. You said that Luke is in the vault. Isn't that a safe?"

"Sorry, I forgot you've never been there. No, the vault is just the name we give to the basement where all the safety deposit boxes are kept. It isn't locked during the day, only at night and weekends. The rest of the time it's just like a big office with lots of metal cabinets in it. It's quite cosy really, not intimidating." Simon looked around at the others, smiling, communicating confidence. "There's an office and everything, bathroom, all mod cons. There's even one of those water cooler things in case he gets thirsty. It's not uncomfortable or anything."

"Not exactly where you'd choose to spend a holiday weekend though, is it?" Vic chipped in. "May be quite comfortable for an hour or so, but not like somewhere you'd want to find yourself holed up for several days. Don't suppose there's any food down there or suchlike."

"No there isn't," Simon acknowledged, his shoulders falling in resignation, "and there's no way of getting out until the time lock switches itself off on Tuesday."

"Time lock?" asked Kenny. "How does that work?"

"The vault has a thick steel door," Simon began, mentally getting things in order. "During the day it's open, so we just need a card to activate the internal glass panel. At night it closes on the stroke of six, just like magic, and it can't be opened until the next business day. When the clock gets round to half past eight, it opens automatically."

"Can anyone override the time lock?"

"Only Metal Mickey."

"You sure of that?"

"Oh yes, certain. Before he arrived, it used to be done manually, you know with a couple of keys held by senior staff, key holders. Mickey introduced a lot of new systems and procedures, including the time lock and the swipe card. Said it would be more secure."

"So now only one person can control it?"

"Yes, Metal Mickey. A couple of weeks ago Luke and I had to work late. One of our clients, firm of solicitors, had some sort of late night closing, big deal with Los Angeles I seem to recall. Meant they might need some title deeds after hours, so we were told to wait behind so we could get them. Mickey had to stay with us as he was the only one with the permissions on the computer system to override the locks. Made a right song and dance about it, I can tell you."

"You said there's an office, does it have a phone?" Erica interrupted.

"Internal calls only," Simon was looking decidedly down hearted now, "and his mobile won't work that far underground. I know, I've tried."

"Where can we find this, Mickey?" Vic asked. "Seems like he's the one we have to get hold of."

Simon shrugged. "I haven't the faintest. He's not the sort that encourages social chit chat, if you know what I mean. Don't even know what part of London he lives in. Could be miles away."

"Who is he anyway?" Vic persisted. "Metal Mickey? What sort of name is that?"

"Metal Mickey is just our nickname for him. His real name is Mike Dalton, the Managing Director. He's been in charge for about six months. Like I say, he's not what you might call pally, keeps himself to himself. He could live on the moon for all I know."

"He might suffocate." Erica was staring into the middle distance, lost in her own thoughts.

"I didn't mean that he does live on the moon."

"What? Oh no, I didn't mean Metal thingy. I meant Luke. If he's left in a closed room for the whole weekend, he could suffocate, couldn't he?"

There was a moment's silence as they all considered the prospect. This time it was Kenny who broke the spell.

"Just how big is this vault, Simon?" .

"It's about the same size as the rest of the floors in the building. It's quite big, though of course a lot of space is taken up with the deposit boxes and so forth. Let me see," Simon began, and then trailed off. "Hang on a minute. I can tell you exactly." So saying he stood up from the sofa, only just protecting his modesty by catching the trailing tails of his bathrobe and wrapping them around his body at the last moment. He pushed past Vic and Kenny and went over to a large chest of drawers that stood by the wall to the left of the bay window.

"What's this all about?" asked Erica as Simon rummaged about behind her.

"When I go on holiday I sometimes go scuba diving," Kenny began.

"Delightful," remarked Erica, in a how the other half lives tone of voice.

Kenny ignored the implication. "When I go diving I take a tank of compressed air. The one I usually take is called an Al 80. The Al is short for aluminium and the 80 stands for 80 cubic feet. That's 80 cubic feet of air." Kenny looked from Erica to Vic and back again, but both were registering nothing more than mild interest.

"Depending on how vigorously you swim, the Al 80 will last up to 75 minutes. We normally dive for an hour to be on the safe side. What I'm saying is that eighty cubic feet of air is good for at least an hour. From what Simon has told us, the vault is unlikely to be ventilated, but it's bigger than the average sized room. What size is this room for example?" Kenny looked around the four walls, and the others followed his gaze, ignoring Simon who was now elbow deep in a drawer which seemed to be filled with scraps of paper. "Must be what, twelve feet by sixteen? Roughly eight feet high. That makes," Kenny paused, his eyes rolling to the ceiling as though looking for divine inspiration, "about sixteen hundred cubic feet, give or take. If eighty cubic feet lasts an hour, there would be enough air in here for about twenty hours or so, say a day at the outside."

Kenny stopped and looked at the others. Vic raised his eyebrows and nodded. "Makes sense to me," he said, "if we know how big the room is at least we can eliminate the possibility of suffocation."

Erica didn't look convinced, but before she could comment Simon let out a cheer.

"Knew it would come in handy one day," he said, passing a creased piece of paper to Kenny. "Pays not to throw things away, that's what I always say."

Kenny looked at his hand. He was holding a piece of ruled paper, which had clearly been torn from a loose-leaf notebook. There were figures on it, written in pencil.

"What's this?" he asked.

"Found it in the lift at work a couple of months ago. Like I say, thought it would come in handy one day. The vault was being redecorated and recarpeted. I reckon that's the carpet fitter's notes estimating the size of the floor from when he measured up. Must have dropped it on his way out."

Kenny looked again at the piece of paper. The numbers now made sense. "It says 40 x 60," he told the others, "and there's a sort of apostrophe after each number, which I assume means feet. That makes the floor area forty feet by sixty. That sound about right to you, Simon?"

Simon gave a slight shrug. "Could be," he said, "but it's hard to tell what with all the safes and that in there."

"How high is the ceiling?" asked Kenny.

This time Simon gave a large shrug, nearly losing control of his bathrobe in the process.

"Search me, I'm not very good at that sort of thing." Simon's manner quickly became defensive, challenged by a question he could not answer. Kenny backed off, rephrasing the question.

"Put it this way, can you stand up straight in there?"

"Course you can. Didn't I say it's like a big office?"

"You certainly did. Sorry. Can you reach up and touch the ceiling?"

"Never tried. But I can't quite on our floor, and that must be about the same height."

"So say, what eight feet? Roughly the same as in here?"

"If you say so. Yes, probably about that."

"So if we want to know the volume of the vault, it must be forty by sixty by eight."

"I'm going to need a calculator and a pen," interrupted Erica. In a trice, Simon was on his feet again. He disappeared for a moment and returned with a small electronic calculator and a biro. He handed them both to Erica.

"Right, give me those numbers again," she demanded. Kenny responded, and Erica wrote them on the back of her hand, before tapping figures into the calculator. She repeated the operation three times before she was happy with the result.

"I make it that the total capacity of the vault is 19,200 cubic feet. If you are right and eighty cubic feet lasts an hour, that means there is enough air in there for two hundred and forty hours, exactly ten days."

"So even if half the room is taken up with safes and equipment and stuff, there should be plenty for five days," finished Kenny. "That means Luke would be fine until Wednesday night, and he will be released automatically by Tuesday morning, so I think we could safely rule out the danger of suffocation, don't you?"

Vic nodded, but still looked dubious. Erica handed him the calculator and he took the scrap of paper from Kenny. After doing the sums himself a couple of times, he seemed happier. He handed the paper and calculator back to Erica. "Like I said, seems logical. You'd think a room that size would be big enough for one human being for a long weekend anyway."

Erica was looking decidedly happier than she had a few minutes earlier. "That means that Luke is in no immediate danger. Seems that the worst that can happen is he'll get a bit hungry over the next couple of days, but that's not exactly life threatening." She heaved a sigh and turned to Kenny. "Thanks for working that out. Sorry if I was a bit snappy."

Kenny smiled. "Glad I could do something useful. I feel a bit of a spare part not being able to help. Which still leaves the question of what to do next."

Simon sat resting his head on his hand, scratching the side of his nose with his little finger. "If I was stuck in the vault," he said as if to himself, "I think the first thing I'd want to do is make contact with the outside world. Can't use the phone, but he has got the Internet."

"What was that?" Kenny seemed to sense that Simon might be on to something.

"The Internet. The office in the vault has a computer terminal that is connected to the bank's system. That includes a 50 meg broadband connection. He may not be able to talk to us, but he can at least send an email."

"That's not much use to me," said Erica. "We haven't got the Internet at home. Luke said we couldn't afford it, not until I get a job at least."

"No, but I've got it here," said Simon, leading them all into the back room where a computer terminal sat in the far corner. It took a few minutes to boot up, but before long Simon was opening his inbox. "One of the things that Mike Dalton introduced was remote Internet access to the company network, so we could check emails from home, that sort of thing. Look, here it is now."

Simon checked through the various messages. "Here's one from Luke," he said, "timed at just after six o'clock this morning." He double clicked the icon and stood back so that they could all read Luke's terse missive.

Erica stood with her fist in her mouth, tears hovering on her eyelashes. "Send him a reply, Si," she said suppressing a sob, " and let him know we're trying to help."

Simon sat down at the keyboard and clicked *Reply*. He thought for a moment, and then began pressing keys.

```
Got your message mate, he typed. Erica is
here, and she's going to try to get you out.
Don't panic, everything will be fine.
```

He looked over his shoulder at Erica, who nodded, so he clicked *Send*.

"With a bit of luck, he'll read that soon, and then he can email back to let us know he's alright. Now if you don't mind, I need to get dressed and make my way over to Farnborough, to see how my wife and daughter are getting on."

"Of course, Simon," said Erica. "We've taken up too much of your time already. You've been really helpful." She was still holding the scrap of paper and she scribbled a number on it. "Here's my mobile. Let us know how Luke is, won't you."

"'Course I will. Soon as I get back from the hospital I'll be in touch with him."

They all said their goodbyes, and soon Kenny, Vic and Erica found themselves back on the street.

"I'd better be getting back to the shop," said Vic. "What are you two going to do?" Erica looked at Kenny, lost for something to say. Kenny took charge.

"We need to go to the police. Time this was reported. You never know, they might have some way of dealing with this sort of problem, emergency call out service or some such."

Erica didn't share his optimism. "Somehow I doubt it," she said. "Not exactly a high priority with the police, I would have thought. Can't see them being much help, myself."

"Well, if we don't ask, we'll never know will we?" Kenny seemed determined to remain positive, but Erica just shrugged dismissively.

"I'll walk up to the corner with you," Vic said. "The police station is just on the right. You can't miss it." They parted at the main road. "Come over to the shop when you're done. Let me know how you get on," said Vic, and Kenny nodded.

Penge police station is a late Victorian building, gothic in inspiration, the traditional red brick style recognisable in libraries, swimming baths and primary schools the length of the country. Except that this red brick building is not red but a rather incongruously pale shade, somewhere between cream and off-white, built from the local Kentish sandstone. As they climbed the steps to the front door Kenny paused momentarily, looking up at the blue lamp suspended above them on wrought iron brackets.

"Second thoughts?" asked Erica, without malice.

"No, just thinking," said Kenny. "It's the lamp. Always reminds me of Saturday teatimes, Dixon of Dock Green. Whatever happened to the friendly bobby who could settle an argument with a few well chosen words or a clip round the ear? I suppose those days are gone."

"Long gone," Erica replied, leading the way. As if to prove her right, they found that in order to gain access to the station, they had first to be allowed through an electronic door by a uniformed security guard who seemed to suspect them of carrying hidden weapons or explosive devices. The body searches were mechanical, but the air of suspicion unmistakable. They were directed to wait on two institutional chairs, propped against the wall.

In place of a counter was an apparently bullet-proof screen, behind which the station staff could be observed, talking on telephones or browsing over desktop computers. A prime example of the South London public was at that moment in vociferous dispute with the desk sergeant. Clearly the worse for alcoholic wear, the man was trying to abuse the officer verbally, while struggling to escape from the iron grip of a burly constable who held him by the scruff of the neck. Were it not for the constable's support, the drunk would probably have collapsed in a heap on the floor, for not only was he unable to find the words to express his opinion of the officer's actions, and in all probability parentage, but his efforts to free himself from his physical encumbrance were uncoordinated and utterly futile.

Kenny looked from the writhing, struggling and incomprehensible, though undoubtedly blasphemous individual to the desk sergeant. Instead of an avuncular Jack Warner figure, he found himself looking at a young woman. Short and blonde, she was clearly used to dealing with this sort of situation and was not going to be put upon. She wore an expression of tired indifference, like a schoolteacher listening to a child who claimed to have left his homework on the bus. I've heard it all before, her body language asserted, and I am not putting up with it for much longer.

Joe Public was now ranting in an incoherent babble, wriggling in the constable's grip. Neither the constable nor the sergeant said a word, but just held their positions, waiting for the storm to blow itself out. After several minutes of gibbering, the man's feet started to slither on the tiled floor, and the room was filled with the unmistakable smell of fresh urine. The man seemed suddenly to realise that the material at the front of his trousers was a shade darker than it had been seconds earlier, and immediately fell silent.

Mistress of cool efficiency, the sergeant took the opportunity to speak. "Stick him in a cell, and then get someone to clear up this mess," she ordered. "I'll see to him when he's had a chance to sober up. Twenty four hour opening? I'll give them bloody twenty four hour opening." And she shook her head, the traditional professional's response to the stupidity of those in higher authority.

A door opened in the wall behind the constable, and the drunk was tugged unceremoniously through it, his failure to control his bladder evidently taking the wind out of his sails. He allowed himself to be dragged away.

"And what can I do for you two?" The desk sergeant turned her attention to Kenny and Erica, the picture of equanimity, as if the drunk had never existed. They picked their way gingerly across the floor, around the spreading puddle, and came together at the screen. They looked at each other, and Kenny spoke first.

"We have come to report a missing person," he began, but got no further before Erica interrupted.

"He's not exactly missing. We know where he is, we just need to get him out."

Erica's look was accusing, stopping Kenny short. He held out his hand to her, palm up, handing over responsibility.

"So is he missing, or isn't he?" the sergeant's smile was still in place, though it had turned slightly patronising. Erica didn't seem to take any notice.

"It's my brother, see," she started, "he's not exactly missing, it's just that he's trapped and we can't get him out."

"Trapped, eh?" The sergeant started to make notes on a lined pad on her side of the screen, "where is he exactly?"

"He's in a safe," blurted Erica.

The sergeant's demeanour changed. Her expression became one of concern. She checked around her, as if preparing for action, seemed to be looking for her hat. Something had obviously touched the adrenalin button. "And how old is this infant?" she said, no longer friendly, now businesslike.

"He's not an infant, he's thirty five." Erica seemed alarmed at the officer's change of attitude, which must obviously have stemmed from something she had said.

"Thirty five? Must be a bloody big safe." The sergeant's manner switched from friendly, to concerned, to suspicious, in a matter of seconds. She seemed to sense a wind up.

"It's not exactly a safe, more like a big office with safes in it."

The sergeant put her pen down and paused for a moment, apparently weighing up the alternatives, somewhere between crisis and practical joke. She took a deep breath and turned to Kenny. "Maybe you would like to explain what has happened."

A junior officer came out from behind the screen with a bucket and mop and began dealing with the mess on the floor. The chairs by the wall had been taken by a woman wearing an oversized man's raincoat.

She had three small children with her. The youngest was in her arms, while the other two fought for possession of the second chair. Kenny was slowly and with a minimum of fuss explaining what had happened to Luke. Erica half listened to references to the bank, the vault, a headache and falling asleep, as she watched the small family. The youngest child, a dummy in its mouth, its top lip caked with dry snot, was wriggling on its mother's lap, eager to join the fight that was developing between its siblings. The sister, probably no more than three, was losing out to her bigger brother. Both wore soiled jeans and torn sweatshirts, evidently hand-me-downs. The baby set up a wail, as its efforts went unrewarded. Erica looked more closely at the mother.

She could have been in her forties, the hair lank and the skin sallow, but was probably no older than Erica herself. Her expression was resigned, defeated, and it was only some mechanical instinct to protect her offspring that seemed to keep her from letting go of the child. Erica realised that she was staring, and turned her attention back to the officer, who was now reading through the notes that she had made.

"So this is what it boils down to." She cleared her throat. "This brother of yours," she turned to Erica, "this brother, one Luke Marshall, works for some bank up in town, had a bit of a headache yesterday afternoon," she looked up from her notes, and Erica nodded mechanically "so went for a kip in the basement, fell asleep, and the upshot is he's still there and won't get out until Tuesday morning. That about the sum total of it?"

Kenny and Erica both nodded. "We don't think he's in any danger, do we?" began Kenny, and Erica nodded again, though rather doubtfully. "Seems that he has water and enough air to last him, but he's going to get awfully hungry unless we can get him out. We just thought you might have some way of getting in touch with his boss to see what he can do."

"Can't help, I'm afraid," the sergeant shrugged. "Not like there's any crime been committed, and as you say, he's not in any immediate danger. Sounds to me like it was his own fault. As for getting in touch with whoever can release him, there's a database kept at Scotland Yard listing all the senior executives of London banks, key holders and the like. If this were an emergency we could search their records to find who to call, but I'm afraid that in this instance we can't help."

"Couldn't you just let us know an address or a phone number? Then we could contact them direct. That way you wouldn't be bothered." Erica failed to keep a note of desperation out of her voice.

"Not a chance." The sergeant shook her head and closed her notebook. "Data Protection Act, you understand."

Both Kenny and Erica looked defeated. The two children were now arguing loudly, and the boy landed a hefty punch on his sister's cheek. She started to scream, and the baby raised its own efforts by several decibels. The desk sergeant peered past Kenny and Erica, looking concerned.

"Here's an incident number." She handed Kenny a slip of paper. "Give us a ring if anything changes, but for now I don't think there's any question of an emergency, do you? If this bloke is stupid enough to get himself locked up for the weekend, I reckon it's his own lookout. Now if you'll excuse me, I have other matters to attend to."

Kenny put the paper in his pocket, and he and Erica left the station, heads low in embarrassment as they passed the security guard, who ignored them with measured indifference.

Outside, Kenny leant against a lamppost. "Sorry to put you through that. Complete waste of time," he said apologetically.

"Don't blame yourself. Like you said, we had to try. At least no one can say we didn't explore all the possibilities."

"Question is, what to do next."

"Well I don't know about you, but I'm going for a long soak in a hot bath. Might help me think of something. But like the lady said, does seem that Luke's problems are largely self-inflicted. I'm starting to wonder whether it's worth worrying about him at all. Let him stew there for a couple of days. Won't do him any harm. Might even teach him a lesson."

"Can't argue with you on that one," said Kenny sympathetically. "Whichever way you look at it, we've spent the best part of a day worrying about someone who should have known better than to get himself in a fix in the first place. I guess we both deserve a little respite."

"I suppose you'll go back to town then. No point you wasting any more of your time on my stupid brother."

Kenny thought for a moment as if weighing up his options. "No," he said at length. "I've got nothing better to do, to be honest, and I hate to leave a job half done. Think I'll go and pay another call on Vic. See if he's had any more ideas. Then we really ought to have another word with Simon, when he's done at the hospital, find out if he can remember anything else about this Dalton character that might be helpful. Why don't we get together again later, compare notes?"

Erica checked her watch. "It's nearly five," she said, " I'm meeting a friend in *The Billy* at eight. If you're still around you can join us."

Kenny nodded. "*The Billy*, you say. Where's that?"

"*The Admiral Bligh*, down the road. We've walked past it a couple of times."

"*The Admiral Bligh*," Kenny repeated, making a mental note "OK, see you later."

When Kenny arrived, Vic was in the process of closing the shop, pulling down the corrugated metal shutters with a long pole, before securing them at ground level with a series of matching padlocks. He guided Kenny to a door at the side of the shop which led to stairs to the flat above. Once inside Vic double locked the door and settled the chain into its groove. Kenny watched patiently.

"Nice security," he remarked. "Mind you, considering what I've just seen of the seamier side of Penge life, I don't blame you." Vic showed the way up the stairs, the plush carpet and expensive wallpaper contrasting with the stark utilitarian police station. The impression was maintained in the living room at the top of the stairs. Everything was clean and comfortable, the paintwork brand new, the furniture in almost showroom condition.

The smell of cooking wafted from the kitchen, and Vic motioned Kenny to sit in one of the overstuffed armchairs. Kenny did as he was bid and drank in the atmosphere. The place didn't exactly breathe wealth, but it was unarguably homely. The room was about the same size as the one in Simon's house, but there the similarity ended. Where Simon's room was untidy to the point of scruffiness, Vic's was well ordered, tidy to the extent that Kenny was concerned about making a mess. He crossed his ankles and lay back, until he realised that his bottom foot was leaving a rut in the carpet. Quickly he sat up straighter so that his feet were flat on the floor, in the process checking surreptitiously that he hadn't walked any mud in on the soles of his shoes.

Vic returned from the kitchen with two cans of beer. He handed one to Kenny, sat down opposite, opened the ring pull and took a long drink. "I guess it's not what you're used to," he said, wiping his lips with the back of his hand, "but I'm afraid it's all that's on offer. Maureen doesn't let me keep anything stronger in the house."

"It suits me just fine, thanks." Kenny opened his own can and followed Vic's example, pausing to lick his lips, remembering.

"So how was the police station?"

"Complete waste of time. They said they couldn't do anything to help, what with no crime being committed and Luke being in no danger. Like I said though, I did get an insight into the sort of people you mix with.

Seems to me that Penge is populated with incontinent drunks and single parents. You know the type, three kids under five and not so much as a matching pair."

"Shouldn't imagine you get a balanced view of any community from the local nick. Not that we don't have our share of problem cases, no argument there, but if you hung around long enough, I think you would find that most of the people round here are like Luke and me, only interested in making an honest crust and keeping the wolf from the door. Any entertainment we get is a bit of a bonus. Still, can't complain, life could be a lot worse."

Maureen came into the room, wiping her hands on her apron. The years had not been unkind to her, and Kenny had no difficulty in recognising the beauty she had once been. Like Vic, she was unashamedly late middle aged, wearing clothes that made no effort to be fashionable. Kenny smiled in recognition, and Maureen returned the compliment without fuss.

"You'll stay for some supper of course," Maureen stated, her attitude honest and unpretentious. "If my husband here is going to bore the pants off you, least I can do is see that you are well fed." Vic and Maureen exchanged a long look of mutual affection, and Kenny watched for a moment, in silent admiration.

"How can I say no?" he accepted with a smile, and then turned to Vic. "Fact is, I may need to find somewhere to stay the night. Looks like getting your young chum out of that bank is going to take a couple of days."

"No problem," Vic was quick to respond, "there's a spare room here. Stay as long as you like."

"I wouldn't want to put you out. I could go to a hotel." Kenny was surprised at the generosity. "To tell the truth, it would be no hardship to go home tonight and return in the morning, not as if I've any other pressing business to attend to. But I really don't fancy going home to north London just now. A bed and breakfast would suit me just fine."

As was clearly the custom, Maureen had the last word. "Spare bed's made up already and there are clean towels. There's a new toothbrush in the bathroom cabinet, and if you want a change of clothing, there's plenty of Vic's things that he never wears. I'll look something out for you after we've eaten. Now come and get it while it's hot."

With a look that said better do as the lady says, Vic rose from his armchair and followed his wife into the kitchen. Kenny trailed behind. There was to be no arguing with this woman, that was for sure.

Dinner was shepherd's pie with fresh vegetables. It was hot and wholesome and there was plenty of it. Kenny tucked in with relish. "Last person who made this for me must have been my mum," he said to Maureen between mouthfuls. "I'd forgotten how good it can be."

"There's plenty more if you want it," she preened, "but leave room for the afters. It's home made rhubarb and custard."

Kenny grinned like a little boy on his birthday. As they ate, he filled Maureen in on Luke's predicament, and then brought both Maureen and Vic up to date with what had happened in the police station. Vic opened more beers, and Kenny noted Maureen's look of mild disapproval, but nothing was said.

"That has to be the best meal I have eaten in I don't know how long," Kenny sighed, as he finally placed his spoon in his empty bowl after a second helping of rhubarb.

"Get away, you must eat at all the top places," said Maureen, though she was clearly pleased by the compliment.

"You name it, I've been there. But they don't serve up food like that, no way. That was home cooking at its best."

"She's a diamond, my missus," said Vic, with genuine pride. The food and the beers had left him flushed and slightly lethargic. He went to pat his wife on the thigh, but she gave him the slip as she collected empty crockery.

"Nothing fancy about my cooking," she remarked. "That young Luke, he's the one for the cordon blue, isn't he? What was it he made us at New Year, beef en croute or whatever he called it? Dead posh stuff if you ask me."

"And remember how he went on about how cooking is like music?" Vic joined in the reminiscence. "Said something about how you needed to know what went well with what, all the ingredients working in perfect harmony, that sort of thing. Got fair lyrical about it, didn't he?"

"Well, he'd had a few, hadn't he." Maureen was stacking dishes in the sink, running hot water and squirting washing up liquid. "That's the way you all get. I've heard you after one of your concerts. Going on like you know what you're talking about. Make me laugh you do."

"A man's got to have a hobby, that's what I say." Vic got up from the table, surreptitiously removing two more beers from the fridge and motioning to Kenny to join him in the sitting room. Kenny lingered a moment, unsure as to whether he should offer to help with the washing up. Maureen dismissed him with a nod of her head. "You go and join him. Not often he gets company. Go and support his hobby."

Kenny and Vic sat and chatted as they sipped beer. "Sounds a talented bloke this Luke Marshall," said Kenny, relaxing in the armchair and stretching his legs. "Musician and chef. Can't wait to meet him."

"You'll get on like a house on fire, you two. Got a lot in common, I reckon. This cooking lark though, not so much a hobby, more making a virtue out of a necessity, if you get my drift."

"Explain."

"Well, as I understand it, young Luke had to grow up sharpish when his parents died, had a little sister to bring up."

"What happened?"

"Can't say I know the full facts, but their mum and dad were killed in the Clapham rail disaster, about sixteen years ago. Luke was still at school, on his way to university by all accounts. Erica couldn't have been more than four; suddenly no parents. The lad brought up his sister on his own. Doesn't say much about it mind you, not the sort to crow, but they have a very close relationship, as you might expect."

"I see why she's so anxious. Can't be easy not having him around all of a sudden. Like roles are reversed isn't it? Now she's the one who has to look after him. The child is father of the man, as it were, or mother in this case."

"You what?"

"Wordsworth, The Prelude. The child is father of the man, like we learn things from the next generation just as much as they learn things from us. Freud said something similar."

"Don't have much time for poetry, or psychology for that matter. But that's just the sort of thing that Luke would say. Like I said, you two would get on."

Kenny checked his watch. "Look at the time. I'm supposed to be meeting Erica in the pub in five minutes. You going to join us?"

Vic seemed to be on the point of saying yes, when Maureen walked in and made the decision for him. "I think you've had enough excitement for one day, don't you? Let Kenny go and sort things out with the girl. You need an early night."

Vic gave a look of exasperation, shrugging his shoulders and holding his hands out in an expression that showed conclusively who wore the trousers in this particular relationship. He walked Kenny downstairs to the front door, handing over a spare key, and asked him to make sure that the door was double locked when he came in, before sending him on his way.

Chapter 8

Simon dropped the carrier bag of groceries on the kitchen table and scurried into the back room. The monitor clicked into action as he moved the mouse, and he quickly logged on to his email. As expected, there was a message from Luke.

```
Don't worry about me, I'm not panicking, just
wanted you all to know I'm safe. Erica must be
going potty by now, what with me not coming home
all night. Let me know what's happening.
```

Simon sat staring at the screen for several minutes, chewing on his top lip. At length he seemed to come to a decision, clicked on *Reply* and typed.

I'm at home now. If you get this message, log on to MSN and then we can chat.

He sent the message, and then clicked the MSN icon at the bottom of the screen, activating the service. He stared at the monitor for a few seconds more, before returning to the kitchen. As he finished making a cup of tea, he heard the unmistakable tone from the back room and sat back down at the computer. On the screen was a message which said simply :

Luke has logged on.

He clicked the box, adjusted the web cam that sat on top of the monitor and typed.

```
Enable vision and sound at your end.
```

He took a long thin microphone from a drawer under the computer keyboard and plugged it into the socket on the back of the base unit.

In the vault, Luke did as he was told and was rewarded with a grainy image of his friend who seemed to be ferreting around somewhere below the camera. At last Simon looked up at him, his lips moving. Luke switched off the music he had been playing and was rewarded with Simon's voice.

"Testing, testing," he said. "Let me know if you can hear me, mate."

```
Coming through loud and clear,
```

typed Luke. Hang on a minute, I've just had a thought.

Leaving the office Luke went back through the vault to the cupboard where he'd found the speakers. He pulled a large box from the middle shelf, muttering under his breath. "Now where were you," he said, running his hands through a variety of electronic odds and ends. "There you are. Thought I saw you earlier." Smiling broadly, he took out a small microphone attached to a USB plug. Back in the office he plugged it into the front of his computer and blew down it, clearing dust and fluff that had settled over the business end. He looked up to see Simon with a surprised look on his face.

"Now can you hear me?" said Luke.

"No trouble," replied Simon leaning to his left apparently to adjust the volume.

"Thank Christ for that," Luke let out a long sigh, "I was beginning to think I'd never speak to a human being again. So how was Erica when you saw her?"

Simon peered through the web cam. "She seemed OK. A bit concerned about you but relieved when she knew you were all right."

"Well that's a load off my mind. I've been worried sick thinking of her worrying about me. We've never spent a night apart before. She must have been going bonkers."

"Well, like I say, she seemed a lot happier once she saw your email. At least she knows where you are now, and that you're alive."

Luke sighed and relaxed back in his chair. Then another thought seemed to come to him. and he sat forward, talking directly into the microphone. "So why didn't you come and wake me up like you planned to? What went wrong? Did you forget all about me or something?" Luke tried without success to keep the accusatory note out of his voice.

"Sorry mate, I got called away. Jeanette had the baby last night."

Luke's tone changed immediately. "The baby, Christ I'd forgotten all about that! How are they? What is it anyway?"

"It, I mean she, is a girl, Emily. Lovely she is, the image of her mother."

"Just as well for her, I reckon. Wouldn't be much of a life if she looked like you, would it!" And they both laughed.

"So as you can imagine, I suddenly had other thoughts on my mind," Simon continued. "Sorry I let you down. I could have killed myself when I realised what I'd done."

"Not your fault really. I'm as much to blame. I've had time to think today, you know, about the nature of accidents, and it seems to me we all contributed one way and another."

"How do you mean?"

"Well, as you can well imagine, when I first realised what had happened, I blamed you."

"Naturally."

"Of course I didn't know about the baby and that, and you were the first thing that came to mind. But then when I thought about it, I decided that it was all Metal Mickey's fault really."

"How come?"

"Remember what it was like before he took over, when George Parker ran the place. Things were a lot more relaxed in those days."

"You're telling me. Life's become serious since the Metal One came to run our happy band."

"Exactly. Dalton introduced God knows how many new innovations, systems and procedures as he keeps on saying, supposedly to make life safer and more efficient. But think about it, under old George this sort of thing could never have happened."

Simon was quiet for a moment, mulling things over. "You mean life before the advent of the swipe card."

"Precisely. When George ran things we had more people for starters. All Dalton's interested in is cutting costs; the only trouble is that with costs he's cut corners. Remember how there used to be a security guard outside the vault, monitoring all the comings and goings. His job was to make sure that we didn't walk off with anything valuable, and to see that the vault was locked and unlocked at the right times."

Simon let out a snort. "You mean old Snowy? He must have been ninety if he was a day! Come off it, Luke, there's no way Snowy was going to stop anyone who wanted to from taking what they liked from the vault. All he was interested in was having a good chat when you needed to get back to your desk."

"That's as maybe, but one thing he was good at doing was keeping a check on who was around. If I'd gone for a nap when he was on guard, he wouldn't have let them close the bloody door until I'd got out, would

and seamanship. The mutineers set Bligh and his officers adrift in a boat in the open Pacific, but he was able to land them safely some three thousand miles away without losing a single life. Later on he was made a member of the Royal Society for his contributions to the science of navigation. Like I say, he may seem like a bully to us, but for his time he was quite a hero. Even won a commendation for bravery at the Battle of Copenhagen, if I remember correctly. So all round, a bit of a success. Died in his sleep at the ripe old age of sixty four."

"So you think that Metal Mickey might turn into a hero if we give him the chance?"

"Not necessarily. He might turn out to be a mindless bully after all. What I'm saying is that until we know what his terms of reference are, what constraints he is working under, it's a bit too early to judge him."

Erica took another mouthful of lager and looked thoughtful for a moment. "I take your point," she said deliberately, "but for the time being I guess I am looking for a scapegoat, and until someone else turns up, he's the best I've got, so I'm blaming him."

Kenny grinned, "In that case, blame away."

Neither spoke for a few minutes, looking into their glasses, each lost in their own thoughts. "Hang on, where did you get all that stuff from anyway?" Erica suddenly looked puzzled.

"What stuff?"

"All that stuff about the Bounty and Admiral Bligh. You been swotting up or something?"

"Song writing isn't what you might call a full time occupation. You end up with a lot of spare time. That's probably why some people take to drugs and that, too much time on their hands. After all, if you get a hangover you can just sleep it off. Not like you have to go to work in the morning or anything. I spend a lot of my time reading. History is my drug of choice you might say."

"So if my Luke was to take up this song writing job, he would have time to do other things. He could take up the degree course that he missed out on after school."

"Certainly could. Don't spread it around, but I did."

"You took a degree?"

"Keep it down. Yes I did. And why not? Just because I write songs for a living doesn't mean I'm stupid you know."

Erica seemed about to protest her innocence, but Kenny interrupted her.

"I thought you said you were meeting a friend here tonight. If you've been stood up, I can easily empathise with you."

Erica smiled. As before, the expression could be taken as no more than a twitch around the corners of her mouth, but it lingered for a split second longer this time, allowing Kenny to enjoy the warmth.

"Joanne won't stand me up, thank you," she said. "But she never was one for punctuality. She'll be late, but she'll be here, trust me."

"Sure you've got the right pub? I must have asked myself a dozen times last night if I was sitting in the wrong restaurant. It's an easy thing to do."

"No problems there either. This is the pub we used to come to when we were at school. You know, under age drinking. Joanne was always the one egging the rest of us on, leader of the pack like, she knows where to find me."

Kenny nodded. "I remember the feeling, that first illicit drink."

"Don't tell me you were a pub frequenter. My, Mr English, I'd started to take you for a bit of a goody two shoes. Hard to imagine you doing anything unlawful." Erica feigned horror, hand over her mouth, eyebrows raised dramatically.

Kenny laughed out loud, swallowing the sound as heads turned. "We used to go to the *Three Tuns* in Beckenham," he said, a little sheepishly. "I was a June baby, so I was always one of the youngest, but by the time I was seventeen, I was already over six foot, and I can't remember having a problem getting served."

"It's all ID cards and driving licences for the kids today, I'm afraid, but the landlady here never bothered with that sort of thing. Just so long as we didn't do anything out of order, she'd turn a blind eye."

Kenny took a mouthful of beer. "I got the impression that she's the mothering sort, wants to look after you."

"Dead right. Salt of the earth, as they say."

"So is this where Vic's band performs then?"

"Sometimes. If I remember rightly they have a live band here every Thursday, and *the Souls* are on two or three times a year. They have a kind of circuit they do, pubs around the area. They play once a week or so."

"Do you go to watch?"

"Are you having a laugh? No way. I find it embarrassing enough to think that my brother writes music for some no hope band without having to spend my leisure time following them from one smoky boozer to another. I'm not some sort of loser's groupie, I'll have you know."

"Some of these pub acts are pretty good. I know Vic wouldn't be involved in anything that was less than professional, so I reckon his band must be a cut above the average."

Erica sipped her drink. "They all say the band's good, but I really wouldn't know. Luke sometimes plays me what he's written, and I have to say, I always enjoy it, but then I would, wouldn't I?"

"Suppose so. Back in the early seventies, when I was savouring my first alcohol in the *Three Tuns,* there was a young singer by the name of David Robert Jones. Used to come up from Brixton with a backing band. He was pretty good."

"Can't say I've ever heard of him."

"Changed his name to David Bowie. I think he's done quite well for himself."

"Now you're teasing me," Erica's smile lingered. "Even I've heard of him."

"There you are. Sorry if I'm late." Erica looked up, to find Joanne standing at her shoulder.

"We were beginning to think you'd forgotten. Pull up a chair."

Joanne hovered helplessly for a moment, until Kenny stood up and found her a chair from the next table. She sat, purring her gratitude and making firm eye contact. Kenny looked away, but Joanne still maintained her glare as she spoke to Erica.

"Who's your friend?" she asked silkily. "I didn't realise we were expected to bring partners."

Erica smiled, the look of someone who has seen this particular pantomime many times before. "Joanne, this Kenny, Kenny English. Kenny, this is my friend Joanne."

Joanne sat with her mouth open for a second, completely blindsided by Erica's mundane tone; a suggestion that she spent all her Saturday evenings socialising with the rich and famous. Quickly she recovered her composure. "Oh, right," she said, finally, giving Kenny's outstretched hand the most desultory of shakes and dragging her eyes back to Erica. "So where's Luke."

"Luke's still at work. Seems he's come over all conscientious and decided to work the bank holiday weekend."

Now Joanne was staring at Erica, who in turn gave Kenny a knowing look. Finally, it dawned on Joanne that she was being taken for a ride.

"All right you two," she said good-naturedly. "Enough of this messing about. What's really going on?"

Kenny stood. "Why don't I go and get us all a drink, while you fill your friend in on what we've been up to all day? What can I get you?"

"White wine, please, dry." Joanne turned the full force of her charm back onto Kenny, who deflected it by turning to Erica. "Same again?" he asked, and when she nodded, he disappeared to the bar.

As he stood at the bar waiting to be served, Kenny took the opportunity to observe the two girls. They were so similar in some ways and so different in others. The clothes for example were almost a uniform: jeans and tee shirt under denim jackets though whilst clearly Joanne's were carefully chosen and in all probability carried designer labels, Erica's had that lived in look, suggesting a more modest wardrobe budget.

The landlady swanned over, and he ordered drinks. Looking back at the girls, he could see them in close conversation, heads bent together over the table in a form of intimacy that could only be bred of long-standing. They were obviously the same age, even a disinterested bystander would have taken them for school friends, but whereas Joanne displayed a worldliness, a sophistication beyond her years, Erica looked shy, childlike, vulnerable. The drinks arrived and Kenny ordered a couple of bags of crisps, which he held in his mouth as he balanced the three drinks in his hands and negotiated his way back to the table. The girls hardly paid him any attention as he distributed the glasses, and he sat quietly, munching crisps, careful not to interrupt.

Erica had apparently decided to take it from the top. She got to the part about Luke's meeting with Kenny, and Joanne turned to him, her look now appraising, interested. It was as if he had finally been confirmed as a celebrity, a famous name sitting at the same table: something to tell the girls about in the office on Monday. Once again there was the lingering eye contact. Kenny ignored it, and Erica went on with her story.

Kenny sipped his beer, only half listening to the story as he watched the comings and goings around him. The pub was filling up steadily, the usual Saturday night crowd, he assumed. In the corner, a group of youths were watching a live football game, cheering and gesticulating from time to time, nudging each other and joking, but quietly, to themselves, so as not to disturb the other customers. A young girl had joined the landlady behind the bar, and Kenny could see a fat balding man from time to time appearing from the back room, changing barrels or replenishing the supplies of crisps and nuts. Most of the clientele, the boys by the TV excepted, seemed to be old, at least Kenny's age, many older, possibly including his own contemporaries from school, maybe even some teachers.

"Oh my days," Joanne exclaimed. Erica's story had reached the point at which they realized that Luke was trapped in the vault. Joanne had her hand over her mouth in shock. Now she placed it on Erica's hand, which was resting on the table. Erica looked stoical, and went on with the story. Kenny turned back to watching The Billy's clientele enjoying their weekly entertainment. A young boy, possibly the landlady's son or more likely grandson, wandered over with a pint pot and a book of raffle tickets. Kenny bought a strip, and then as the boy hovered over the two girls, he bought two more. Smiling shyly, the boy moved on to the next table.

Kenny finished his pint and noticed that he had also eaten both bags of crisps. The girls were too involved in their conversation to notice, and since their glasses were both more or less empty, he made another trip to the bar. He ordered an identical round of drinks, this time substituting a bag of pork scratchings and some dry roasted nuts for the crisps.

Back at the table, Erica was relating the episode at the Police Station with a passable impersonation of the station sergeant, much to Joanne's amusement. Kenny sipped, and waited patiently for the story to end. At that moment, Erica's mobile rang.

"Excuse me," she said taking the phone out of her handbag and checking the display. "It's Simon," and she clicked on. Erica put one finger in her ear and turned her head away from the general din in the pub, but still she couldn't seem to hear.

"I'll have to take this outside," she said. "You two just talk amongst yourselves."

Kenny and Joanne sat staring at each other for a few seconds, before Joanne spoke. "So how did you come to be a famous songwriter then?"

Kenny smiled. "Not so hard as it sounds, actually," he said. "Back in the early seventies things were a lot more, shall we say, fluid than they are now. There were lots of opportunities in the industry, always people on the look out for something new. I suppose I just got lucky."

"Didn't you ever want to be a performer though, you know, singer songwriter, that sort of thing? There were plenty that did, or so I've heard."

Kenny sipped and thought for a moment. "I don't think it ever appealed to me. I was always more interested in writing. Can't honestly see me getting up in front of thousands of screaming fans and strutting my stuff; bit on the shy side I suppose. To tell the truth, I can't sing."

Joanne giggled, her eyes laughing over the rim of her wine glass. "So what's so interesting about writing? I always thought people bought records for the music, not the words."

"It's an intriguing conundrum. I guess it's fair to say that it's the music that attracts in the first place, but the lyrics, if they're any good, will retain the attention for longer. People often quote lyrics to me, things that they have remembered for decades and which they say have stayed with them in some way; you know, either they're particularly meaningful or they remind you of a certain time and place. I think that on balance people can recall the words more readily than the music."

Joanne thought for a moment. "So you're a words person first and foremost."

"It's a personal thing. I've always been into words, you know, books and poetry, that sort of thing."

"Really?"

"Yes, must come from being an only child; no one to play with at home, so I tended to lose myself in books. These days I might have got into computer games or some such, but back in the sixties it was either books or television, and my parents didn't hold with the box, so it had to be books."

"Only child, eh?" Joanne was toying with her glass. "Sounds rather lonely."

"It was alright, it was all I knew. My parents were older than most when I was born. I think I was a bit of a surprise, to tell the truth. Whatever, there was never likely to be a sibling, so I just got on with things. In some ways I suppose I was spoilt, had more of my parents' time than your average child."

"What about school friends, don't tell me you didn't go to school."

"Of course I went to school. But to be honest, I was a bit of a misfit. I wasn't bullied or anything like that, I was just ignored. I was never any cop at sport, and the only subject I was good at was English, but I guess I was always big for my age so the bullies tended to leave me alone. I don't think anyone really noticed me until the sixth form. That's when I started to come out of myself."

"Tell me more." Joanne's tone suggested that she sensed a scandal.

"Nothing really, but I noticed that I had a knack for putting words into verse. I could take an ordinary conversation and work it into a rhyme. I started doing it one day in a biology lesson. Can't remember what the teacher said now, but I do recall that in my head I heard it as a poem, just by turning the words around. So I said it out loud and everyone laughed."

"Even the teacher?"

"Funnily enough, yes. Once he'd got over the shock of yours truly making a contribution in class, he thought it might be a useful way of remembering things, so he encouraged me. Word must have got round, because before I knew it all my other teachers were demanding something similar. I became like the unofficial school poet laureate, contributing to assemblies, school magazine, even sports day. Overnight I became a minor celebrity."

"So from there it was a short hop to stardom," Joanne drained her glass and put it down on the table.

"More or less. There was a band in the year above me at school, and they somehow got a recording contract when they left, when I was in the upper sixth. They needed a song and asked me to help. Easiest day's work I ever did, to be honest. The song was a minor hit, and whilst the band lapsed into obscurity, I carried on. All it took was a couple of commissions, and suddenly I was famous."

"Sounds really exciting."

"I guess it was when I tell it like that, but when it happens to you, it's just the way it is. Nothing special."

Erica pushed her way through the throng around the table and sat back down. She put the phone in her bag and looked up expectantly.

"So what's the news?" asked Kenny.

Erica took a deep breath, as if collecting her thoughts. "Like I said, that was Simon. He's been talking with Luke."

"I thought he said the phone wouldn't work." Kenny was frowning, trying to concentrate through the combined effects of the background noise and several pints of lager.

"He did. Apparently they've been talking over the internet."

"You can do that?"

"I do it all the time," interrupted Joanne. "I've got a mate in Canada. We talk for hours and it's all free. Lots better than phoning; you can even see each other if you've got the right kit."

"Well I never. So what has Luke got to say?"

"Well, that's the disappointing thing, nothing much. Seems they chatted for half an hour or so about the nature of accidents and how he doesn't hold Simon to blame." Erica stopped for a moment, trying to recall exactly what had been said. "He's not panicking or anything and he's quite safe. Apparently he was more worried about me than he was about himself, which is Luke all over. Obviously he can't get out and he's glad that we're making some sort of an effort on his behalf, but he didn't have any ideas."

Kenny rubbed his chin. "Did Simon have anything to offer? Has he remembered anything about this Dalton character that might help us out?"

"No, nothing about Dalton, but he did suggest that if we couldn't get hold of him we might try getting in touch with the bank's owners."

"Who are?"

Erica sighed and sipped from her glass. "That's the problem, he doesn't know. It's some big corporation or other, but Simon can't remember which. It appears that the company has changed hands from time to time, and whoever the parent is doesn't seem to take much of an interest in what goes on."

"I could find out," said Joanne. Kenny and Erica turned to her.

"You could?" said Erica.

Joanne looked haughty. "Easy peasy. You're forgetting that I work in corporate finance. In the office we've got a direct link to Companies House, you know, a register of all the companies in the UK. Tells you what they do, how much they are worth and, if they are privately owned, who owns them. Might even get a phone number if you are lucky. We've even got access to most European countries and the US."

"Really?" Kenny sounded impressed.

"Joanne's a high flying city lawyer, or didn't I mention that," Erica added. "There's not much she doesn't know about business."

"Get out of it. I'm no more than a glorified secretary. Most of the time those lawyers talk in language that I can't even begin to understand. But while I may not know much about business, I do know where to look if I need to find something out." She reached into her handbag and took out a pda.

"But it's the weekend, surely the office is shut." Erica tried to control her enthusiasm at this new opportunity.

"Are you mad? Time is money, or don't they teach you that at university? Tomorrow is just another day in the office to a lot of the guys that I work with. Most of them would have been in work today, and they often carry on over the weekend so tomorrow will be no different. Our office is manned twenty four seven, and all I need is my security pass and I can be at my desk any time you like." She sprung the stylus from its port on the palmtop and switched to notebook. "You give me the name of the company, and I can let you know who owns it before lunch tomorrow. Fire away."

Erica shrugged. "The bank is called Rousseau Frères, but I don't know if it's limited or anything. "

Joanne put the stylus away without using it, switched off the machine and sat looking smug. "Why on earth didn't you say that before?" she asked. "I don't even have to look that one up. Rousseau Frères is owned by Consolidated Capital."

"Are you sure?" asked Erica, bemused "How do you know?"

"About six months ago we were asked to help in selling it, that's how." Joanne was now beaming like the cat that got the cream. "Consolidated Capital is owned and run by Lord Winsloe. It's massive, fingers in every pie. You must remember a couple of months ago they made a bid for that cable TV company, caused quite a stir." Erica nodded vaguely. "Oh come on, don't you read the papers? Had to be referred to the Competition Commission because of all his other media interests. He's got a real reputation as a nasty piece of work."

"I've heard of him," said Kenny quietly.

"Well whatever, seems his lordship had decided to rationalise his portfolio, get rid of the dead wood, wanted us to help him find a buyer. Anyway, to cut a long story short, we fished about for a bit, contacted the usual suspects, as you do, and then the old goat decides he doesn't want to sell after all. Pulled out and walked away. I tell you my boss was well pissed off on account of he had agreed a success fee. He was convinced the old boy would do a deal, so he waived the usual time based alternative and went for a percentage instead. Left us with nearly four weeks work for nothing. Cost me half my Christmas bonus it did. I'm not likely to forget Lord Winsloe in a hurry."

Erica looked impressed and optimistic for a few moments but then her face dropped. "We still don't know how to get in touch with this lord person. He might not even live in this country, for all we know."

"I can help you there." This time it was Kenny's turn to look smug.

"You can?" Erica still looked doubtful, prepared for further disappointment.

"I can, because I know exactly where Lord Winsloe lives. He's my next door neighbour."

"He lives in London?" Erica asked.

"Not exactly. I have a little place out in Surrey. His lordship's estate is the next one to mine. Can't say that we are exactly the best of friends, but I do know where to find him. I've also heard that he never leaves his country seat these days, bit of a recluse apparently, so if we go down there tomorrow, there's a good chance we'll find him at home."

"Let's go now," Erica half rose from her seat, knocking into the table and slopping beer onto the varnished top. She sat straight back down again and fished into her handbag for a tissue to mop up the mess.

"It's a bit late for house calls," said Kenny, looking at his watch. It was a quarter to eleven. "His lordship's no spring chicken, must be well into his seventies, so by rights he'll be tucked up in bed by now. Anyway, I've had rather too many of these to drive tonight, so I think the morning would be a better bet."

Erica thought for a moment. "You're right," she said, "no point frightening the life out of the old geezer, specially if we want a favour. Tomorrow will have to do."

"What say I pick you up at ten? It will only take us an hour or so from here. We can be there and back by lunch with a bit of luck."

"Sounds good. Do you want to join us, Joanne?"

Joanne thought for a moment. "Ten on a Sunday might be a bit early for me. I need my beauty sleep," again she looked at Kenny. "Let me know how you get on."

Chapter 9

Eaton Row is little more than an alley, a blind turning that runs along the back of Grosvenor Gardens. There's a pavement along one side, and just enough room to park a car. Unlike the surrounding streets, there are no fine porticos here, merely the back doors of the buildings which front the streets on either side, the servants' and tradesmen's entrances from when the buildings were private residences.

The quiet suited him perfectly. There were few passers by, rarely any traffic and he could sit and think. He looked at the list of words, the first six deleted along with the longer efforts. He chose two at random, using combinations of letters and numbers. Each time he pressed Enter he jumped a little, and each time he immediately got the same negative response.

Before the third attempt he paused even longer, aware that this would be his last chance tonight. He rubbed his hands together as if the sweat was preventing him from coming up with the right word. He muttered under his breath, possibly a curse, maybe a prayer; it was impossible to tell, and in all likelihood he himself was unsure of the nature of the imprecation. He stared at the screen, willing it to change, but once again the system locked him out.

He slammed the lid of the machine, scattering the empty coffee cups and burger boxes that littered the passenger seat. He started the engine but then had to wipe tears from his eyes before he could drive.

"I'll get you," he said clearly through gritted teeth, "I'll fucking get you."

And then he was gone.

Chapter 10

Luke sat at the computer, staring at the messenger screen. It was clear that Simon had not yet logged on. He thought for a moment, and then typed a message.

```
Sorry to see you're not up yet, I suppose it
was a bit much to expect you to be on line at
half past six on a Sunday morning. When you get
this message feel free to chat, I don't plan to
go anywhere today.
```

He clicked *Send* and sat swinging aimlessly in the desk chair, looking around at his little cell. The sofa showed clear signs of the fitful night he'd spent tossing and turning on it, and his jacket lay crumpled on the floor. He ran a hand over his stubbled chin and sniffed, wrinkling his nose as he inhaled his own body odour. For something to do he started exploring the various drawers in the desk.

In amongst an assortment of paperclips and drawing pins, he found a broken calculator, a couple of biros and a pad of A4 paper.

Ruling 3, it said on the front cover, *Single lines 8mm apart with margin.* Luke rubbed his chin again and opened the pad. The first page was littered with scribbles from some long forgotten calculation, numbers written apparently at random, some crossed out, the final answer underlined, but the rest of the pad was empty, virgin territory.

Folding the pad open at a blank page Luke drew a vertical line linking the first five horizontal lines, along the left hand margin and then tried a treble clef, starting on the fourth line, curling up and then down in a rough circle before shooting up and above the first line, forming an anticlockwise loop back on itself and finishing below the fifth line with a curly tail. He completed it with dots either side of the fourth line and then held it up for consideration.

"Blast," he muttered, shaking his head, "too big."

to dress, and before long he was heading for the kitchen, guided by the smell of toast and fresh coffee. Maureen was sitting at the kitchen table, browsing over a cookery book and apparently making a shopping list of ingredients.

"Vic at work already?" Kenny asked. "I didn't realise he opened the shop on a Sunday."

"He was up hours ago. Gone to recycle the rubbish, and then there's some things to collect from the electricians. He's got his chores to do even on his day off, you know." There was a slight edge to Maureen's voice but Kenny chose to ignore it.

"Mind if I help myself to coffee?" he enquired, trying to be polite, sensing the atmosphere in the room.

"It'll only go to waste if you don't. There's some toast there as well."

Kenny poured coffee into a mug and buttered some cold toast. He sat down at the table. "We had a bit of a break last night," he said. Maureen only half looked up from her list. Kenny persisted. "Yes, could be quite a break. We worked out who owns the bank, and we know where he lives. With a bit of luck and a following wind, we could get Luke out today, if this bloke tells us where to find the right person."

Maureen seemed engrossed in her cookery book, and studiously ignored him.

Finally Kenny could stand the silence no longer. "Thanks for putting me up last night, I hope I haven't been a nuisance," he began.

"You've been no trouble, no trouble at all." Maureen's answer was just too quick, too pat. Kenny said nothing, waiting for the punch line. After a long pause it came. "Don't take this personally or anything," Maureen began, closing the cookery book with an air of finality. Kenny braced himself. "It's not you, it's Vic." Maureen seemed to be wrestling with the words, trying to find the right assortment of expressions to make her point. Finally, she just blurted it out.

"I don't want you coming round here any more. It's not fair on Vic. It gets him confused." Kenny stared blankly, not understanding.

"Gets him confused about what?" was all he could manage.

"Gets him confused about his life, that's what. You forget that Vic chose a new way of life when he gave up the music business. He put all that behind him, the wild life, the drugs, all that sort of thing. He's happy, we're happy. But we both know that if I hadn't wandered into his life, Vic would be dead by now. He couldn't handle it, the fame, the money, the success. Went to his head, didn't it? All but killed him."

Kenny raised a hand to interrupt, to protest, but Maureen was in full spate, and his attempted interjection only seemed to spur her on.

"When I met Vic, he was a wreck, barely human. I picked him up, dried him out and took him home. That's the way it is with us. Now we've got a new life, but the past is always lingering there in the shadows, waiting to pounce. Somewhere in the back of his mind Vic still wonders what it might have been like if he had carried on, if he'd gone back to the business. We get by all right, what with the shop and the occasional royalty cheque, but I can see it in his eyes when he hears a record or someone from the past is interviewed on the radio. He harks back to the good old days and wonders how things could have been." Maureen paused and Kenny took the opportunity to speak.

"How can that be, Maureen? The good old days nearly killed him, didn't they? What you've got here is worth more than money in the bank, it's more valuable than fast cars and expensive hotels. What you two have is happiness, and it may be an old cliché, but money can't buy it. Vic must be mad to imagine giving this up."

"That's easy to say when you have all the trappings of success. Believe me, Vic looks at you and sees glamour. He looks at you and sees all the things he could have been. Trust me, Kenny. You being round here is no good for Vic and me. I'm asking you to go away and not come back. Just let us be."

Kenny thought for a moment. He looked embarrassed and saddened, guilty. "I only came here by coincidence in the first place," he said, making an effort to explain himself. "I didn't mean to make things difficult for either of you."

"Like I said, it's not personal, Kenny. I know you meant no harm. I don't think you're a bad person, but for Vic and me, what you stand for is like a poison. We had our first row for years last night, and all because he started a sentence 'Just imagine if…'. I don't want to 'imagine if'. I'm happy with our life here, and I don't want it spoiled. What you don't understand is that the old life didn't include me. I came after. I'm the one who picked up the pieces. All I saw was the damage that too much money, too much fame and too much time on your hands can do to a person. I don't want to see that again, and I don't want you here putting thoughts into my Vic's head."

Kenny finished his coffee in silence and stood to leave. He paused. Maureen looked up at him.

"Yes?" she said.

"I was just going to say, see you, but I guess that's not what you want to hear is it? Be lucky, Maureen. Look after Vic. I won't bother you again."

Without waiting for a reply, Kenny turned and left the room. He picked up his coat and walked slowly, a little sadly, down the stairs.

At the street door he stopped, getting his bearings. He dithered for a few seconds, as if expecting Vic to show up, but eventually he shrugged his coat on, and in so doing shrugged off all feelings of guilt. "Let them get on with their lives," he muttered to himself. "Time to get on with mine."

The streets were still wet from last night's rain, but a plucky spring sun was making a valiant effort at drying things out. The pavement shimmered slightly, as Kenny retraced his steps to the side turning where he had parked his car. Miraculously, it was still their, ticketless and apparently with all its features still intact. Kenny drove the now familiar few yards to Erica's house.

The door opened as soon as he pressed the bell. Clearly Erica had been waiting for him.

"What time do you call this?" she asked by way of introduction. "I thought we agreed ten o'clock. It's bloody nearly afternoon."

Kenny half lifted his arm to check his watch, about to argue that he was only a few minutes late, that she was exaggerating, but he instinctively realised that this was no time for pedantry.

"I'm sorry," he said limply, and then added by way of mitigation, "I was held up talking to Maureen. There were a couple of things we had to sort out."

Erica shrugged helplessly, deflated by Kenny's abject surrender.

"Well, we'd better be on our way then and not waste any more time. Where is it we're going anyway?"

"Farnham. It's in Surrey. Near Aldershot." Kenny spoke over his shoulder as he unlocked the car.

If Erica was impressed by their mode of transport, she didn't show it. She opened the passenger door and climbed in as if she was chauffeured around in an Aston Martin every day of the week. As Kenny sat behind the wheel, she made herself comfortable, dropping a small sling bag onto the floor behind her seat and buckling her belt. "How long will it take?"

"Depends on the traffic." Kenny started the engine and pulled away from the pavement. "An hour probably, maybe an hour and a half. Should be there by twelve."

They drove in silence, Kenny making a conscious effort to relax. As the road became a dual carriageway, punctuated by the occasional roundabout, he seemed to be enjoying the sheer pleasure of driving. The sun was shining, the hedgerows were in bud, he was in control of a superb piece of engineering. He turned onto the M25 and accelerated effortlessly to seventy, a smile coming to his face as his temper changed as smoothly as the automatic gearbox.

"You could at least talk to me, you know." Kenny was shaken back to reality. Erica had been so quiet that he could almost have forgotten she was there. He glanced across at her briefly, to see her looking straight at him. "I'm sorry?" he said.

"That's the second time you've said that this morning, and I'm still not sure what you're sorry about. All I want is a bit of conversation. Is that too much to ask?" It appeared that if Erica was prepared to forgive him for being a few minutes late, she had decided that he should pay for his lapse by providing her with entertainment.

"You could put the radio on, if you like." Kenny offered.

"I don't want the radio thank you. I want a bit of human interaction. I want you to talk to me." She folded her arms resolutely.

Kenny couldn't fail to notice a touch of humour in her voice, a slightly girlish teasing, as if she were winding him up, being unreasonable on purpose, but the expression on her face was deadpan and gave nothing away about her inner emotions.

"It's not that easy you know, making conversation." Kenny tried to keep it light, playing along, but at the same time playing for time, desperately trying to think of something appropriate to say.

"Thought you were a writer, thought that sort of thing came easily to you. Isn't language your speciality? Surely words are the tools of your trade. I'm sure you could make a very interesting conversation if you chose to." Again the teasing tone, almost flirting. Kenny suppressed a smile.

"Well, I suppose we are having a conversation now, aren't we?"

"That doesn't count, and you know it. You can't call a conversation about having a conversation a conversation." Erica paused for a moment, mentally rewinding that last sentence to make sure she had said what she meant to. "Yes that's right, isn't it? Talking about a conversation isn't the same as having one. And I think that it's down to you to come up with a topic that we can sit here and discuss like educated human beings, so there." Kenny looked across and caught the smile. Just for a moment the atmosphere in the car warmed appreciably, and then the look was deadpan again. Kenny assumed a look of deep thought, as if trying to find the inspiration to come up with something really profound.

"What star sign are you?"

"Is that the best you can do? What bloody star sign are you? God help you if that's your number one chat up line. Come off it, I'm sure you can do better if you try hard."

Again the hint of a smile, and then it was gone.

"No really, what sign are you?"

It was Erica's turn to pause. "Don't know," she admitted at length. "Never bothered to find out."

"Really. You must be the only person on the planet who doesn't know their star sign. Didn't you know, it's one of the great paradoxes of our time? No one in their right mind believes their horoscope, but everyone knows their star sign. So you are trying to tell me that you have never read your horoscope."

"Well, if I don't know my star sign, it sort of follows, doesn't it?"

"So when's your birthday?"

"April fourth, so if you were planning to buy me a present, you're too late."

Kenny frowned. "How old are you?"

"Didn't they teach you never to ask a lady her age?"

"I thought that only applied to ladies of a certain age. And anyway, I wasn't sure that you were a lady."

"Ouch! What did I do to deserve that? I am every bit a lady, I'll have you know. But since you ask, I'm twenty-one. Luke made us a special dinner to celebrate."

Kenny looked at her for just a little too long and had to brake sharply to avoid running into the car in front. He recovered control and spoke again. "Really, I guess that explains the name."

"What?"

"Erica. If you're twenty one this year it means that you were born in 1984."

"Correct."

"Which is the name of a famous book."

"Written by George Orwell. I know, I read it."

"Whose real name was?"

"Eric Blair. So you reckon that my parents named me after the author of a book just because I was born in the year in the title. Sounds a bit far fetched to me."

"Not just the year. The day. April fourth is the day that 1984 opens. It's the first date that Winston Smith puts in his diary. You were born on the day that the story starts. Still far fetched?"

"Maybe not. I'm reliably informed that both my parents were well into books. Sounds like the sort of thing that might've amused them."

"I'll tell you something else amusing. The fourth of April 1984 was a cold crisp day: bright sunshine but a heavy frost. The pavements were still white at lunchtime."

"So?"

"The opening lines of 1984 read: *It was a cold crisp day in April and the clocks were striking thirteen.* Orwell's vision of a future totalitarian dystopia may have been some way wide of the mark, but his weather forecast was perfect."

This time Erica laughed out loud. The sound filled the car, a rather masculine laugh but a natural sign of genuine pleasure, the sort of sound that you can only make when you are truly relaxed and comfortable in yourself and with your company.

"You are potty."

"It's true."

"I don't care if it's true," Erica wiped a finger under her eye as if brushing away a tear. "What is really potty is that you can remember what the weather was like over twenty years ago."

"Ah, that's because that day was a very special one, special to me, anyway. It was the day of my first divorce, and you tend to remember days like that. I can remember the weather. I can remember what I was wearing, dark blue pinstripe, since you ask. I can even remember what I had for lunch."

"Go on, impress me."

"A magnum of Bollinger followed up by a bottle of single malt."

"Aren't you the health freak? And did you do all this drinking on your own?"

"Couple of mates helped me with the scotch, but the Bolly was all my own work. We ended up crashing at someone's flat in Soho, and then went on a four day bender, none of which I remember at all. Come to think of it, I don't recall seeing the mates again either. Reckon they just buggered off when the money ran out."

"Some mates."

"Well, it was all my own fault as usual. Never have been much of a one for choosing my friends. Never been much of a one for picking the ladies either." Kenny paused long enough to notice that Erica was giving him a strange look. "Present company excepted of course."

"Of course, not that you chose me as a friend exactly, no more than I chose you." Erica stared forward out of the windscreen as Kenny made a left onto the A3. They lapsed into silence as they sped along the Guildford bypass until Erica spoke again.

"Hang on," she began a little too loudly, making Kenny jump. "Hang on," she repeated more quietly, "did you just say your first divorce? How many have you had?"

"That's rather a personal question isn't it?"

"Please yourself. I was only being polite."

Kenny sighed inwardly. "If you must know, I've had three."

"Three? You're dead right about not being able to choose your friends. You must be going for some sort of record."

"Yes, well we all make mistakes. I suppose I just took longer than most to realise the error of my ways. You can rest assured, it won't happen again. Marriage and I are no longer on speaking terms, as you might say. The way I feel at the moment, if you asked me to take a vow of chastity, I would do it without a second thought."

Erica went quiet again, unsure as to what to say next, concerned that she had hurt Kenny's feelings.

"Where are we anyway?" She said at length, looking out of the window at the seemingly endless rows of skeletal hedges, which permitted occasional glimpses of the brown fields beyond. "How can anyone live all the way out here? Where are the shops?"

"Bit of a townie, are we? Lost without our concrete and asphalt fix?"

"Yeah, something like that. Give me roads and pavements any day. You know where you are with a good dollop of inner city blight. All this countryside looks the same to me. You sure you know where we are?"

"Don't worry, we're here."

Kenny slowed the car and pulled over to the centre of the road, indicating right.

He turned the car into a narrow country lane and then sharply up a hill to the left. For a moment they seemed to be pointing straight at the sky, until the lane levelled out and they turned around a small copse of trees, gaunt in their spring nakedness. The road ahead meandered between tall hedgerows, and after a couple of hundred yards they turned left again into a drive blocked by a five bar gate. Kenny stopped and slipped the car into neutral.

"This is it," he said. He climbed out and opened the gate. Without comment he got back in the car, drove through and then repeated the process, making sure that the gate was secure. The road followed a short rise and a right turn over the brow of a hill. As they completed the turn, the sun burst through the thin cloud cover, lighting the view into the valley beyond, adding a sudden splash of colour to the drab scenery and highlighting the large house in the middle distance.

"Welcome to my home from home," Kenny remarked, as he manoeuvred the car slowly over the rutted track, making every effort not to snag the Aston's undercarriage on the regular outcrops of rocks and weeds. There was a note of self deprecation in Kenny's voice, but it was a few moments before Erica understood why.

From a distance the house looked impressive. Built on three floors in red brick with a pitched roof of dark grey slate, Erica counted six chimney stacks along the ridge of the roof, and some twelve tall windows set in the upper floor. The architects had clearly chosen the position carefully to provide the best setting, framing the mansion against the backdrop of a low wooded slope, and providing the residents with uninterrupted views over the rolling Surrey countryside; even a born and bred city dweller could appreciate that in high summer the picture would look utterly stunning.

As they neared the house, however, the irony became clear. The first thing Erica could see was the boards at the windows. Not all of them, just here and there like rotting teeth. Closer and she could see the missing tiles on the roof, gaping holes in places, and the areas of damp on the walls where the pointing had given way and the rain leaked in. Finally, as Kenny pulled the car into a small courtyard near the main entrance, Erica could clearly make out the peeling paintwork on the doors and window frames, the grass sprouting from the gutters and the fallen plasterwork that littered the area.

Chapter 11

Luke scribbled a few more notes onto a piece of his homemade manuscript paper, then stuck the pen behind his right ear. Reading from the score, he whistled a tune, stopped and then whistled the first line of the harmony. Frowning slightly, he changed a couple of notes on the sheets, and then repeated the whistling process, trying to ignore the rumbling accompaniment coming from his stomach. He nodded to himself, smiled and retrieved the pen.

Luke seemed lost in his own world, concentrating on his work, pausing every so often to check what he had written, sometimes whistling, occasionally singing, often laying his hands on the desktop and playing his imaginary keyboard. When the computer chirruped to tell him that Simon was back on line, he jumped and looked at his watch.

"Blimey, it's after one," he said, as Simon's image appeared in the window on his computer monitor. "Don't know where the time's gone. How's Jeanette?"

"She's fine. They're both fine, thanks. She sent me home to get some things for her, so I've only got a few minutes, I'm afraid. She's making demands already, so you can tell she's on the mend."

Luke grinned. "Sounds like Jeanette."

"So what have you been up to?"

"I've been writing music. Helps to keep my mind off things, you know, like how hungry I am."

"Suppose it's just as well you've got a good supply of water. People go without food for weeks on end, but you'd be really up against it if you didn't have something to drink."

"Tell me about it. I've been thinking that things could be a lot worse. At least this way, maybe I can lose those difficult couple of pounds. Don't suppose you've heard from Erica since we last spoke."

"Sorry. You have to switch your phone off in the hospital. Hang on a sec. I'll see if she's left a message." Si fiddled with his mobile for a moment. "No, nothing. I guess she's still on the look out for the big boss or whatever. No doubt she'll be in touch when there's something to say. Tell you what, why don't you break into a couple of safety deposit boxes while you're down there, see if they've got anything in there worth having? You never know, someone may have deposited a bar of chocolate or something."

"Don't imagine I haven't thought about that. I've got my swipe card, and I can get into the system to check on the individual codes. Would be easy as pie to open most of the boxes down here, but where would it get me?"

Simon thought for a moment. "Pile of title documents, I suppose," he said glumly. "There's nothing in those boxes of any real value, not in itself, just lots of pieces of paper."

"Not so long ago there would have been the occasional tiara or box of cash, but even that's not there anymore, and if it was it wouldn't do me much good."

"All in the inner vault now, I suppose," Simon nodded in agreement. "All part of the latest master plan. What was it Mickey was going on about at the staff meeting last month?"

Luke thought for a moment. "Something about attracting a new type of customer, friends of the chairman or whatever. Put all the valuables in the inner vault, more a question of appearances than security, make it look impressive."

"That why it's got that bloody great combination lock on the door? That why you have to open it manually instead of through the system?"

"Something along those lines. Mind you, they must have spent a small fortune on the conversion."

"King's ransom, if the mess they made was anything to go by. That's why they had to recarpet. And have we seen any new business?"

"No, not a whisper. Waste of time, just like every other pie Dalton gets his fingers in."

Luke could see Simon shaking his head on the screen. He looked at his watch again. "So am I right in thinking it's early Sunday afternoon?"

Simon looked at his wrist. "Yeah, that's right. I'm afraid you've missed your Saturday night for this weekend."

"That's no great loss, Erica and I aren't really into clubbing or the like. She sometimes gets invited to a party with her university mates, but I don't go. Not after the last time."

"Meaning?"

"Some prat thought I must be her dad and that was a laugh, but then some other prat decided I must be her sugar daddy. You know, older bloke younger bird sort of routine. Well he'd had a couple and started mouthing off about how disgusting it was, and how I probably had a wife and family at home and that. All rather embarrassing and totally unnecessary, but that's the way it is with some people, isn't it? Couple of drinks inside them and they come over all evangelical."

"So what do you normally do then?"

"Nothing much. Saturday evenings for the Marshall household tend to be nothing more than me cooking a nice meal for the two of us, bottle of wine and a video. I normally end up falling asleep before the video ends and wake up just in time for Match of the Day, which is Erica's cue to doze off; sort of built in complementary body clocks we've got. Must be much the same for households up and down the country."

"Sounds like Jeanette and me, except she's the cook."

"Yeah, well getting into cooking for me was a case of making a virtue out of a necessity. When the old folks popped their clogs, I had to learn fast, had to learn to look after myself and, as luck would have it, my little sister."

"You've never talked much about losing your parents."

Luke stopped, chewing his bottom lip, coming to a decision.

"I suppose it's something I've put to the back of my mind over the years," he said slowly as if unsure how far he wanted to go. "It was all rather traumatic. Burying your parents is something most of us have to do one day, I just had to do it a bit earlier. My mum and dad weren't exactly spring chickens, but they had a good few years left in them, and by rights I should have had plenty of time to get used to the idea that they wouldn't last forever. Not only that, but under normal circumstances you only lose one parent at a time; that way you're forewarned that the other one is nearing their sell by date, so that it's less of a shock when it happens."

"So that's when you started looking after Erica?"

Luke paused for a moment, thinking back. "Social services wanted her to go to an aunt and uncle, lived out in Dorset. As far as they were concerned, I was an adult and could fend for myself, but they made a big fuss and to do about Erica. To tell the truth I wasn't that bothered at first. She was that much younger than me that I'd hardly taken any notice of her really. But when I started thinking about her being brought up in the country, all those miles away, I sort of decided that she'd be better off at home."

"And the authorities agreed?"

"You are joking. They were outraged and tried to think up all sorts of alternatives, but that just made me more determined to make a go of it. I left school, and then got a job back there working in the library, so that I could earn some money and still have the holidays at home. The house was bought and paid for, so we didn't need that much to get by. Bit by bit, I must have demonstrated that I was sufficiently responsible to look after a four year old, because gradually the social workers lost interest. I suppose they had a lot on their plates, and we just became less of a problem. In the end, they left us alone, probably had bigger fish to fry.

"Mind you, it meant I had a lot of learning to do in a short time. Cleaning, washing, ironing, cooking; they were all new to me, but somehow I worked out what needed to be done. Cooking was the only area that I found really fulfilling. My mum was a good cook, in a safe undemanding sort of way, and I tried to follow in her footsteps. These days Erica takes the lead when it comes to the housework, but shopping and cooking are still my areas of responsibility, and though I say so myself, I have developed into a mean chef. Sod it, Simon! Why have you got me talking about food? Can we change the subject please?"

"Sorry. Erm, what do you think Kenny English does with his Saturday nights?"

"Partying and clubbing, no doubt. Probably the same every night."

"You reckon?"

"I reckon. Take it from me, the rich and famous lead a totally different life to the likes of you and me. I'd lay serious money that at this very moment Kenny English is half way between sleeping off last night's excesses and getting himself in shape for another evening's debauchery. Normal people work the week in order to play at the weekend. For Mr English and his ilk, every night's party night."

"Surely even Kenny English has to work some time."

"That's what I was thinking about earlier: how my day to day existence would change if I became a famous composer. The hours would be different for a start, and I have to say the thought of getting away from the drudge of the early morning commute does have its attractions. But the flip side of drudgery is the security of routine, knowing that you are doing the right thing simply because it's what you do every day and everybody else is doing it as well. Could I take the buzz of fame, I ask myself, the feeling that a writer must get when they see their efforts come to fruition? Kenny English must spend a lot of time working on songs that no one ever sings, or refining his creations over and over again to get just the right effect.

"There must be hours of frustration built into the creative process, seeing something that looked promising end up on the musical equivalent of the cutting room floor, not knowing whether you're wasting your time or not, never sure that you are making something happen until the whole process is over. The payback of course comes with the final production, seeing the record in the shops, hearing the music on the radio, seeing your name in lights. That has to be a hell of a feeling, but even then, could I cope with it? Would fame go to my head the way it went to Vic's? Would it destroy my life the way it so nearly did his?"

"There's only one way to find out."

"Yeah, but at what risk? Anyway, the way things stand, I'm not likely to find out. The chance has gone and maybe it is all for the best, maybe I am better off not being tempted. My life may be ordinary, but at least it's safe; at least you know where you are with predictability."

"Well your next few hours are predictable at least, unless Erica finds a way of releasing you that is. What are you going to do this afternoon, young sir?"

Luke pouted. "Could take the roller for a spin, or perhaps a round of golf. Thought I might go hang gliding if the weather holds, or perhaps I'll just sit here and play computer games."

"That sounds like fun. What did you have in mind?"

"I've taken rather a shine to Hearts, as it happens, a bit more demanding than Solitaire."

"That's the one like whist isn't it?"

"Correct. There's a certain symmetry to card games, I always find."

"How do you mean?"

"Well for a start, there are only four suits, and only thirteen cards in each suit, so that the playing area, as it were, is finite. Fifty two cards equals the number of weeks in a year, four the number of weeks in a lunar month and thirteen the number of lunar months in a year. The faces on the court cards are all different, and if I recall correctly, are all supposed to represent a real individual from history. I remember that the King of Diamonds is supposed to be Julius Caesar, but I forget the rest."

"There's a similar order in music, although instead of thirteen cards there are twelve notes."

"Hang on. I can't say I know much about music, but didn't I hear that it's made up of octaves? Surely that implies there are eight notes."

"Well you'd have thought so, wouldn't you, what with oct standing for eight? But I'm afraid that if you look closely, you will find that an octave actually contains twelve notes. Sure, from middle C to top C on the piano, you can play eight white notes, and you would be playing the major tonic scale, from doh to doh. Think of Julie Andrews in the sound of music, doh a deer and all that, and you will find that there are indeed eight."

"So I was right!"

"But that only works if you count the doh, or the C, twice. In reality the tonic scale only consists of seven notes, because the eighth is the first note of the next scale up. In the major version of the tonic scale, the notes are set out at intervals of tone, tone, semitone, tone, tone, tone, semitone. Since a semitone is half a tone, the total scale therefore covers six tones, or twelve semitones. Look at the keyboard of a piano and count the notes from middle C to the next B, the note before top C, including the black ones. You will find that there are twelve, one for each semitone."

Simon was starting to look bewildered, eyes moving from side to side as if trying to visualise what he had just been told. Finally it seemed to sink in. "If that's the major scale," he said, carefully, "what about the minor?"

"Since you ask, the minor scale is also a total of twelve semitones, but the steps are different, namely tone, semitone, tone, tone, semitone, tone and a half, semitone. This applies to any minor scale, no matter which note you start on. All that changes is the position of any sharps or flats, the black keys on the piano."

"I think I'm following."

"Now, I always think that Julie Andrews sold the von Trapp children short. Not only did she fail to teach them the minor scale, thus limiting the number of pieces that they could sing, but she only taught them the tonic names rather than the notes. Remember that bit in the song where she tells them that now they know the notes to sing, they can sing most everything? Well, apart from the abominable lyrics, what she doesn't tell them is that if they can't sing a particular song, probably because it's out of their range, they can soon put that right by transposing it. Move the note to the next one up or down and you have exactly the same piece of music but in another key, one that may be more suited to your vocal chords."

"So you can make any tune higher or lower just by starting on a different note? All that will change is the number of black notes you have to play?"

"You're not as green as you're cabbage looking, are you? That's the magic of music: its symmetry. Take any note that you care to mention, and you can construct its major or minor scale simply by following the formula, by applying the appropriate steps in terms of tone or semitone and locating the relevant note. The key of C is the simplest because it contains no sharps or flats, that is if you play in the major. In the minor on the other hand, you need to flatten the E and the A, and it is this latter flattening, the A, that leads to the unnaturally large leap of a tone and a half to the B that then completes the scale with a final semitone to the C which is the beginning of the next scale."

"If you say so, I'm starting to feel a little out of my depth."

"You don't need to follow the detail. All you need to realise is that it goes on, octave after octave, each octave symmetrically identical to the next and to the previous. It's just like counting. Think about it, numbers have their own symmetry as well. When you pass one hundred you just start all over again, except this time with the preface of a one. You can dream up the longest number ever, and know automatically what the next number is going to be if you add one to it, because it will follow the same rules as if you took all the numbers to the left away. Like numbers, music is an international notation. Give a piece of music to a Japanese musician, and he or she should produce the same sound as if you gave that piece to a Russian or Brazilian."

"Doesn't music still have some words written on it?"

"You have been paying attention. OK, so the instructions are written in Italian, and you have to learn them sort of by rote, but that's splitting hairs. The musical notes themselves have a meaning to musicians which transcends language and which make sense to all musicians no matter what their mother tongue. If you can read music, you are in effect bilingual, because you can look at a sheet of dots and lines and hear what the writer intended you to hear. Communication without words. It's fascinating."

"Sounds it. But now, if you'll excuse me, I really must be getting back to Jeanette. She's waiting for a fresh nightie."

"One more thing before you go: music is better than numbers because it is a natural phenomenon."

"Go on then."

"The numerical system that we use is based on the number ten, apparently because we are born with ten fingers and ten toes, or so the story goes. However, there is no reason why we should use ten any more than we should use twelve or fourteen or eight. There just happen to be ten symbols that we use. Computers use number systems based on two, eight and sixteen, known as binary, octals and hexadecimals, and I seem to remember reading somewhere that the natural logarithm is thirteen point something, but now we are getting into rather rarefied atmosphere. The point is that the decimal system is the one we use because we find it convenient.

"The octave on the other hand is a fact of nature. Take a piece of string and pluck it. You will get a note. Halve the length of the string and pluck it, you will get the same note but one octave higher. Try it next time you see a guitar. Pluck any string and then put your finger half way along it and pluck again. If you have estimated half way accurately you will get the same note one octave higher. Now half the distance from your finger to the bridge and pluck again. Another octave up."

"Remind me to try it sometime, but now I really have to be going."

Luke grinned at his friend's image. "Give them both my love, then come back and talk to me again. Give me a chance, and I'll make a musician out of you."

"I can't wait."

Kenny stopped the car and switched off the engine, looking over at Erica for a reaction.

"What a dump," was all that Erica could manage, unable to hide the disappointment of finding that such a beautiful house was nothing more than a wreck, like a child who has been shown a delicious birthday cake, only to discover that it is made of cardboard. As they got out of the car, Kenny took a ring of keys from the glove box.

Erica found herself standing in a pool of wet gravel. She watched as Kenny found the correct key and opened a small door on the right edge of the house's front elevation. He indicated to her to join him. The door led into a small kitchen, complete with table and chairs, gas cooker and sink. Kenny tossed the keys on the table and idly flicked through the stack of mail he had retrieved from the doormat.

"Can't go through the front door," he said, putting down the letters. "It's still blocked with plaster from where the ceiling fell in. All due to the tiles missing from the roof, apparently."

"This place is freezing. Can't you put the heating on or something?"

"Not much point. The boiler gave up years ago, and most of the pipe work has rotted through, so we had to drain the system to stop it leaking everywhere and bringing even more ceilings down. You can have a look around if you want, but I wouldn't recommend it. Some of the floors are a bit iffy, and some rooms haven't got any floors at all. This used to be part of the servants' quarters and now it's the only part of the house that is even remotely habitable. There's a bedroom next door with a fan heater that works, and there's even a shower room, although the water tends to come out a light tan colour. I still come down here from time to time, when I want to be alone, but otherwise it's a bit of a white elephant, I'm afraid."

"What on earth possessed you to buy it in the first place?"

"Ah, that would be wife number two. She had this idea that we should live in the country, would be healthier for the children she planned us having together. I think she saw herself in full gymkhana kit, taking the young ones for hacks across the downs, then rubbing down the horses in our very own stables. That and a bit of lady of the manor. It wasn't quite so decrepit then, could have made a very nice family home if you're the sort that likes living in the middle of nowhere."

"So what went wrong?"

"She caught me in bed with the Estate Agent." Erica raised an eyebrow. "It's OK, she was a female Estate Agent."

"That's all right then."

"Anyway, caught *in flagrante*, end of marriage number two. It tends to be the way things go, I'm afraid."

Erica ignored the note of indulgence in Kenny's voice and quickly changed the subject. "How much is this pile of old brick worth?" She hugged her arms about her, as if to emphasise the cold.

"About two."

"Million?"

"That's what the last valuation said. I know what you mean. I find it hard to credit myself, but the local agent, and before you ask, I made sure this one was male, reckons that property in this area is in high demand. The scenario he painted went something like this: it's hard to find substantial houses in this area, so someone with more money than sense, and probably with a wife that wants to take the kids horse riding, would buy the wreck and then spend a million or so doing it up. Result: a country mansion that is worth upwards of five mill, and a good investment for the buyer."

"Be it ever so humble." Erica looked about her in mock admiration. "So why don't you sell?"

"Seems the estate agent's theory doesn't hold much water in practice. While there should be people clambering over themselves to get on the Surrey country mansion property ladder, it's taking time to find exactly the right combination of money, need and foresight. Most buyers are looking for something they could move into and then add to. As you can see the usable living accommodation here is somewhat limited."

"So it's all a matter of time?"

"Got it in one. It's been on the market for nearly a year now. We've had a few sniffs, serious ones too, and at the right sort of price, but nothing as yet you could hang your hat on."

"So in the meantime you are the proud owner of a complete dump in the middle of nowhere."

Kenny nodded. "That's about the sum total of it. Now come on, let's see if his lordship's at home."

Kenny let Erica out of the back door and turned to lock it. Erica moved across the courtyard to where the car was parked, assuming that they would drive to the neighbouring estate, but when she looked over her shoulder Kenny was strolling in the opposite direction, towards the back of the house. Cursing under her breath she broke into a trot to catch up.

"I take it we're walking," she said, as she drew abreast.

They followed a paved path that led to the back of the house, and came into a small garden, sheltered between the house and the rising land. For a few moments they walked in shadow. "There are sixteen acres attached to the house," Kenny began, as they emerged into the sunlight and started to climb, the land sloping upwards. "For some reason they built the house in this corner, rather than more centrally. That means that whilst it is a two mile trip by road to Lord Winsloe's front door, it is only a matter of yards round here until we get to his property."

At the top of the slope the land levelled out and they were confronted by a low wooden fence. "This side of the fence is me, the other side is him." Kenny led them to a stile set in the fence.

"There's a public right of way that runs across the two stretches of land. Technically there is nothing to stop ramblers from wandering around the side of my house and over this fence onto Lord Winsloe's estate. In practice, I can't remember anyone actually bothering. What it means, though, is that we can take this short cut without fear of accusations of trespass."

"If he's your next door neighbour, how come he would object to you coming to see him? Where I come from we try to get on with our neighbours, or do they do things differently out here in the sticks?"

"To tell the truth, I've never so much as met the bloke." They crossed the stile and continued down a winding path that led across open fields. The sun had cleared the sky of clouds by now and was shining brilliantly in a blameless blue sky. Kenny shrugged off his coat and hung it over his shoulder on the index finger of his left hand. "We may be neighbours, but it's not as if we bump into each other when we're hanging out the washing. I am looking forward to meeting him though. From what I hear, he's what you might call a colourful character."

"What, just because he's a peer of the realm? Can't say I find that a particularly attractive proposition. Ask me, they're a bunch of parasites."

"But this one is a bit different. When I bought the house, the previous owner told me all about his lordship." Kenny paused, as they took a short detour to avoid a particularly muddy area of track, caused by the recent rain. The silence of the countryside was punctuated by the cawing of crows from nearby trees.

"This place smells," said Erica, her nose wrinkling. "Sort of combination of rotting vegetation and drying mud. Give me Penge High Street any day. Even choking on traffic fumes would be better than this. So what's the story about his lordship?"

"Well, it's nothing special, just that he's not what you might call a royal as such, not exactly old school. He got his peerage for services to industry, then bought himself this estate to live the lifestyle, as it were. Seems he grew up in the East End and made a small fortune from selling second hand cars. There's all sorts of rumours about him being involved with, shall we say, the seamier side of life, you know, the criminal fraternity, but nothing's ever stuck. It's like he wants to prove he's legitimate."

The track took a left turn, and Erica found herself walking on tarmac.

"Seems he looks after his property rather better than you do."

Kenny grinned. "Well he can afford to, can't he? Worked his way up the corporate ladder, bought a business here, made a fortune there. Now he's chairman of Consolidated Capital, major shareholder. I guess that one way and another it is possible to buy a good reputation, but as I say, he does seem to have the odd skeleton in the cupboard."

"He sounds a delight I'm sure. And what else does he do, apart from investing his ill gottens in an outsized property in the middle of nowhere?"

"Buys jewellery, so I'm told."

"What, to decorate the equally undesirable Lady Winsloe."

Kenny paused for a moment. "No, I don't think so. I seem to recall that she passed away some years ago. I think the Winsloe diamonds are another attempt to buy respectability, establish a name as a collector."

"The Winsloe diamonds, eh? That does sound impressive. I suppose his property is like Fort Knox, twenty four hour security that kind of thing."

"Not so as you'd notice. I can't imagine he'd keep the diamonds out here. They're worth millions, by all accounts."

"Well, I have to say, Mr English, life is never dull when you're around."

Kenny grinned to himself at the shrouded compliment. "We're here to help your brother, if you remember. Lord Winsloe may be one of the country's more interesting individuals, but he must be pushing eighty by now. I think we can handle an octogenarian between us."

The road opened out onto a view of ploughed fields stretching to the horizon. In the middle distance they could see a group of trees, and as they watched the air above the trees seemed to explode in a cloud of red dust. Immediately after the explosion they heard the unmistakeable crack of gunfire.

"What the bloody hell is going on now?"

"With a bit of luck, that'll be his lordship. Seems we've come across him at play."

"At play? What sort of games does he get up to, for Christ's sake?"

"Clays," said Kenny bluntly. Erica continued to look bemused.

"Clay pigeons," Kenny explained. "I think you'll find that his lordship is engaged in a simple and harmless country pastime, clay pigeon shooting. Come on, there's nothing to worry about."

Erica continued to look doubtful, as Kenny strode on down the path. There was another explosion of dust, followed by a loud report and she hurried to catch up, as if to confirm that there is safety in numbers even if those numbers only amount to two. The explosion happened again, and Kenny nodded in appreciation.

"He's good," he said. "That's three out of three."

It took a couple of minutes to get close enough to the trees to make out the two figures, and in that time, three more clays went to meet their maker. By the time the seventh target was despatched, Erica could see that there were two old men, both wearing long overcoats and flat caps. One was carrying a double-barrelled shotgun, and the other was crouched over a strange metal contraption that seemed to be some sort of catapult. The one with the gun shouted, and the croucher pulled a lever which sent a disc flying into the air away from them. This time they heard the crack of the gun before the disc exploded.

The standing man turned towards them as they approached, and for a moment the gun was levelled at them. The man seemed to realise what he was doing and flicked a lever on the gun's side, breaking it in the middle so that the barrel pointed to the ground and the remaining cartridge was exposed clear of the hammers. A faint curl of smoke rose from the opening.

"What do you want? Don't you know this is private property?"

The man was a little over average height, thin and gaunt. The coat he was wearing spoke of quality, but must have been made for a man of considerably greater girth, hanging on him as it did, flapping in the slight breeze. The accent was unreconstructed east London.

"You must be Lord Winsloe," Kenny began, stepping forward, his right hand outstretched in greeting, apparently undeterred by the brusque welcome. "I'm Kenny English. I live on the next property. This is a friend of mine, Erica Marshall. We've come to ask a favour."

"I know who you are, Mr English," the thin man remarked with what could only be described as a sneer. He took a packet of cigarettes out of his coat pocket, lit one and inhaled hungrily without taking his eyes off Kenny. "Bit of a celebrity by all accounts, or so I hear."

"Not the only famous person around here, from what I've been told," Kenny replied, without missing a beat, "though in your case infamous might be a better word."

The thin man took another drag on his cigarette, flicking ash onto the muddy ground, and eyed Kenny suspiciously for a moment. Erica gazed at him uncomfortably, but suddenly he opened his mouth and roared with laughter. He stopped abruptly, his eyes filling with tears and then threw his head back and roared again. This time his laughter was cut short by a sudden attack of coughing, a hacking dry paroxysm that left him doubled over in pain, wheezing for breath. The man at the contraption made as if to rise, to come forward in support but the thin man waved him down, slowly unwinding back to his full height. He hawked violently and turned his head to spit into the trees. Wiping his mouth with the back of his hand, he turned back to face Kenny, appraising him as if seeing him for the first time. "Nice one, English," he said. "Like your style. Celebrity, notoriety; famous, infamous; not much difference these days, eh?"

"Not sure there ever has been."

"Probably right, probably right." The man took a final drag on the cigarette before dropping it on the ground, where it fizzled out in a small puddle. Without pausing, he took another full strength unfiltered from the packet and lit it, sucking hard and making the tip glow red.

"Leastways, gets doors opened as you have no doubt found out," the thin man continued, "and since you have obviously done your homework you can dispense with the lordship crap. I'm Lenny Hodgson, my friends call me Len." This time it was Len who held out his hand, wedging the cigarette temporarily between his teeth. Kenny stepped forward and shook, wincing slightly at the strength of the older man's grip. The hand looked no more than skin and bone, but the handshake warned him not to take too many liberties. He may appear frail but this was clearly still a man to be reckoned with.

"Nice to meet you, Len," Kenny said politely.

"My pleasure entirely I'm sure," there was a slight mocking lilt to Len's voice. "Now what can I do for you?"

"Well," Kenny began, not quite sure where to start.

"It's my brother." Erica suddenly found her voice, clearly deciding to dispense with the preliminaries and cut to the chase." He's locked in the safe at your bank, and we need your help to get him out." Len turned slowly towards her, as if he had forgotten that she was there. He took another drag on the cigarette and through the smoky haze he studied her slowly. As he stared, she could make out every bone in his skull, the leathery skin stretched like a drum over his frame. Erica suppressed a shiver.

"And who did you say you were again?" Len said at length.

"Erica, Erica Marshall," Erica repeated. "My brother Luke works for Rousseau Frères. He got himself locked in the safe on Friday, and we need to find out who has the key or whatever, so we can get him out. We thought that you might be able to help us."

"Oh, you did, did you? And why might I want to do a thing like that?"

"Because it's the human thing to do?" Erica seemed unprepared for the question.

"Serve the sod right, if you ask me. I know why he would have been down in the vault on a Friday afternoon: skiving, that's why. Don't think that you can fool me. I've been robbed blind by those lazy good-for-nothings for years. Decent day's work for a decent day's pay, that's all I asked, and what did I get? Fucking layabouts, that's what. Down the pub the minute your back's turned. I'll bet he was pissed, wasn't he?" Erica stood with her mouth open, unsure what to say, completely flummoxed by the old man's outburst. Kenny intervened.

"As it happens, Len," he waited while Len turned back to face him, "we can't be sure how the accident occurred. All we know is that while he isn't in any immediate danger, he's not going to be too comfortable. It's not exactly good publicity for your employees to get locked in the premises over the weekend now, is it?"

"Don't talk to me about fucking publicity," Len roared, his face reddening as his temper rose. This time the croucher got to his feet and moved towards his master, clearly sensing trouble. "I've had more publicity than you've had hot dinners, as you well know. Think I give two shits what they write in the papers." As he spoke his voice grew gravelly and he was wracked with another vicious coughing fit. This time the servant was at his arm, supporting him and turning him away from the visitors. After what seemed like minutes, the storm abated and Len finally regained control of himself.

When he turned to Kenny, his skin was deathly white and his eyes where filled with rheumy tears. Len spoke more quietly now. "Sorry about that, not very neighbourly, I'm sure. Not been feeling myself lately." Both Kenny and Erica made sympathetic noises. "Truth is, I couldn't help you if I wanted to. No day to day responsibility, if you know what I mean, non-executive director." Len paused to take several deep breaths, before standing unaided. "I haven't had anything to do with the bank for nearly a year now, not since my Seymour took over. Couldn't figure out why he wanted it in the first place. Like I said, I could never make it pay, too many idlers on the payroll, if you pardon me saying so," this last comment directed at Erica, "but the boy comes back from cutting his teeth in Hong Kong and decides he wants a piece of the business. I was all for selling it, get shot of it while you still can, thought I, but no, for some reason he thinks he can make a go of it. Fancies himself as the young executive. So I says, if you want it, you can have it, but don't come crying to me when it all goes tits up. Last I heard he'd been sacking people left right and centre, brought some hot shot in from the Far East to do the dirty work. Only senior people I knew there have all gone now, and good riddance to them, I say."

Len paused again and took several more deep breaths. Kenny spoke. "So you have no idea who is in charge, don't know anything about where we might find this Mike Dalton."

"I've met Dalton, but that's as far as it goes. Where to find him, search me. To be honest with you, English, I would help if I could, but I'm afraid I'm pretty useless these days. You need to speak to my Seymour."

"Do you know where we might find him?" Erica asked a little shyly.

"My man Harry here will give you the address. Can't help you with the phone number, I'm afraid. Don't speak that often, if you know what I mean." He nodded to the servant who took out a pad of paper and quickly scribbled on it. Tearing off a page, he handed it to Kenny.

"Do you have children of your own English?"

"No, Len, I don't," replied Kenny, folding the paper and putting it in his shirt pocket. "Probably just as well, given my track record."

"Oh yeah, I heard about you splitting up. Bit of a lad, eh? Well, take my advice and avoid them if you can. They can be a blessing and a curse. When they're little you love them because they're blood, but when they grow up, you have to judge them as people. You bump into my Seymour, you'll know what I mean," and he smiled. "Anyway, best get on. It's been nice talking to you."

"And you, Len. See you around. Thanks for this." Kenny tapped his breast pocket, and he and Erica turned and headed back the way they had come. Before they had walked a hundred yards they heard the crack of the shotgun and turned to see the pink dust spread across the sky. His lordship had returned to his sport.

Back on Kenny's side of the fence they both instinctively made for the Aston, the house had no more to offer. Neither spoke until they were settled in the car.

Erica shivered. "Nice company you keep, Mr English," she said, "Now what do we do next?"

Kenny drove in silence for a moment. He switched on the car's headlights and took the piece of paper out of his shirt pocket.

"Have a look at this," he said. "I think we should go and pay young Seymour Hodgson a visit."

Erica read the address scrawled in a random collection of upper and lower case characters on the page from the notebook.

"24 Eaton Place," she recited, carefully enunciating the words as if reading a foreign language. "Where's that?"

"Victoria," said Kenny flatly. "I suppose they'd call it Belgravia, but to you and me it's Victoria. I used to work with a recording company that had offices just round the corner in Buckingham Palace Road. It's what you might call a well posh area. If young master Hodgson is funding his mortgage from the bank's earnings, he can't be doing so badly."

"Is it anywhere near Grosvenor Gardens?"

"A hop and a skip, why do you ask?"

"That's where the bank is."

"So he lives over the shop does he? Well, you never know, he might just be able to let us in."

Kenny turned to Erica and smiled optimistically. She was looking tired as if the meeting had taken a lot out of her in nervous energy. "Come on, look on the bright side," he said. "If we can track down Seymour, and he can open the bank, Luke might be free in a few hours." Erica rewarded his buoyancy with a small smile, and then relaxed back in her seat.

As they headed up the A3, she turned to Kenny. "If that was your country house, where do you normally live?" she asked.

Kenny blinked as if not expecting the question. "St John's Wood, since you ask."

"Why there? It's a bit of a hike from Farnham."

Kenny shifted into the outside lane to overtake a truck. "You could put it down to sentiment, I suppose: a promise I made to my old man."

Erica looked interested. "Go on," she said.

Kenny paused before answering, his head tilted to one side as if he were thinking about events a long time ago. "When I was a kid, the first thing I remember about my dad was his passion for cricket. If I cast my mind back to our house in Beckenham, I can smell my mum's cooking and my dad's pipe, and invariably the sound on the radio is the Test match commentary. Cricket mad we was, and whenever he got the chance he'd take me to the Oval to see a match. Tell the truth, it was the only time we really did anything together."

"Not my idea of entertainment, but how does that link you to St John's Wood? Even I know the Oval is in south London."

"I'm coming to that, be patient. Like I said, the Oval was sort of our spiritual home, our special place. Then one day he tells me he's got tickets for a test match at Lords."

"I'm starting to understand."

"1968 it was, England against McKenzie's Australians. All in all it was a brutal game. The pitch was badly affected by the rain and batting was a hazardous occupation, but that didn't stop Ken Barrington. Even though he took several blows to the body he was never less than stylish, scoring 75 runs that effectively put the game out of reach of the visitors. That was the day I stopped being Kenneth and turned into Kenny. He was my hero."

"You boys never do grow up, do you?"

"Not so as you'd notice. Anyway, more rain meant that play ended early, but dad and I were so engrossed in talking about the game that we turned right instead of left through Grace's Gates and had to take a detour along Hamilton Terrace to make our way back to the tube station. I tell you, I was absolutely spellbound by the architecture, captivated by the neo-Georgian splendour, the colonnaded pediments behind forbidding wrought iron gates. That's when I promised myself that one day I would live there."

"Nice story, now let's get on."

They crossed the M25, each lost in thought, and it wasn't until they approached Kingston that Erica broke the silence. "Why do you think his coat was so big?"

Kenny snapped out of his reverie. "Who? What coat?"

"Lord Winsloe, or Lenny Hodgson, whatever you call him. Surely he could afford a coat that fit him."

"I think you'll find that he was a bit larger in his youth. Apparently there was a time when he was known as Fat Lenny."

"So he's been on a diet has he? Or do people naturally waste away as they get older?"

"Cancer," said Kenny, "lung cancer, if you ask me. Probably not got more than a few months to live, if I read the signs correctly."

"So now you're a medical expert as well. You never cease to amaze me." Erica's voice took on that teasing, slightly flirty tone.

"I speak from experience. It's how my old man died."

Erica pursed her lips. Maybe she had overstepped the mark. "Oh, I'm sorry," she said, "I didn't know."

"No reason you should," said Kenny, touched by her contrition. "It happened more than thirty years ago. I'm over it. Did for my mum though. She never recovered. That's when I was left all alone, an orphan." Kenny tried to sound upbeat, uncomfortable with the morbid turn the conversation was taking. "Tell me about your parents."

"They're both dead."

Kenny cringed, angry with himself for forgetting what Vic had told him in the shop the previous morning.

"They both died when I was little. It was an accident. I don't remember anything about it, and I don't want to talk about it thank you. I have no doubt that it left serious scars on my personality, and that I should go in for some counselling or some such other crap, but if you don't mind, I'm OK as I am, so if it's all the same to you, can we let the matter drop?"

It all came out in one go, almost as if it was practised, a much rehearsed monologue. Kenny took the hint and changed the subject.

"So tell me, what you do for a living?"

"It's not very interesting, I'm afraid."

"Come on, you know what I do. It's only fair that you tell as well."

"I'm a char lady."

Kenny raised an eyebrow, but only briefly. "And your day job?"

Erica smiled inwardly: he wasn't going to fall for that one. "I'm a student, if you must know," she said, with an air of finality intended to close this particular chapter. This time Kenny missed the implication.

"Really, what are you studying?"

"Business Administration. I'm majoring in Finance and should graduate next month, if I ever get home to finish my dissertation that is."

"Finance, eh? You sound like just the person I need to be talking to."

"Why do you say that?"

Kenny took a deep breath. "As it happens, I am in a bit of a pickle financially, and I need someone I can trust to show me the way out."

"Thought you were rolling in it: flash car country mansion and all that. Don't tell me you're on your beam ends." Erica seemed determined to make light of the conversation. So far they had stuck to fairly meaningless topics, safe. But Kenny just ploughed on.

"I should be rolling in it, and to be perfectly honest, I'm not exactly signing up for income support, but I do have a problem with money at the moment, and it might help to talk it over with someone who knows what they're on about." Kenny looked over at Erica, giving her his best little boy lost expression, trying to elicit a positive response.

Erica was still uncomfortable. "Surely you have an accountant for that sort of thing."

Kenny sighed. "I have an accountant, a banker, a lawyer and an agent," he replied, his eyes now fixed firmly on the road, an air of resignation settling around him. "And not one of them is interested in me." Much as he tried not to sound churlish, the weeks of frustration were too much for him, and there was a slight whine to his voice.

"They are only interested in what they can get out of me, the ten or fifteen percent that they can latch on to. To them I am the goose that lays the golden egg, and the more trouble I get into, the more eggs I lay. To be honest, they wouldn't piss on me if I was on fire, not unless they were sure of getting paid. What I need right now is a friend, not an apparatchik, someone who will tell it like it is, who will be honest with me." Kenny stopped talking as the traffic slowed for road works.

Erica was silent for a moment, weighing up the options. Finally she seemed to come to a decision. "Go on then, try me," she said. As they crawled towards a set of temporary traffic lights, Kenny carefully listed the chain of events that had led to him being deeply in debt. Erica's eyes widened when he mentioned the figures involved, but she said nothing, allowing him to unburden at his own pace. She took an old envelope from her jacket pocket and started making notes.

"Like you said, not exactly income support time is it. Most of us would be happy to be worth six million or so. Mind you, giving the ex half the estate seems somewhat on the generous side. You couldn't have been married that long, is that normal?"

Kenny looked rueful. "Not exactly, but I'm afraid she had me over a barrel."

"How?"

Kenny swallowed hard. "If you must know all the gory details, she found out I'd been having an affair." He paused. "With a married woman."

Erica shrugged. "Happens all the time from what I've heard, or don't you read the tabloid press?"

"Yes, well it's different when it happens to you. The married woman decided that she wanted another chance to make a go of her marriage, decided I'd been a bit of a mistake, I suppose. My ex made it clear that unless she got exactly what she wanted, she'd go to the press, name names, make it all rather ugly. I didn't have much of a choice really. If Monica wanted another shot at married bliss, then I had to do as I was told."

Erica put down her pen and half turned towards Kenny. "That was rather benevolent of you, wasn't it?" she asked slowly.

Kenny dismissed the question with a tilt of the head as he braked, waiting for the lights to turn green. Erica resumed her position and looked down at her notes.

"I still don't understand why you took out the loan though. You must have been mad. Surely you could just have mortgaged the house or something."

"Twenty-twenty hindsight is a marvellous thing. If I had known then what I know now, I might have had second thoughts. Fact is, I just wanted the whole thing over and done with. I wanted that old cow off my back and out of my life. She wanted half of everything and she wanted cash. The loan seemed the best way out at the time."

"I can see that, but why for six months. Like I say, you could surely have raised a mortgage on the town house."

"Time was the other problem. You see, in my line we don't get a regular salary. The banks want to see income to service the loan, not just assets to secure it. Given time, I could have come up with income statements to support a reasonable level of debt, royalties that sort of thing, but even, then I don't think I would have got away with six mill."

"So you could have liquidated some of the property and then raised the remainder of the money. It's not rocket science, is it?"

"It isn't, you're right. But again, the problem was time. Like I told you, the house in Farnham is on the market, but there's no real sign of it shifting. The basic idea was that the loan would give me the time to sort things out, but now I've got it hanging over my head, six months doesn't seem so long after all."

"Which begs the question as to what you are doing out here with me, when you could be getting your affairs in order. You should be having serious talks with an Estate Agent, not chasing around trying to get my stupid brother out of a locked room."

Kenny nodded at the irony, as they passed the road repairs and began to pick up speed again. "I have to admit, I've been asking myself that very question. Why am I here doing this?"

"And the answer is? Oh, hang on a moment, I see it." Erica was looking straight ahead, as if talking to the windscreen, but her words were indisputably aimed at Kenny.

"You just want Luke out of the vault so that he can write your bloody music and make you some money. Now who's laying golden eggs? You see my brother as a way of repaying your debt and getting you off the hook. I was just starting to think that you may have had some higher motives, like you cared or something, but I get it now. Writing that musical must be worth a fortune to you, more than enough to settle what's owing and let you get back to your celebrity life style. Work with an unknown like Luke, and you can decide on the share out. You can rip him off to your heart's content: all he wants to do is write music. You money grubbing bastard. You'll take all the credit and the lion's share of the proceeds. Well thanks for nothing, mate. If it's all the same to you, you can drop me here, and I'll carry on alone." Erica put the pen and envelope back into her jacket and made as if to open the car door. Alarmed, Kenny reached over and pinned her by the arms to prevent her leaving the seat.

"Just stop there," he said firmly, only releasing his grip as he felt her relax. "If you jump out at sixty miles an hour you'll kill yourself." Erica returned to looking straight ahead and they sat in silence.

When Kenny eventually spoke, his voice was calm and quiet. "I asked for honesty, and it's only fair that I should be honest with you," he said, his tone measured and careful, walking on thin ice. "The main reason that I came looking for Luke yesterday was because I thought we could work together. That much is true, I did think of him as a possible way out of the mess, but only if the chemistry was right. Remember, at that stage I had no idea why he stood me up. As far as I knew, he was sitting in bed with the flu and gagging for a chance to start a new career. It was only after I got here that we found out the truth. If I'm honest, the sensible thing to do at that stage would've been to cut my losses and hightail it back to St John's Wood. Maybe with a bit of negotiating, I could have done like you said and got a better deal on the loan, maybe I still could. But the fact is I stayed on, didn't I? Went to the police station and all, because I got this feeling that I could help out in some way. And I was right, wasn't I? Without me you would have no idea how to find Lord Winsloe and would be sitting at home wondering what to do next. As it is, one thing led to another, and now we have a real chance of getting Luke out. Yes, I did get into this for purely business reasons, but I kept on it because I saw an opportunity to do some good, and I wanted to help. If you still want to walk home, I'll pull over, and you can leave in safety."

Erica continued to stare at the road. "Thank you, but that won't be necessary," she said finally. "I'm sorry, I guess you have been very kind." There was a slight crack in her voice, the echo of a tear maybe, but she swallowed hard and continued. "Since you asked for it, my advice would be to sell the house in town and repay the debt. That would leave you with money in the bank and time to decide what you want to do with the rest of your fortune. It's the only sensible alternative."

Kenny shrugged. "That isn't about to happen," he said with an air of finality, and they headed for Belgravia in silence.

Chapter 12

It was dark by the time that Erica and Kenny arrived at Eaton Place. The road was quiet and Kenny had no difficulty in finding a parking space close to number 24. Eaton Place is a terrace of Georgian town houses, and Kenny stood on the top step as he looked for the bell push. The small porch was illuminated by light from the half moon above the door and there were sounds of muffled voices coming from inside. A woman laughed loudly.

"Looks like they're home," said Kenny, as he gave up the search for a bell and rapped the knocker, set in a brass lion's head. He stepped back. The sounds from inside grew more distinct, an internal door opening, music playing, Phil Collins, footsteps muffled by carpeting, a light came on in the porch above Kenny's head and finally the door opened. On the threshold stood a young woman dressed in a light blue cheongsam and wearing white sling backs. She leaned against the door teetering on her heels, and looked fuzzily in Kenny's direction.

"Can I help you?" she asked, slightly blearily, as if she had just woken up. "Are you expected?"

"I don't think so," Kenny replied. In the harsh glare of the porch light he could see that the woman was heavily made up, the mascara under her left eye running slightly, as if she had been crying. "We are looking for Seymour Hodgson." The woman looked at him for a long time, as if weighing his words, before responding.

"Oh, you want Seymour, do you?" she said, as though the thought was a profound deduction. "Well, he's inside, but he's ever so busy at the moment," the words *ever* and *so* merged into one "What shall I say it's about? Is it important?"

"We need to speak to him about the bank, about Rousseau Frères," Kenny enunciated his words carefully, "and yes it is rather important. We won't take long." This time the message hit home at once, and she rolled her eyes to the ceiling.

"Business, why didn't you say so to start with? I'll go get him. You just wait here now."

She shambled back into the house, touching the wall for support and turned left into a room at the far end of the hall. As she did so, she lost control of the heel of her right shoe and her right ankle hit the floor. She expleted loudly as she opened the door, her words drowned by *No Jacket Required*. Kenny heard her call to Seymour, and a muffled, brief conversation as the door closed behind her.

After a few moments, the music crescendoed once more as the door opened, then diminuendoed as it closed behind a tall man in a grey two-piece suit, who came into the hall and walked purposefully towards the front door. As he approached the threshold, he stuck out his right hand.

"Good evening," the left held a crystal tumbler, quarter filled with amber liquid, "I am Seymour Hodgson. I understand you wish to speak to me." His tone was neither warm nor rude, a sort of practised formal pleasantness, like a campaigning politician.

"Kenny English," Kenny said, taking the proffered hand which gave his a perfunctory shake and quickly returned to its owner. Standing at street level, Kenny had to look sharply up at Seymour Hodgson on the doorstep. At this distance, and in this light, it was hard even for the expensively cut suit to disguise the spreading waistline stretching the equally expensive shirt as it disappeared beneath his belt. Seymour Hodgson clearly enjoyed the good things in life, and apparently had inherited the weight gain gene.

"Sorry to bother you, we were given your address by your father."

"How is the old man? Still breathing?" Seymour interrupted, without a hint of sympathy. He took a silver box from his pocket and extracted a hand-rolled, untipped cigarette, another inherited trait.

"He seemed well when we left him this afternoon," Kenny continued, as if Seymour had made a genuine enquiry after his father's health. "He told us that you may be able to help us with a little problem concerning the bank."

Seymour lit the cigarette with a heavy gold Dunhill that he then slipped into the inside pocket of his jacket. He blew smoke and the air was thick with the unmistakeable fragrance of seriously good weed. Kenny leant his head back to avoid inhaling.

"Fire away. What seems to be the problem?"

"My friend's brother." For the first time Kenny indicated Erica, who was standing rather sheepishly behind him. Seymour gave her a small nod, in recognition of her presence. "My friend's brother seems to have become locked in your vault. We were wondering if there was any way you could help us to get him out."

Seymour's groan was almost imperceptible, but it was there all the same. God save me from little people, it said, why do I have to deal with all these petty problems? "How on earth did this happen?" he said out loud, the politician's voice desperately trying to sound sincere. Erica stepped forward.

"Seems he went into the vault on Friday afternoon and must have fallen asleep or something, because he's still there, and we're very worried that he may suffocate, and anyway, he hasn't had anything to eat for more than two days now, and he'll be worried and everything." It all came out in one breath, almost as one word, and Kenny could see that she was close to tears. She was obviously overawed by Seymour's manner, his aura of confidence, intimidated by his self assurance. Seymour's demeanour changed from politician to lord of the manor, slightly condescending, as if talking to a servant.

"So you don't know for certain that he is actually in the vault?"

Erica looked unsurely at Kenny. "We had an email from him, begging us to help get him out."

Seymour closed his eyes patronisingly. "My dear girl," he opened his eyes again and took a long pull on the reefer, "he could have sent that from anywhere; doesn't prove a thing. For all you know he's having a joke at your expense."

Erica was speechless. She looked blankly at Kenny.

"We have no doubt that Luke is where he says." Kenny's tone was firm and confident. "He's made contact with one of his friends and they've discussed his predicament. There can be no reasonable doubt about it he's locked in your vault."

Kenny looked Seymour firmly in the eye, holding the stare. Seymour was the first to blink.

"And you say that he fell asleep. What the bloody hell was he doing there?"

"We are guessing that he fell asleep. We haven't had a chance to talk to him about the exact circumstances yet. Whatever the reason, it is only humane to try and get him out."

"Don't try to tell me what is humane, chummy," Seymour's tone was now openly hostile. "It's my bloody business, and I'll decide what's humane and what isn't, is that clear?" Without waiting for a reply, he carried on. "I'll have you know that I am a very busy man, and I really don't have time to bother with some stupid clerk who has got himself stuck up a tree or whatever because of his own ineptitude. I'll have you know that I am in the middle of closing a very lucrative deal with some gentlemen from abroad, and I am buggered if I am going to put that at risk for some ignorant non-entity. If he's stuck in the vault, it's his own fault, and he can suffer for it, teach him a lesson."

Seymour half turned as if to return to the house, but Kenny was still on the case.

"As it happens," he began, and Seymour reluctantly turned back, "as it happens, we don't need you to be there personally. We just need to know how to get hold of Mike Dalton. We understand he's the Managing Director. Maybe he can take care of things."

Seymour took a swig from the tumbler, switching it to his right hand and running his left through his thinning hair in exasperation. "My dear fellow," he said, slowly, as if talking to a particularly stupid dog, "this is my home, do you see? I may do some business entertaining here from time to time, but it is not my place of work understand?"

Kenny's hands were clenched into fists, the knuckles glowing white.

"I am not in the habit of communicating with my employees when I am at home, and I am afraid that I do not count Mr Dalton as a close friend. I am therefore not in possession of his personal details about my person at present, nor are they available to me in my abode, which you see herewith." The combination of alcohol and dope was having an obvious impact on Seymour's ability to string words together. He was losing it, and Kenny recognised the symptoms. "Now, why don't you and your daughter here be a good fellow and just piss off and leave me to my business."

Kenny gritted his teeth and stared at Seymour, whose mottled features were now no more than a foot from his own face. Erica tugged at his sleeve, apparently calm and in control. "Come on, time we were going," she said. "Let's leave the nice man to his business meeting. Best we were getting along." Kenny stared at Seymour for a few seconds longer, establishing the ground rules, in case there was a next time, and then allowed himself to be guided back along the street to the waiting car. By the time they were seated in the Aston, the door to number 24 had closed and the street was quiet again.

Kenny looked across at Erica, who sat pale and shivering, staring silently out of the window. "You look shattered," he said. "What you need is a warm bath, a change of clothing and a hot meal." Erica didn't comment, so Kenny started the engine and pulled out into the road.

"We'll go to my place. It's not far," he said as he turned right at the end of the road, heading north. Erica finally spoke.

"What a dreadful man," she said quietly.

Kenny smiled to himself as they joined the traffic turning towards Piccadilly, making a left up Park Lane.

"Typical product of a public school education, if my experience is anything to go by." Erica turned to look at him.

"Can't say I've met that many public schoolboys. They're a bit thin on the ground in Penge, if you know what I mean. Come to think of it, I do seem to recall Luke mentioning that the new chairman had been to Eton."

"Proves my point. The music business is riddled with the chinless wonders, though most of them try to cover it up: not exactly street cred to have daddy paying for your education. I do remember one though, old Etonian, I mean." He looked at Erica, who raised an eyebrow, encouraging him to continue.

"He worked for a recording studio, can't remember which one, or his name, come to that, but he was assigned as my account manager, you know, sort of liaison with the company, made sure that everything went OK while I was producing lyrics for an album for some immediately forgettable band."

"You're a mine of information today."

"It was during my substance abuse period. I was pissed most of the time, and memories get a bit blurred. I'm not so bad these days."

"Glad to hear it," Erica remarked, as Kenny weaved through the traffic around Marble Arch and made for Edgware Road.

"Anyway, I do recall the conversation we had quite clearly. He told me that all the time he was at Eton, the teachers and such like impressed on the pupils what a great heritage they were heirs to. When they were leaving they had a meeting in the main hall surrounded by portraits of old boys who had gone on to be Prime Ministers or the equivalent, and they were told that they were the next generation who would make Britain great, carry on leading the country. Imagine it, the whole conquerors of the universe bit. Hardly surprising that they end up thinking that the world owes them a living. He even told me how lucky I was to have him managing me, the spotty oik."

"So what happened to him?"

"I got him sacked. Told his boss that he was useless, which he was."

"That wasn't very kind."

"Think of Seymour Hodgson."

"OK, you're forgiven."

"Anyway, the story doesn't end there. When he found out that he was getting the boot, guess what happened."

There was a pause, as Erica waited for the punch line. "Go on then, tell me."

"You're supposed to say what."

"All right, what?"

"He burst into tears, completely fell apart. I learned something then. I learned that he and all his sort are nothing but bullies. They think that they can intimidate you with their fancy accents and their self-confidence. Some of the better ones do give off this air of invincibility, but at the end of the day they're bullies, and like all bullies when it comes down to it they're cowards. Face them up and they crumble, put their tails between their legs and go running home to mummy. Young Seymour will be the same: he'll just take a little longer to break down. "

They stopped in traffic at Paddington Green, and Erica returned to staring out of the window. "I thought you were going to hit him," she said. Kenny thought for a moment.

"He was starting to get to me. Yes, maybe I would have had a pop. Just as well you stopped me."

"Because you might have hurt him?"

"No, more likely I would have hurt myself. I've never hit anyone before."

"What, never?"

Kenny thought for a moment as the traffic carried them forward. "No, I don't think I ever have. When I was young, you know, when most boys have play fights and that, I was always the smallest, so it seemed sensible to avoid confrontations. I started a growth spurt when I was about eleven, but by the time I was big enough to look after myself any fighting would have been for keeps, and since I didn't have the experience of the play fighting, I always reckoned that I'd come off worst. So again, I tended to favour discretion. I have to say though that tonight was as close as I've come to a real ruck. I might have enjoyed it, you never know, he was really getting under my skin. Come to think of it though, he was bigger than me, and a good deal younger. Probably best to walk away."

Kenny nodded to himself, as if seriously considering the options, and Erica smiled again. This time the smile remained long enough for Kenny to turn to her and return it. They took a right at the lights into St John's Wood Road and then left into Hamilton Terrace. About two hundred yards along, they turned into a driveway. Kenny pressed a button on the dashboard, and the tall wrought iron gates opened. An up-and-over door opened as they drew close, and a light came on automatically overhead. Kenny parked the car between a Bentley convertible and a red Porsche, slipped the gear shift into park and pulled on the hand brake. "Home, sweet home," he said, and opened the door.

Erica followed Kenny out of the garage through a door set in the side wall. They went up a short flight of stairs, through another door, and into what was clearly the entrance hall of the house. Erica stopped for a moment to take in her surroundings, the high ceiling with ornate cornices, the chandelier set into the elaborately carved ceiling rose, the neutral wallpaper, and the black and white tiled floor. The walls were littered with photographs, mainly black and white, and mostly of Kenny together with an array of celebrities, like a who's who of popular culture from the previous thirty years.

Doors led off the hall to various rooms, and to her right, an impressive staircase with polished mahogany banisters led to the floors above. Taking hold of one of the newel posts, Erica swung her head into the stairwell so that she could see upwards, and was met with the dizzying prospect of at least five floors, each tidily shrinking in perspective towards infinity.

Erica whistled softly. "Be it ever so humble," she said with an admiring nod, "I can see why you don't want to sell it."

"Like I said, it's my home."

"And very impressive it is too, I mean it. But is it still worth risking everything for?"

"That's my decision. Let's see what there is to eat. I don't know about you, but I'm starving."

Kenny led them along a passage that ran behind the staircase and ended up in a large kitchen, dominated by a farmhouse-sized pine table. He opened cupboards and explored the fridge, before announcing: "Looks like there's steak and salad, if you fancy it. Otherwise, we could ring for a takeaway. What do you think?"

Erica cocked her head to one side, considering the options.

"Steak suits me fine," she said, "but you'll have to cook it. I'm completely useless in the kitchen."

"I'm not exactly Jamie Oliver, but I should be able to cope with steak and salad without poisoning us. What we first need, though, is a shower and a change of clothes."

Kenny caught Erica's look of discomfort. "Wife number three was a bit bigger than you in the chest department, but otherwise she was about your size. She left some of her things when she walked out, in a bit of a hurry, as I recall, so there must be something suitable for you to wear. Come on, you can use one of the guest bedrooms."

They left the kitchen, and Kenny led upstairs, along a landing, and opened a door into a bedroom. Erica peered into the room, with its floor to ceiling windows and king-sized bed. Kenny drew the curtains and switched on the bedside lights. "The bathroom's over there, and there should be some clothes in the wardrobe. Come downstairs whenever you're ready. I'll be in the kitchen."

Thirty minutes later, Erica returned to the ground floor, a little self-conscious, but warmer and cleaner. The smell of cooking would have led her to the kitchen, even if she didn't already know where it was. She found Kenny cooking steaks on a griddle pan over the stove, a huge extractor fan above him efficiently wafting the smoke out of the room. He had changed into clean jeans and a grey shirt, his hair was still wet and he had a glass of red wine in his hand. He turned around as Erica walked in.

"You look great," he said. "Help yourself to wine."

After taking a bath, Erica had found a pair of beige combat trousers in the wardrobe that, when she put a couple of turns into the legs, fitted her OK. Kenny's ex had indeed been several sizes larger, and a couple of inches taller, if her clothes were anything to go by, but she had managed to locate an olive green sweater that was probably intended to be worn baggy. She had towelled her hair dry, and it now stuck out at all angles in its usual disarray. She poured a glass of wine and topped up Kenny's, as he put it down to turn the steaks.

"This is all rather cosy," she said. "I could get used to this."

Kenny grinned. "Trappings of success. Just relax and enjoy it. I reckon you've earned a bit of pampering. Makes a change for me to have someone to cook for."

"Don't go in for entertaining then?"

"Not so you'd notice. To be honest, I can't remember the last time I invited anybody home, let alone cooked them a meal. I don't normally do the cooking."

"So who does?" Erica looked about her.

"Gordon, my butler. He's got the weekend off."

"Butler, eh? Well I should have guessed. He keeps the place nice and tidy."

"I'll take that as a compliment, you being a professional. He keeps the place looking spick and span, does all the cooking and generally makes sure I'm well seen to."

Erica toyed with her glass as Kenny set the table. He put a bowl of salad in the centre and fished a loaf of French bread out of the oven where it had been warming. Finally, he slipped the steaks onto plates and put them on the table. "Dinner is served," he said. "It's not much, but it should be wholesome."

"Looks good to me," said Erica and they both sat down.

For a few minutes, they ate in silence. Erica was the first to voice her thoughts.

"What are we going to do about Luke?" she said.

Kenny stopped with his fork half way to his mouth. He sat and thought for a few moments before answering, his food untouched.

"Seems we've reached a dead end," he said, with a note of resignation. "All that running around after Lord Winsloe and his delightful progeny got us precisely nowhere."

"We could still try the phone book," said Erica cagily, as though grasping at a particularly thin straw. "You know, see if we can track down Mike Dalton."

"And how many M Daltons do you think there are in London? It's not as if we can ring directory enquiries. There must be dozens. We don't even know for sure that he lives in London, and even if he does, he's only been here a few months. He might not even be in the directory yet." Kenny put his food into his mouth and chewed morosely.

"We could try Simon again," suggested Erica, lamely. "Make sure Luke's still all right. Perhaps one of them will have remembered something."

"He's probably still at the hospital. Didn't he say he'd ring, if he had any news?"

Erica chewed on her steak and sulked. "We could go back to the police," one final straw to grasp at, "maybe they'll take it more seriously now he's been missing for two days."

"Guess we ought to try at least," said Kenny, without any enthusiasm, "but if last time is anything to go by, we'll be lucky to get past the desk sergeant. What we need is to get hold of someone in authority who can…" Kenny stopped talking and stared straight at the table, just beyond the edge of his plate. For a moment he seemed to be having a heart attack or a seizure, but then he suddenly stood up, rattling the cutlery and slopping wine from the glasses.

"Oh, what a stupid twat I am!" he yelled, slapping his forehead. "Why didn't I think of that before?"

Erica stared in amazement, as Kenny leapt to the sink and opened a drawer, rummaging through its contents as if his life depended on it.

"Is there something you should tell me?" she enquired, with exaggerated politeness. Kenny turned and looked at her as if he'd forgotten that she was there.

"Frank Blaney," he said, as though it were the most obvious thing in the world, and appeared slightly surprised when the words failed to elicit a reaction. "Francis Blaney, Deputy Assistant Commissioner Blaney of New Scotland Yard, one of the Met's finest. He's a neighbour, sort of nodding acquaintance, if you like. If anyone can do something about Luke, surely he must have the pull. Can't believe I didn't think of it earlier."

"But will he help? I mean, even if he can, how well do you know him? It's the weekend, after all. You can't just barge into Scotland Yard and ask for him on a Sunday night. He's probably at home by now."

"That's just the point: he only lives down the road. And I reckon he owes me a favour. Anyway, if I can find his number, it's certainly worth a shot." Kenny carried on rummaging in the drawer until he came up with an old, rather battered address book. He turned to Erica. "Here he is," he said triumphantly. "Now where's that phone."

The search for the phone book transmogrified into the search for the phone. Kenny returned to rifling through drawers, opening and closing cupboards and looking under chair cushions, until he finally found a small metallic handset under a pile of what could only be unpaid bills.

"Whatever happened to real phones?" he asked, as he sat down again at the table, phone in one hand, address book in the other. Erica looked blankly at him, bemused by the question and rather hoping that it was rhetorical. Kenny looked up at her, clearly anticipating a response.

"I don't suppose you remember real phones do you?"

"Meaning?"

"Real phones, you know, with a wire that attaches to something in the wall. And a real dial, one that makes a sort of whirring sound as it returns to its origin. You know, something that you can relate to."

"I think I know what you mean. But weren't they rather cumbersome? Didn't you find it a bit limiting to have to make a phone call standing still, always in the same place?"

"But that's just the point: they were cumbersome, so you always knew where they were. The trouble with the phones today is that they

The rest of the band returned and the set continued, *Tie Your Mother Down*, if I remember correctly.

"All the eulogies and tributes that I have heard paid to John Lennon in the intervening twenty something years haven't come close to the poignancy of that moment. Like I say, no fuss, no flannel. Just one great musician showing his respect for another. I'll never forget it, and I doubt if anyone else who was there could."

Kenny picked up his glass and drank. Erica sat and watched him, warm tears pressing against her eyelashes, a lump in her throat. Pulling herself together, she sniffed and swallowed. "You're just a great big softy at heart, aren't you?"

"Guess I must be," Kenny acknowledged with a shrug.

Erica finished the last mouthful of wine and stood up. "Well, I don't know about you," she said, "but this old girl's ready for bed." Kenny stayed seated.

"You'll find everything you need in the bathroom. I like to keep my guest rooms kitted out, even though no one ever stays these days. There's an alarm clock by the bed, but you probably won't need it. I'll see you at breakfast."

Erica left the kitchen and climbed the stairs to the room she had used earlier. She yawned as she undressed and climbed in between the crisp clean sheets, unused if she was any judge. It had been a long day and she was more tired than she had imagined. Within seconds of switching off the bedside light she was fast asleep.

Kenny sat for a few moments, drinking wine and thinking. He emptied the second bottle and ambled a little unsteadily over to the wine rack. He ran his fingers over the serried ranks, pulling bottles out at random, checking the labels. Finally he selected a 1988 Chateau Talbot and took it over to the table. He picked up the corkscrew and was about to cut the foil when he stopped. He looked at the empty glasses, the two finished bottles, the dribble of wine left in Erica's glass. He held the fresh bottle in one hand and stared at it as if unaware how it had got there. Finally he shook his head, returned the bottle to the rack and left the room.

He switched out the lights as he walked through the house, admiring his surroundings. As he climbed the stairs, trailing his hand along the smooth surface of the banister, he passed a selection of framed gold and platinum discs.

"I'm not selling," he muttered to himself, as he closed the bedroom door behind him. "This is my home, and I'm keeping it one way or another. They'll have to take me out in a box."

It was just after three, when the pressure on Erica's bladder woke her. After stumbling groggily to the bathroom to pee, she brushed her teeth, trying to get rid of the taste of stale red wine. She sat on the bed and rolled her tongue round her mouth. Now she had the thick taste of toothpaste, but still her mouth felt grungy. Erica was by no means a heavy drinker, and two large glasses of wine had been more than enough to stun her into a deep sleep, but had left her with a mild hangover. What she needed now was a glass of water.

Borrowing a towelling robe from the back of the bathroom door, she tiptoed out of the room and along the passageway to the stairs. A door to her right was slightly ajar and she could hear Kenny snoring gently. There was no need to switch on a light as there were no curtains on the windows at either end of the landing and there was more than sufficient light filtering in from the world outside for her to see where she was going.

The kitchen by contrast lay in darkness. Erica found the switch beside the door jamb and flipped it on. She stood blinking as her eyes slowly became accustomed to the glare, the impact intensified by the array of white kitchen units and worktops. The two empty wine glasses still stood on the table and their plates still lay in the sink. Erica rolled up her sleeves and started filling the dishwasher. She hesitated for a moment with the glasses, flicking the rim of one to confirm it was indeed crystal. With a shrug she added it to the machine.

She poured a glass of water and drank it in one, before replenishing it. Immediately she felt better and made her way back to bed. As she approached the bedroom, she was stopped in her tracks by the sound of a gunshot. She stood still for a moment, listening hard. Just as she started to move it came again, not one shot but two, distinct cracks. She cocked her head to identify the source, somewhere further along the passage.

Erica would never have claimed to be a brave woman, but she was acutely inquisitive, not exactly nosy, just the sort of person who can't let things rest. Putting her glass down on a table inside her bedroom, she crept along the corridor. She held her breath to hear better. There it was again, a shot, and this time accompanied by the sound of a horse neighing. She came abreast of a door to a room on her left and heard again sounds from within. Carefully she turned the knob and pushed.

The sight that met her eyes was so staggering that she could do nothing but stand and stare.

Rather than another guest bedroom, Erica found herself in what appeared to be the sitting room of a small suburban house. A grey haired old woman was sitting in front of a three bar electric fire, watching a western on a black and white television. In front of her was a small coffee table, on which there was a cup of tea and a plate of plain biscuits. She was munching on a biscuit, spilling crumbs down the front of her knitted top. The walls were papered in fading patterns and decorated with an eclectic array of photographs and cheap prints. In one corner stood an upright piano, not unlike Luke's. The room smelt warm and musty, but it was light, the window in the far wall showing that outside it was apparently daytime. Erica looked at the window. Not only was it daytime, but she could see houses across the road, just like at home.

As Erica watched, the woman turned her head. She peered myopically in Erica's direction, trying to make out who this visitor might be. Erica opened her mouth to speak, but no words came. Instead it was the old woman who reacted first. She let out a scream, a scream of such velocity that Erica instinctively stepped away as if pitched backwards by the blast. She held out her hand in an effort to pacify the woman, who simply screamed again.

From nowhere, a white-coated young woman appeared. She looked briefly at Erica, and then turned her attention to her patient. Taking out a small hypodermic, she settled the woman firmly but gently in her chair, rolled up a sleeve, with practiced dexterity, and injected. In seconds, the old woman was calm and had returned to watching the television. The nurse turned to Erica.

"You have to go now," was all she said, as she extended her arm and pushed Erica into the hallway, closing the door firmly behind her. Erica heard the sound of a key turning.

"What's going on?" Erica turned to see Kenny standing outside his bedroom door. He didn't sound angry, just bemused and befuddled. His hair was messy from sleep and he was wearing a robe that matched Erica's.

"I was rather hoping that you might tell me. Who was that woman? What is she doing here?"

Kenny sighed. He pressed the wall next to the bedroom door and a concealed panel slid noiselessly open. "I didn't really want you to know about this," he said, switching on a light inside the door, "but now you're here, you might as well get the whole story."

The panel led to a staircase. The treads were metal, like you might expect to find inside a factory, utilitarian in stark contrast to the sumptuous carpeting elsewhere in the house. Kenny led upward.

"That woman is my mother, and she is here because this is her home."

Erica followed in silence up four flights of stairs. Kenny opened a door and they entered a small room. Three white-coated orderlies sat at monitors while a fourth, the nurse that Erica recognised from the room downstairs, appeared through a door on the far side of the room. She opened her mouth to speak, but Kenny raised his hand to silence her.

"After my father died, my mother had a nervous breakdown, complete collapse, the works. She never recovered. They had been together all their lives, you see, childhood sweethearts, relied on each other totally. There were times, when I was a child, I felt like an outcast. Apart from the occasional cricket match, Mum and Dad seemed happier when I wasn't around. I guess that was why I became a bit of a loner; they were just so self-contained. Dad's death hit her hard. She didn't know what to do on her own.

"The doctors say that she is now suffering from dementia. She has no idea what day or even what year it is. She exists from one day to the next." Kenny paused.

Erica peered at the monitors. The one closest to her showed an image of the old woman still watching television in the mock up sitting room.

"Shouldn't she be in a home or something?" she asked, trying to come to terms with the situation, trying to understand.

"That would be the normal course of action, I suppose. Put her in a home, lock her away. Have you ever been to one of those places? I have. Believe me, I checked them out, best that money can buy. Some of them are real hellholes, but most of the time they do try to make the patients comfortable. Trouble is, there are too many patients and not enough nurses. No matter how hard they try, they can't exactly provide an individual service, now can they? What my Mum needs is personal care in her own home. Live in nurse, or better still nurses. Trouble is, there's was no room in the semi where I grew up, certainly not for the number of people that she needs to see to her. And what would she want with strangers fussing around her all the time, not exactly dignified is it?"

Erica looked at the other monitors, which showed a bedroom and a kitchen. One of the orderlies flicked a switch and the bedroom became a bathroom, quickly followed by a garden. The truth suddenly dawned on her.

"You've built a replica of your parents' home inside your own house?" she said quietly. "It must have cost a fortune."

"Not as much as you might imagine, not in the greater scheme of things. Needed a few structural alterations, but otherwise it's mostly cosmetic, you know, a few interior walls and a bit of decorating."

"Rather you than me. Just as well you can afford it."

"What's the point of having money if you can't spend it on the ones you love? What sort of son would I be if I packed my old dear off to a crappy nursing home while I lived in the lap of luxury? I may be slightly embarrassed in a financial sense at the moment, but I can still support my own. She's the only living relative I've got."

"Bit like me and Luke."

"I hadn't thought of it in that way, but since you mention it, yes. You should understand how I feel."

"I think I'm just starting to. Tell me, why is she still up at this time of night?"

"One of the symptoms of her condition is that she loses track of time. Sometimes she sleeps for days on end, and others she hardly sleeps at all. That's the main reason that this lot are here." He indicated the orderlies, still quietly scanning the house within a house.

"They cost an arm and a leg, but I can't do without them. She might get up in the middle of the night to make a roast dinner, as if she's expecting company. Someone has to watch, because she is more than likely to leave the gas on or the tap running, or to forget about the meal all together. When that happens, one of the guys here has to pop down an internal stairway and tidy up."

"Does she ever go out?"

"There's nowhere to go, and she doesn't seem inclined to experiment. She can look out on the garden, but it's all an illusion, computer generated graphics on a grand scale. Sometimes she sits down and writes a shopping list as if she is going to the supermarket, and so we make sure that what's on the list appears in the fridge. It's a bit pointless because she never seems to remember what it was she was going to buy. When we think she thinks it's a mealtime, we simply leave something to eat in the kitchen. Most of what this lot spend their time doing is predicting what she is going to want next, guessing what time of day she thinks it is and making the environment as comfortable for her as they can. They do a fantastic job."

"Isn't it a bit like being in a zoo?"

"Not really. It's not as if we use her for entertainment. She just gets on with her life. The observers are only here to look after her without her knowing it. The alternative is a home or a hospital. At least this way she thinks she is still living at home and looking after herself. At least she has some dignity."

"I suppose so." Erica nodded. "Do you ever go and talk to her?"

"No point. She doesn't recognise me. If I walked in there, I'd get the same sort of reception as you did. I do come up here from time to time to do my share of the observation, to check on how she's doing."

"What's the prognosis? How long does she have?"

"Doctors can't say. She's only 82 and physically she's in pretty good shape for her age. Dementia as such isn't fatal, but since it affects the elderly most people don't have to suffer for long. Old age gets them in the end. Realistically, she's probably got no more than four or five years, but theoretically it could be ten plus. Whatever. As you can now appreciate, there's no way I can sell this house while she's still alive."

"I thought you were just being pig-headed. I suppose it would make this a difficult property to market."

"That's not the issue. Like I said, most of the alterations are cosmetic, and it wouldn't take a lot of money to put it all back together again. Someone buys a house of this size and they expect to do a bit of refurbishing, so I shouldn't think a new owner would be bothered. There's enough nutters out there with money who might actually find this type of house attractive. They could play real life Big Brother, or some such. The real problem is mum. If I have to move, what will happen to her?"

Erica looked at Kenny. "I think I need to go back to bed. I've had enough surprises for one night."

Kenny nodded resignedly and led the way out of the room and back down the stairs. He closed the panel behind them. "You won't tell anyone about this, will you? It's sort of private."

"You can trust me," said Erica and disappeared into the bedroom.

Chapter 13

He gnawed on a grubby thumbnail, as he looked at the sheet of paper. It was torn now along one of the creases made from constant folding and refolding, spattered with stains. Some of the alternatives were now faded and all but indecipherable, but he scanned them carefully, as though there might be a clue in the way they were written.

"No time, no time," he muttered under his breath. "Too many options, no time."

He wiped a hand across his face and tried three passwords, seeming to anticipate failure and to be almost relieved when his expectations were realised. With a sigh he carefully closed the laptop and started the car. He sat holding the steering wheel in both hands, staring ahead through bloodshot eyes.

"Has to be another way," he said clearly. "Got to find another way."

Still he sat motionless, his eyes unblinking.

At last he seemed to come to a decision. He put the car into gear, released the handbrake and slowly, calmly let out the clutch. As the car pulled into Hobart Place, he smiled.

Chapter 14

Luke sat dozing in the chair, his head lolling on his chest, arms folded in his lap. He moved his head fitfully from side to side, muttering incoherently in his sleep. Pages of music were scattered across the desk in front of him, a few littering the floor at his feet. A patina of sweat covered his forehead. When the computer warbled to tell him that Simon was on line, he woke with a jerk.

"Luke, Luke, are you there?" Simon asked across the ether.

Luke shook himself awake, rolling his neck and wincing in pain as the stretched muscles creaked. "I'm here," he said grumpily, moving the mouse to clear the screen. "Not likely to be going anywhere, am I?"

Simon's face peered at him from the monitor, an anxious look. "Sorry, did I wake you?"

"I was just having a nap, that's all. Seem to keep nodding off, must be the boredom." Luke was awake now, his natural good humour returning. "I've got a thumping headache, mind you. Feels like a hangover."

"That vault must be better equipped than I thought."

"Ha, bloody, ha. I didn't say I had a hangover, just that it felt like one. To be perfectly honest, I could murder a pint though. Doesn't seem natural going a whole weekend without a drink. What time is it anyway?"

Simon looked down in the direction of his wrist. "Just after six thirty Monday morning. I was at the hospital all day yesterday. Didn't get home until midnight. Emily's not been too good, so I had to stay with Jeanette. I'm off back there now, but I thought I'd check on you first."

"Nothing serious, I hope."

"No, the doctors seem to think it's pretty normal, some kind of everyday post-natal thing, but you worry when it's your own flesh and blood. So what have you been up to?"

"Nothing much, as you can well imagine. I've been writing some music, but I'm finding it hard to concentrate. Probably lack of food."

"You must be hungry, mate. When did you last eat?"

Luke scratched the stubble on his chin. "Thursday, I think. To tell the truth, I can't say as I miss the food. I reckon I've gone past that stage. To start with, it was constantly on my mind, but now you mention it, I've hardly thought about eating since we last spoke."

"Maybe it's your body's way of coping, you know, switching off. I know if I hadn't eaten since Thursday, I'd be starving by now."

"You think so? I'm not so sure. Most of us in the western world have no idea what starving really is. I read an article a couple of weeks ago about obesity, about how overweight the population is becoming. This journalist made the point that people have become sufficiently affluent not to have to worry about where their next meal is coming from."

"Makes sense, I suppose. These days you're hardly like to run short, what with twenty four hour supermarkets, and that."

"Exactly what he was saying, but is it natural? Apparently the human body is designed to take on food as and when it's available and to store anything that is not needed right away. Hence fat. Our ancestors would kill a mammoth and gorge themselves stupid, because it might be days or even weeks before they got their hands on another meal. The higher the calorie content of the kill the better, which kind of explains our preference for fatty foods."

"So we're hot-wired to eat anything that comes within range."

"Seems like it. Prehistoric mankind would survive on their reserves of fat while they tracked down the next mammoth. The problem we have today is that most of us have enough money to keep the fridge well stocked so that we can get our hands on a mammoth steak, or more likely a microwave pizza, at the drop of a hat. We don't eat because we are hungry anymore: we eat out of habit."

"So if you get out of the habit, you don't miss it. Is that what you're saying?"

"Something like that. All I know is that if I don't think about food, I don't feel hungry. I guess I'm using up my reserves of fat the same way the caveman would have done when he couldn't find a mammoth for a couple of days. I can't imagine I'm doing myself any permanent harm since my body's designed to cope with it."

"So what have you been doing to while away the hours?"

"Talking to myself mostly."

"Sounds to me like you're going potty."

Luke smiled. "Not out loud, in my head. You know, thinking."

"About what?"

"Well, just before my last nap, I was thinking about accidents. Do you remember Mr Henderson?"

"Our old art teacher? How could I forget? But what's he got to do with the price of cheese?"

"We must have been about twelve or thirteen, I suppose, at big school. Remember, we were mucking about in art?"

"Can't say it rings a bell. We were always up to something."

"Right, and this wasn't anything special, just the usual low level stuff, flicking paint at each other, bit of pinching and poking. Everyday childishness I suppose, but then again we were children after all."

"Hang around. You're not talking about the time we knocked the display over?"

"The very same. Right pile of odds and sods it was. Bloody mess, if you ask me, old kettle, broken guitar, few dried flowers."

"I remember. There was a bird box in there and all, wasn't there?"

"You may well be right. All I know was it looked like a heap of shit. Henderson on the other hand seemed to think it was the Holy Grail, protected it with his life."

Simon beamed at the memory. "It's all coming back to me now. You knocked it over and he went apeshit!"

"We knocked it over actually, and you're right, he completely lost it. Started calling us irresponsible, juvenile delinquents, hooligans, that sort of thing."

"Rather unprofessional of him, if you ask me, but I guess he was upset."

"You can say that again. But to be fair, he wasn't a bad sort, and when he calmed down a bit he tried to explain. If you recall, his A-level students had been working on the display as part of their coursework, and our stupidity meant that they'd have to start all over again."

Simon was nodding. "I do remember, Made us think a bit didn't it? Winding up the teacher is one thing, fair game like, but letting down your own, well that's just not on. We were really ashamed, weren't we?"

"You went all quiet, like you always do when you're in the wrong, but of course I had to try to make excuses. After all, we hadn't done it on purpose, it was just an accident."

"Yeah, and you should have learned to keep your mouth shut. For a moment, I thought Henderson was going to launch into another rant, but he didn't did he?"

"No, this time he kept it under control, just took us to one side and told us that there was no such thing as an accident. Just like that, as if it was one of the basic laws of nature, like the world is spherical and water is wet. You know, when you're young, you tend to take things that adults tell you at face value, tend to believe them without question. I recall thinking at the time that if Mr Henderson said it was so, then it must be true. He told us that there is no such thing as an accident, and that they could all be prevented with a little foresight. Humans cause accidents because they don't think things through, that's what he said, and for the next few years I believed him. He was a teacher after all, and that particular accident could have been avoided if we hadn't been messing about, so all things considered he did have a point. These days though, I'm not so sure."

"Meaning?"

Luke took a deep breath. "Take me and Erica, for example. Our lives were changed irrevocably by an accident."

Luke paused and after a few moments Simon felt the need to fill the void. "You mean when your parents died?" he said, a little awkwardly.

"In December 1988 I was still at school, in the upper sixth, studying for my A-levels. Dead normal like thousands of others, when a stupid accident changed everything."

"You've never spoken to me about this before, Luke."

Luke continued, as though talking to himself. "I remember how I felt the day I came back from school and my parents told me that they had to go and see my gran, and that I had to stay in and look after my sister until they came back. Gran was seriously old, must have been pushing ninety, and she had been on the way out for some time. I still have vague memories of her when I was little, when she still made me cakes on a Sunday, and let me stay up late when she was baby sitting, on the rare occasions that my parents went out for the evening, but by the time I was ten or so she had become old and doddery, couldn't look after herself.

"There was a real fuss and to do when my dad, her son, had to sell her house and make the arrangements for her to go into a home. They found her a nice place though, just outside Bournemouth, and we took her down there one Saturday afternoon. Guess I must have been eleven or twelve. It was the last time I saw her."

Luke turned to the screen and saw Simon settling down to listen. He looked away at the office door and continued. "By 1988, I had all but forgotten about her, so when dad told me that they had to go and see her because she was dying, I was taken a bit by surprise. He explained that the home had rung to say she only had a few hours to live, and that they should be there to say goodbye. He sort of made a token gesture to me, asking if I would like to come with them, but I didn't really want to, and anyway someone had to stay behind and look after Erica.

"You can imagine how I felt, proud to be treated as a grown up, saddened that my gran was dying, concerned for the feelings of my parents? Dream on, I felt right royally pissed off, that's how I felt! Imagine it. I was seventeen years old, and here I was tied to the house, looking after a toddler. How embarrassing is that?

"What's more, I had things to do. It was December, the school concert was the next week, I was performing, directing and conducting. Without me, and I say this without a hint of conceit, the show would not go on. We had rehearsals planned for every evening in the run up to the performance, and now I had to cry off. As your average footballer might say, I was gutted, but what could I do?"

Simon made sympathetic noises.

"The call came from the home on the Tuesday evening, and the plan was that mum and dad should go down to Bournemouth the next day. It was unlikely that gran would survive more than twenty-four hours, so they reckoned they'd be back by Wednesday night. All I had to do was take one day off school to look after Erica. With a bit of luck they might even get back in time for me to go to rehearsals that evening, so I was somewhat appeased, but still not happy at the thought of being stuck with my little sister for a whole day. They decided to go down on the train because my mum didn't like to think of my dad driving there and back in the same day; said it wouldn't be safe. There's irony for you."

Luke turned to the screen for a reaction.

"Go on." Simon's voice was no more than a whisper.

"So mum and dad took the train up to Waterloo first thing Wednesday morning. As it turned out, the day with Erica was more fun than I had imagined. She was a lot of laughs, in a toddlerish sort of way, and I got to do things that I had forgotten all about. I suppose the same thing happens when grown-ups have their first kids. They find that they have an excuse to relive their own childhood. We went to the park and kicked a ball around. Well, I kicked She just kept falling over and giggling. We played on the swings. I hadn't been on the swings for years, and to tell the truth, I was rather relieved that all my mates were at school and not around to see me. Erica had her first go on the slide. She was petrified to start with, but by the end of the day she found it a complete hoot, just like everything else.

"When we got home, we had chocolate sandwiches, something mum would never have allowed, and Erica got chocolate all around her mouth and all over her hands. I had to clean her up with a flannel, before she redecorated the house. She just laughed and laughed. Then it was getting late, and mum and dad weren't home. I started getting Erica ready for bed. To tell the truth, by now I was enjoying the parent bit, and I was making a pretty good job of it, even if I say so myself. The phone rang, and it was mum to say that they had been delayed. Gran had died in the afternoon, but they had lots of arrangements to make, like the funeral, settling up with the home, that sort of thing. They were too late for the last train, but they would be on the first one in the morning, should be home in time for me to go to school.

"I wasn't that bothered, to be honest. I felt in control, and I told mum not to worry, I'd look after Erica, and I'd see them in the morning. I put the phone down, and that was the last time I spoke to either of them."

"Oh, Luke." Simon sounded helpless.

"It didn't really register when I heard the news on the radio the next morning. A rail crash was just another disaster, a bit close to home maybe, but still, just another example of someone else's misfortune. When mum and dad hadn't been in touch by nine o'clock, though, I started to get the feeling that something must be wrong. I listened more closely to the next bulletin. Seemed that two trains had collided just outside Clapham Junction, one coming in from Basingstoke, the other from Bournemouth. My blood ran cold as I heard the name. I listened more intently. Now it seemed the train had left about six o'clock. They'd promised to be on the first possible train, and getting up early was nothing to my parents. They were never the sort to linger in bed.

"The trains had collided, but then the situation worsened when an empty train coming out of the station ploughed into the wreckage. I sat in stunned silence. I tried to tell myself that there were bound to be survivors, but something inside me told me to expect the worst.

"The police arrived at about quarter past ten, and then I knew. Apparently, they had been killed in the first crash and were among the first to be identified, being in the front carriage. I remember that the vicar turned up with the police to bring the news. I couldn't work out why he was there, at the time. It wasn't as if we were religious or anything, never went to church, but I suppose he just thought he could bring some comfort. Can't blame the bloke for trying. They told me that mum and dad had been found holding hands, that they had died together and that both had been killed instantly. Suppose we should be thankful for small mercies."

Luke's voice cracked and he took a few moments to compose himself. Simon was lost for anything to say.

"Thirty-five people died in the crash, and over a hundred were injured. There was an inquiry and everything, not that I took a lot of notice, I had a life to get on with, but I did check it out a few years later. They blamed poor signalling for the accident, that and the fact that there were too many trains on the lines, what with so many rails being out of service because they had been badly maintained. The enquiry made recommendations, as enquiries do, but few of them were implemented. Subsequent events at Purley, Southall, Paddington and Hatfield should have shown that things still needed to be done to make the railways safe, but as far as I am aware, the full proposals have still to be implemented.

"I don't know what Mr Henderson would say about it all. If he thought that all accidents could be prevented, then Clapham would seem to support his hypothesis. You'd have thought that after thirty-five people died they would have made sure it couldn't happen again. After all, we learned our lesson and stopped messing about in art. But the powers that be simply carried on as if nothing had happened, and more lives were lost in more crashes, and I suppose people will still be dying in avoidable disasters long after I'm gone."

Simon found his voice. "I've never really thought about it before, mate," he said slowly. "I guess at the time I was so wrapped up in my own life, I didn't give much consideration to what you were going through. How on earth did you manage?"

"I know it's a horrible cliché, but the next few weeks really were a blur, what with the arrangements and the funeral and everything. Somehow I hung on to Erica. From being a pain in the neck, she became my entire family, and in a sense my reason for living. Neighbours were fantastic of course. We couldn't go short of food if we'd tried. Every day brought a new donation from someone. People can be very kind. That Christmas Erica had more presents than all her previous Christmases put together, and somehow we made it through to the New Year. Things settled down after that. You know, people start to forget about you and get on with their own lives, and we just got into a routine."

"All I remember is you left school. Seem to recall being slightly envious."

"Bang went the A-levels, of course, and the place at university. Turns out that wasn't to be. I had responsibilities and I had to grow up fast. Not that I resent it, don't get me wrong. Sure, I wish that my parents hadn't been on that train. I wish that I had gone to university, had my chance at a real career. Who knows where I'd be now. Not in this bloody vault, that's for certain. But to be fair, I have enjoyed the last seventeen years, really I have. I've got a great relationship with my sister, and I think she's a smashing person. If it hadn't been for the accident, she would be quite different, I'm sure, and we would probably hardly know one another."

"That's one way of looking at it. But how did the accident affect Erica?"

"She's never really spoken about the crash and the impact that it had on her life. A few days after it happened, she asked where her mummy and daddy were, and I just mumbled something about they weren't going to come home and it was just her and me and don't worry because everything would be all right. That seemed to satisfy her, and she just got on with things. But I have no doubt the whole incident affected her profoundly. When I think back to that first day together, I can't help but remember her laughing, cackling, giggling uncontrollably. That's how she was in those days, nothing fazed her, everything just seemed funny.

"After the crash she changed, became serious, almost introverted to the extent that a smile was a rare event and a laugh hardly ever heard. Don't get me wrong, it's not that she's unhappy or anything, just doesn't seem to have the confidence to let herself go. It would have been a couple of years later, when she was at school and she had somehow figured out that everyone else had at least one parent and no one in her class lived with their brother, that she came home one day and rather coyly asked if she had a parent, or was I really her dad and just didn't want to admit it. Then of course, I had to tell her the whole story, about the crash and how her parents and mine were both dead and that they had really loved her and they were up in heaven; forgive me, I did the whole heaven thing, don't ask me why, and that now it was just the two of us and that I would look after her and so she had nothing to worry about."

"How did she respond?"

"I'll never forget what she said next. She sat on the floor and thought for a few minutes, mulling things over in her solemn, serious way, and then she stood up, put her arms around my neck and kissed me on the cheek. 'I don't need a mummy or a daddy,' she said, 'because I've got you, and brothers are best.' And she ran off to play. Still cracks me up when I think about it even all these years later. I wonder what she's up to now."

Simon coughed, making slightly more of it than was probably necessary. "Listen, mate," he said, "you just hang in there and in a few hours you can ask her what she's been up to yourself. No doubt she and Vic are still on the case."

A thin pall of blue grey smoke welcomed Kenny as he walked into the kitchen, accompanied by the unmistakable smell of freshly minted carbon. Erica stood at a work surface buttering toast, a small pile of blackened remains bearing witness to her earlier efforts. Kenny coughed and she turned around sharply.

"You made me jump, creeping up on me like that," she said.

Kenny raised a hand. "Sorry. It's one of the drawbacks of living alone, forgetting to announce yourself." Erica followed his gaze to the stack of charred bread.

"Cooking isn't what you might call my forte," she started defensively, "but I think I've finally got the hang of it. And I've made coffee, how do you like it?"

"Black please, no sugar."

Erica handed Kenny a plate of toast, light brown, done to a turn. She poured coffee into mugs and led the way to the table. Kenny followed.

"That toaster's always been a bit temperamental," he said, as he picked up a slice of toast. He looked at it carefully, while trying not to appear critical. The butter had gathered towards the centre of the slice, as if afraid of falling off the edge, but otherwise it looked OK. He munched contentedly.

They sat eating in silence for a few moments. Erica broke the spell.

"What are you thinking?" she said.

Kenny smiled. "I was just trying to remember the last time somebody made me breakfast in my own home," he said. "Apart from Gordon, of course, but then he's paid to do it."

"Surely that would have been the last Mrs English."

"Not exactly. What you've got to remember is that my late lamented spouses were what I think is referred to in the popular press as trophy wives. You know, eye candy to grace the arm of the rich and famous. Your average trophy wife doesn't consider it her role in life to make breakfast. Even if she wakes up before lunchtime, which is not always guaranteed, she expects someone to make breakfast for her, preferably delivered to her in bed, on a tray, with a single long stemmed flower in a crystal vase. You get the picture."

"Vividly. Can't say it's ever happened to me, though."

"Well, I wouldn't exactly have you down as the trophy wife type. For a start you've got a brain."

"I'll take that as a compliment. Would be nice to be pampered from time to time, though."

"You'll just have to train your husband then. And from what I've seen, that shouldn't be beyond your talents."

Erica smiled briefly, a moment's warmth. Kenny paused to enjoy the experience.

"I'm sorry about last night," he said tentatively. "You shouldn't have had to witness that."

"You're afraid I'm going to go running to the press." Erica said it as a statement rather than a question, immediately defensive.

"No, not at all. Like you said, I can trust you. It's just that it is rather private, you know, personal. No one else should need to know anything about the skeleton in my cupboard."

"What are you, ashamed or embarrassed?" Erica offered the two as exclusive alternatives. Kenny thought for a moment.

"Neither really. It's not as if I'm doing anything wrong or harming her in any way. You know we supposedly live in a civilised society. In my book the principal characteristics of civilisation are that we educate our young and protect our weak and elderly. It's pretty basic stuff, when you think about it, not exactly radical politics. So what does our so called welfare state offer my mum? A place in a home or a hospital, that's what. The only alternative is that I look after her myself, and that's what I'm doing. And does anyone out there care? I don't think so. As far as social services are concerned, my mother doesn't exist. I could keep her chained up in a dungeon for all they know. I don't even draw her pension. She's disappeared off the official radar, and they don't give a damn. In a way, I can't blame them, too many other things to do."

"I'm the last person to criticize you," Erica's spoke quietly, her tone affectionate. "You do what you have to do. Sure, it's a rather small skeleton and a bloody big cupboard, if you don't mind me saying, but that's your prerogative. Bit like me and Luke in a way. He broke all the rules when he chose to bring me up, and after a while the powers that be forgot all about us. I guess officialdom saw that I wasn't in any immediate danger and went off to fight fires elsewhere. Don't worry. Like I said last night, your secret is safe with me. If anything, I'm rather proud of you. Now let's get this table cleared and be off. Your friend the Bill will be waiting."

Shortly before midday, Kenny and Erica were on the pavement in Hamilton Terrace. The drizzle had given up for the time being and the sun filtered through the skinny clouds, providing no more than a modicum of warmth. Erica had foraged in the various drawers and wardrobes at her disposal and come up with a pair of cords, a cotton shirt and an old denim jacket, all of which fitted her more or less. Kenny had a faded University of Michigan sweatshirt to complement his perennial jeans, and had shrugged on the leather coat as they left the house. They walked the few yards up the road, in silence.

The Blaney's house was in Marlborough Place, a turning off Hamilton Terrace. Though smaller than Kenny's by some way, it was still impressive. The tall gates stood open, and Kenny led the way, climbing the steps to a large black front door.

Erica paused at the foot of the steps, looking up at the façade.

"Something up?" asked Kenny.

Erica shook her head. "I was just thinking. Before yesterday, this would have been the largest house I'd ever been inside. I used to think the houses in Park Langley were grand, now they seem small and insignificant. I suppose it all comes down to what you're used to."

Kenny nodded sympathetically. "It's nothing to worry about," he said, ringing the doorbell. "We all have to live somewhere; the only difference is size."

Erica shrugged and joined him.

The woman who opened the door was the archetypical middle class, middle-aged white housewife. Brown hair flecked with grey and cut into a neat bob, long neck graced by a single string of pearls. Erica checked her out as only a woman can, noting the careful make up that camouflaged but could not fully disguise the lines, the slight sagging of the breasts and swelling of the waistline that the pale cashmere sweater if anything exacerbated. The overall impression was of an attractive woman maintaining her appearance in the face of the twin challenges of age and motherhood.

"Hello, Monica," Kenny said, a note of trepidation in his voice. His manner had changed. For once, he seemed unsure, apprehensive.

"Good morning," Monica replied, "or is it afternoon already?" She too seemed flustered, unclear as to whether she should be pleased or not. She turned to Erica.

"You didn't say anything about bringing a friend."

"Monica this is Erica. Erica, Monica." Kenny performed the introductions, and the two women nodded at each other. "Erica is why we are here. Her brother is in a bit of a fix, and we thought that Frank might be able to help. Is he home yet?"

Monica stepped back into the hall. "He phoned about twenty minutes ago to say he was leaving the motorway. Should be here shortly. You'd better both come in."

The hallway was carpeted in rich burgundy, giving an effect far warmer than the tiles at Kenny's house. The walls were decorated with photographs, mostly of two small children, charting their growing up. Monica led through the house to the back and into a sitting room, strewn with the day's newspapers. A pair of French windows stood open. A small girl appeared from the garden, the corners of her mouth marked with a brown substance that had to be chocolate.

"Have you been at those chocolate biscuits again, young lady," teased Monica, in mock scold. The child opened her mouth to say something and then, noticing the visitors, she quickly closed it again, her eyes large and wary.

"Don't worry about these two They're here to see your father. Now where's that brother of yours?"

The little girl took a moment to compose herself before replying. "He's out by the summer house," she said, her voice prim and official, a little girl playing the grown up. "He's pretending to hunt for tigers."

"Well, tell him to come in and get cleaned up. Daddy will be back soon." The little girl turned and ran into the garden, seeming pleased to be relieved of her unaccustomed role.

"She's lovely," said Erica, turning on her warmest smile.

"They both are," replied Monica, pleased with the compliment. "They are my pride and joy. Now can I get you two some coffee?"

"Yes please." Erica was the first to respond, the smile fixed in place. "White without, if it's not too much trouble."

Monica turned and left the room without asking Kenny what he wanted. Erica looked around at the eclectic mix of furniture, the collection of popular prints on the wall. "This is all very cosy. She's nice."

Kenny seemed distracted, uncomfortable. "Yes, she's lovely, isn't she? Like I said, the children are everything to her. She'd never do anything to upset them."

"You mean like run off with a songwriter? No, I can't see her doing that exactly. Hard to think of her having so much as a minor liaison let alone a full blown affair."

"Yes, well let's just say that appearances can be deceptive; there's a lot more to Monica than meets the eye. The marriage is effectively over, but she'd put up with all manner of suffering for the sake of the kids. If she was honest with herself, she'd admit that her relationship with Frank was a mistake from the outset, but that would in turn deny the children, and she could never bring herself to do that."

"So what did you see in her? She's nothing like a trophy wife. Can't see her lying in bed waiting for breakfast on a tray. Not your average Mrs English wannabe if you know what I mean."

"Maybe that was the attraction, is the attraction. She's just so different. She never made any demands on me; you know we could just sit there and chat, no hassle. It felt right somehow. Oh shit, I don't know."

Kenny turned and stared out of through the French windows, clearly unhappy. Erica stepped forward as if to comfort him, but then changed her mind and relented, giving him space.

Just then Monica returned, carrying a tray loaded with three mugs, each one painted with a different herb. "You did say white without, didn't you?" Monica handed her a mug inscribed *Petroselinum Crispum*, a picture of Parsley. Kenny was given Thyme, his coffee black the way he liked it. As Monica handed him the mug, their fingers touched briefly, and their eyes locked. For a moment electricity seemed to surge through them, and then Monica pulled her hand away and the spell was broken. Erica realised she had been holding her breath.

"Please sit down," said Monica, her voice cracking slightly as if she was making a physical effort to control herself. "We don't stand on ceremony in this house." There was the sound of a key turning in the lock.

"That'll be Frank." And she was gone.

Kenny and Erica stood uncomfortably, hearing the murmurings from the hall, the muted greetings, the perfunctory kiss, the mention of company in the sitting room. Finally, Frank Blaney appeared in the doorway.

"Kenny boy, nice of you to drop round. Haven't seen you in months. Not since last summer." Frank gave Kenny a conspiratorial wink as they shook hands. "And who's this young charmer? This your latest girlfriend, you old dog?"

Erica's smile remained fixed in place, but all the warmth drained away.

Kenny turned to her and then back to Frank. "This is Erica. She's a friend, and she's the reason we're here. I'm afraid we're in a bit of a fix, and we thought that you might be able to help."

"Well, make yourselves comfortable and out with it. You know me, I'll do anything I can to help a mate. What are friends for and all that, eh?"

They all sat, and with an occasional word from Erica, Kenny laid out the story. Frank listened without interruption until the tale was finished and then sucked noisily through his teeth, like a plumber confronted with a particularly expensive leak. He shook his head.

"Hard to see what I can do for you at this stage, old sport." He clasped his hands together as if inviting them to join him in prayer. "Look at it from my perspective. It's not as if a crime has been committed or even threatened, now is it? This chap seems to be doing no one any harm, he's on private property and in no immediate danger. Sounds to me like he'll get out as soon as they open up tomorrow. He'll be a bit hungry, I suppose, but unless he's got some medical condition you haven't told me about, I don't see that would be life threatening. Not a good thing to get the police involved with the private sector, could give us a bad name if we were seen to be interfering, if you see what I mean."

Kenny looked to Erica, whose smile had now completely disappeared. "Looks like another dead end, I'm afraid," he said to her quietly. At that moment there was a cry from the garden. The little girl came up to the French doors.

"Mummy," she wailed, pointedly ignoring her father as only the very young can, "Nick's fallen in some nettles. He's in awful pain." Monica was on her feet in an instant.

"Excuse me," she said politely, "minor domestic crisis."

Nobody spoke for a moment after Monica left, and then Kenny turned to Frank.

"Conference was it this weekend, Birmingham was it?" Frank seemed a little blind-sided by this unexpected turn in the conversation.

"Yes, it was as it happens." He didn't add what of it, but the question was there all the same.

"Did you take Constable McEntyre with you? Tracey wasn't it?"

"What are you inferring?"

"I think the word you want is implying. I imply, you infer. And anyway, I wasn't implying anything, just asking a polite question. As I recall, she wasn't too well last time I saw her. You can infer what you like."

Frank looked nonplussed, vaguely aware that his intelligence had been insulted but not quite sure how. He went on the attack.

"Now look here, English, what I get up to in my spare time is between me and my conscience. There's no need for you to go telling tales out of school. You're not exactly a saint, if what I've heard's anything to go by." Frank had started to sweat. Kenny stayed calm.

"All we want is an address or even a phone number for this Mike Dalton. I'm sure that the data banks at New Scotland Yard can come up with that sort of information in a matter of minutes."

"It's Bank Holiday Monday." Frank was no longer denying he had the capacity to help, now he was dissembling.

"I have no doubt that the offices are fully staffed, even on a bank holiday weekend. All it takes from a man in your position is a quick call to the right person."

Frank gave up arguing. He stared at the floor for a few moments. "It could take a couple of hours. I'll have to check who's on duty and owes me a favour," he said quietly. "Leave me a number, and I'll get back to you."

Kenny quickly scribbled his mobile number on a scrap of paper and handed it to the other man. He and Erica rose to leave.

"Say thank you to Monica for us. We had better be going."

Frank stood up, and the activity seemed to give him renewed strength.

"Better make that thank you and goodbye, eh Kenny? I don't think you and I have anything more to say to each other. I'll do this one favour for you and then we're quits. Don't bother calling round again."

Kenny met his glare full on. "Suits me fine," he said.

"What was all that about Constable McEntyre?" asked Erica, when they returned to Kenny's kitchen. Kenny made more coffee.

"Let's just say that Monica is not the only one of the Blaney ménage who's been playing away."

"You mean Frank? Ugh, that's horrible. Who'd want to do it with him? He's a louse."

"Power can be a potent aphrodisiac, or hadn't you heard? I'm sure our Frank is a very attractive proposition for a young police officer with the right mix of low morality and high ambition."

"And you knew about this? Why don't you tell Monica? It might change her attitude to her happy family home."

"I don't think Monica would thank me or anybody else for pointing out that Frank is a nauseating scumbag. She knows that, she is married to him after all. I know her well enough to be certain that she wouldn't run into my arms simply because she finds out that she can't trust her husband. Remember, she's done the whole adultery bit herself, she can't exactly claim the moral high ground. Anyway, I want her to love me for myself, not because she ditches the current model."

"She loves you all right. You can see that from the way she looks at you."

"You reckon?"

"Without a shadow. A woman can tell these things, you know. That said, you'd have to be blind, deaf and dumb not to notice the chemistry between you two. I'm amazed that filthy Frank didn't twig. Guess being a copper, he hasn't got the same refinement of the senses as the rest of us. Believe me, Kenny, she is just as miserable as you are that you can't be together."

"If you say so. Guess I'll just have to wait until the children are grown up and then try again. Way it is at the present, I am about as welcome in that house as a paedophile on speed. And that goes for husband and wife."

"Oh well, course of true love." Erica sipped her coffee, and then a thought struck her. "Hang on a minute," she said, pausing to give Kenny time to look up from his mug, making sure she had his full attention. "How come a policeman can afford a house like that. Must be worth a couple of million at least?"

"And then some," said Kenny reflectively, as he blew on his mug, "but that's where Monica came in. She comes from old money."

"What, you mean like aristocracy, daddy got a place in the country?"

"I don't think you could call it that, can't remember any titles being mentioned, but Monica's family apparently are dripping with it. The way she tells the story, they were less than impressed when she announced she was marrying someone as ordinary as a copper. Seems they had rather hoped she might do better for herself, a Duke maybe, or an Earl at least. She was a bit of a rebel in her youth, it seems, because she put her foot down and said it was Frank or nothing. That might explain the attraction, not so much in love with the man as with thumbing her nose at her people. The house was a wedding present from daddy, sort of peace offering you might say, but as you can imagine, it did nothing to blunt the Blaney ambitions."

"Must have been quite a feather in his cap, rich missus, big house for entertaining. Makes it even more revolting to think that he plays around."

"That's Frank for you. I guess Monica knows what he gets up to and ignores it. I got the feeling that she rather regretted her rebellion and saw Frank's infidelities as a punishment. I guess her feelings of guilt made it harder for her to accept our relationship, gave her an excuse to break it off."

Erica looked at Kenny, as he stared gloomily into his coffee, as if the answer might be there somewhere in the steaming blackness.

They both jumped as Kenny's mobile sprang into life. Kenny picked it up and pressed the green button.

"Hi, Frank, that was quick," he said, trying to sound friendly.

"It was easier than I expected. Mate of mine was doing some overtime. I've got an address and a phone number. But listen, you didn't get any of this from me. Like I said before, from now on we don't know each other."

"As you wish, fire away."

Kenny scribbled the address and phone number on a piece of paper as Frank dictated.

"Petts Wood," said Frank. "Must be somewhere south of the river. Never heard of it myself, way off my manor."

"I know where it is. Thanks for your help, Frank." Kenny clicked the off button and turned to Erica.

"Mike Dalton lives in Petts Wood."

"But that's just down the road from…"

"Penge, exactly." Kenny finished the sentence. "We've been up and down and round the houses, and all the time he was a couple of miles away, on the outskirts of Orpington."

"Small world," said Erica. "Shall we give him a ring?"

"That's the general intention," said Kenny and he tapped the number into the keypad. He held the phone to his ear and they both waited in silence as the call connected. Kenny let it ring for a few moments, but nobody answered. He clicked the red button, with an air of resignation.

"Nobody home."

Erica sighed with disappointment. Not for the first time, she wore a look of dejection.

"What shall we do?" she asked in a small voice.

"We've got the address. I suggest we pay Mr Dalton a visit." Kenny tried to sound upbeat, for Erica's benefit if nothing else.

"But what's the point if there's no one at home?"

"Just because they don't answer the phone doesn't mean they're not in. Remember what happened with Simon. Frank may have given us the wrong number or I might have written it down wrong. They might have popped out to lunch, or the garden centre, or the supermarket. They might be in the garden, for all we know, and didn't hear the phone. There's no end to the possible explanations. We can't do anything sitting here can we? May as well climb back in the car and go check things out in person. What do you say?"

Erica seemed to make a physical effort to appear positive. "Come on then," she said. "Let's go."

Chapter 15

The house was as tidy as the car. Cushions had been pulled from the settee and matching armchairs, drawers lay upturned on the furniture. Everywhere there was paper.

An old bureau stood to one wall, drawers missing and the desk open, strewn with it's contents.

He sat in the middle of the mess, picking up handfuls of old bills, bank statements and junk mail, scanning each of them briefly before discarding one batch in favour of the next. Finally he picked up a small leatherette address book and gave a childlike cry of pleasure. He stood up with his prize and took it over to the window to get the benefit of the weak daylight that filtered through the tatty net curtains.

He fumbled with the book, almost tearing the cover, before taking a deep breath in an effort to calm down. He found the tab with the letter D and opened the page.

Running a finger down the handwritten entries, he stopped just before the end.

He smiled again.

Chapter 16

The drive through central London and across the river couldn't have been easier. The traffic was so light as to be virtually non existent, and this time Kenny took the most direct route, straight through Victoria and over Vauxhall Bridge. As they neared Penge, Erica's phone bleeped.

"It's a message from Simon," she said, reading. "He says Luke's fine but bored. Trying not to think of food, and spending his time writing music."

"That sounds positive. Should help the hours pass."

"You're right. Luke seems to lose all track of time when he's composing. Sometimes, it's like he goes into a trance, you know, forgets about everything else, gets so absorbed."

"Tends to be the way when the creative juices are flowing. I suppose it can make a bloke rather difficult to live with."

"Doesn't bother me, so long as he's happy."

"Is Simon at home? We could pop in, and you could have a word with Luke yourself."

Erica paged down. "No, he says he keeps having to go to the hospital. Must be doing a kind of shuttle service between his two responsibilities."

"Sounds like a good friend."

"He is." Erica put the phone back in her bag.

"Do you want to stop for a change of clothing?" Kenny asked.

Erica thought for a moment.

"No, let's not bother," she replied. "I don't want to waste any more time. I'm starting to get an uncomfortable feeling."

"Meaning what?"

"I don't know exactly, but I'd sort of got it into my head that Luke wasn't in any real danger. You know, we worked out that he had enough air to survive on, and there's plenty of water. He seems to be fine from what Simon says."

"So what's the matter?"

"I'm not sure. Maybe it's just that time is moving on, and we don't seem to get any closer to him. I can't help thinking that we may have underestimated the problem. Maybe he is in more danger than we imagine. I've started worrying that we're never going to get him out."

Kenny looked across at Erica, who seemed close to tears. He tried to sound upbeat. "You may be right. So the best thing is to get to Mike Dalton as quickly as we can. Grab the A to Z from the glove box and check out where Pastor's Avenue is."

Erica busied herself with the map, the activity seeming to take her mind off things, to alleviate her pessimism. She found the road and pointed it out to Kenny as they stopped at traffic lights in Beckenham. Kenny took a brief look and nodded.

"I know where it is," he said confidently. "You can put the map away."

Kenny drove assertively, and Erica sat back and did her best to enjoy the ride. As they pulled up outside Mike Dalton's house she checked her watch.

"Crikey," she said, "it's nearly four. Where's the day gone to?"

Kenny climbed out of the car. "Time flies when you're having fun."

Erica joined him on the pavement. "And are you?"

Kenny looked at her, noting the signs of strain, the dark smudges under the eyes, lines at the corners of the mouth. "I suppose I'd be enjoying myself more if the circumstances were a little different," he said carefully.

Erica gave a grunt that could have been taken as agreement, and Kenny led the way to the front door. He rang the bell and the sound echoed through the house. No response. He rang again, more in hope than expectation, with the same result.

Erica exhaled. "Nobody home," she said quietly.

"Let's check round the back," said Kenny.

Petts Wood is a typical south London suburb, consisting almost entirely of three bedroomed semi-detached houses. Mike Dalton's home was no different to thousands of others in the area. Built in the fifties, it had a front and back garden and a garage on the unattached side. Beyond the garage, a wooden gate guarded a short footpath to the back garden. The gate had no lock and squeaked on its hinges as Kenny opened it. He walked past the garage to the back of the house. Not surprisingly, the garden was also typical of the neighbourhood. Predominantly lawn with a shrubbery border, a washing line and a shed. It was identical to those on either side. A swing and a tricycle bore evidence to the presence of children in the household, and a plastic table with matching chairs sat on the concrete patio, but otherwise it was a clone of every other garden in the street. It was also empty of people. Kenny looked briefly up at the back of the house, but once again there were no signs of life.

Kenny walked slowly back down the path, to where Erica was waiting patiently on the crazy paved drive. She looked at him expectantly. "Nothing," he said, hating himself for letting her down again. She just nodded her head, as if it were no more than she expected, and turned back to the car.

"Can I help you?" a voice seemed to come from nowhere. Kenny looked around for the source and saw a figure standing in the doorway of the house next door.

"Hi, yes, maybe you can," Kenny said, walking across the small patch of grass to the low wall that divided the properties, thankful of any hint that the journey had not been entirely in vain. "I'm looking for Mike Dalton."

The door opened and the figure stepped out. He was as tall as Kenny and about the same age. His hair was greyer than Kenny's, and he had a short stubble beard; they could easily have been taken for brothers. He eyed Kenny suspiciously.

"Are you friends of the Daltons?"

"Not exactly, but we have a mutual acquaintance who is in a spot of bother, and we thought that Mike might be able to help." Kenny kept the explanation short, not wanting to scare off what could be their last chance.

"Well, they're not in, as you can see." The tone was still mistrustful, cagey, but at least they were talking.

"Any idea when they might be back?" Kenny's maintained the air of friendliness in his voice.

"I can't be sure, but I think they went down to the coast. Probably won't be back until tonight."

"Any idea where?"

"Poole, I think. They've got a boat or something down there. Probably just staying for the weekend."

"Don't suppose you've got a phone number or anything?"

"I think they stay on the boat, sort of camp out like. Haven't got a mobile number or anything like that. Don't really know them that well. They've only lived here for a few months."

Kenny nodded sympathetically, thinking. "Could you do me a favour please?" he tried, aware that he was now running out of options. The man seemed unsure, but he looked over at Erica, who had been listening to the conversation, and she gave him an encouraging smile. It seemed to do the trick.

"Sure, what can I do?"

"If I leave you my number, can you ask Mike to call me when you see him?"

"Course I can." He ducked inside the house and came back with a small notebook and a pen. "Here you go. Write it in the book, and then I won't forget."

Kenny took the book and pen and wrote his name and mobile number.

"Shall I tell him what it's about?" asked the man, as he took the book back.

"Just say that there's a bit of trouble at the office, and he could probably sort it all out in no time."

"Will do," said the man, and walked back into his own house. Kenny and Erica headed once more for the car.

"Where to next, madam," Kenny asked, as he settled behind the wheel. Erica closed her eyes. "Just take me home, will you. I need a strong cup of tea."

"As you wish," said Kenny, and pulled away from the kerb.

Neither noticed the old Vauxhall parked across the road; the middle-aged driver slumped low in his seat, watching them curiously.

They had just passed through Bromley, when the knocking sound started, seeming to come from somewhere near Erica's left foot. She looked into the well of the car and then up at Kenny's face, frowning.

"Blast!" said Kenny, and he drew up at the side of the road.

"What's up?" asked Erica, as Kenny pressed the boot release and climbed out of the car.

"Flat," he said, over his shoulder, and wandered round to the front, to survey the damage. He kicked the front passenger's tyre, which had indeed assumed pancake proportions. Kenny rolled his eyes to the sky, and then went to the back of the car, to collect the wheel brace, jack and spare. Without further comment, he started loosening nuts, and as he grimaced with the effort, found himself looking straight into Erica's face. She was smiling.

"What's so funny?" he asked, sliding the jack into position.

"Oh, nothing."

"No, come on out with it. What do you find so amusing?"

Erica thought for a moment. "I don't know really. I suppose it's the thought of you having to fix a puncture."

Kenny frowned and started cranking the jack. "It might help if you got out," he said. "It's bad enough lifting a couple of tons of metal, without you adding to it."

"Sorry I'm sure," said Erica, doing as she was asked. She stood behind Kenny as he raised the car so that the flat was clear of the road surface. Four young men in a Fiesta passed on the other side of the road, windows down, hooting in derision.

"Seems I'm not the only one to see the funny side," Erica remarked.

Kenny stood with the damaged tyre and dropped it in the boot. "Can't say I share your sense of humour."

"Oh come off it, Kenny, it is rather silly. I mean, how much did you pay for this car?"

Kenny positioned the spare. "If you have to ask the price, you can't afford it."

"Got to be at least a hundred thousand."

Kenny grunted. "So what?"

"Well, you pay all that money, and you still get a flat. You'd have thought they'd have unpunctureable tyres or something."

"Even an Aston Martin runs on pneumatic tyres. Christ, even an F1 does."

"Yeah, but all the same. And you look silly doing, I don't know, everyday things you know like ordinary people."

Kenny started tightening bolts and then lowered the car before finishing the job. For several minutes he said nothing, seemingly immersed in the activity. He put the tools back in the boot and scrubbed ineffectually at his hands with a piece of cloth.

"I do lots of things that ordinary people do," he said sulkily, as he got back into the driving seat.

"Such as?"

Kenny sat staring ahead. "Well," he began and then stopped again.

"Let's see. How about shopping, do you go shopping?"

Kenny turned to Erica. "I sometimes go and buy a few clothes, or books."

"No, I meant real shopping, you know, for food and that."

"That's what Gordon's for."

"And I suppose he does all the housework and the cooking as well."

"Naturally."

"So what else do you occupy your time with, just like ordinary people. Going to work, that's what ordinary people do. But then again I don't suppose that's high on your list of everyday activities."

"You know it's not."

"Gardening, DIY?"

Kenny started the engine. "Can't say I've ever been that way inclined."

Erica giggled. "You're not trying. I bet you could convince me of your ordinariness if you really wanted to. Go on, what is the average day like in the life of Kenny English?"

Kenny grinned back at her. "Most days I try to sober up before I go out and party, if you really want to know." He checked over his shoulder before pulling out into the road.

Now Erica laughed aloud. "And there was me thinking you were a complete waster. I'm so glad to hear you've found plenty to fill your time."

"Yeah well, you can only play the cards you're dealt. Let's get back to your place so I can clean up a bit."

It was nearly six by the time that they returned to Penge. Erica opened the door and switched the lights on, ushering Kenny into the kitchen. Without asking, she filled the kettle and set it to boil. While Kenny washed his hands in the sink, Erica busied herself with mugs and tea bags. When she spoke she caught Kenny unawares.

"He's been in that vault for three days now," she said.

Kenny thought for a moment, rinsing the dirty suds away and mentally confirming the arithmetic. "That's right, about seventy two hours."

"And if we don't get to him, he should be released in fourteen hours or so."

"So he's over the worst of it. Is that what you are saying?" Kenny tried to follow Erica's line of thought. She passed him a towel.

"Something like that. I was just trying to imagine how I would feel if the roles were reversed. I would make every effort to look on the bright side. If it were me, I suppose that I would try to sleep through as much as possible. That might help to ease the boredom and the hunger. By now, I would be counting the hours till tomorrow morning. At least there is light at the end of the tunnel."

Erica squeezed the tea bags and dropped them in the bin before adding milk to the mugs. She handed one to Kenny who accepted it gratefully.

"I'm ready for this," he said, sitting at the kitchen table. Erica flopped into the chair opposite. "Do you still get the feeling that we've missed something, that Luke could be in more danger than we think?"

"It's at the back of my mind, but I can't quite work out what it is. It's like a premonition, a feeling that I should know something, that there is something else we should have thought of. It's getting to me, like an itch I can't scratch. Do you know what I mean?"

Kenny nodded supportively. "Probably women's intuition," he offered.

"You think I'm being neurotic, don't you?"

It was a statement rather than a question, but Kenny still felt obliged to respond.

"No," Kenny lied, "but I do think that you're tired, and that you've been under a lot of stress. You may have something, or you may just be imagining it all."

Erica opened her mouth to object, but Kenny's calm authority combined with his good sense were too much for her to challenge.

"I need to get into some of my own clothes," she said, picking up her mug and heading for the door. "I won't be a moment."

Left alone with his mug of tea, Kenny looked around the kitchen, so different to his own in Hamilton Terrace. He stood and wandered around the small room, staring out at the patch of garden, opening cupboards randomly. In the hall he looked through the doorway at the through lounge, the original wall between the two downstairs rooms no more than a couple of thin pillars on either side. He sighed and walked over to the piano that stood next to the front bay window. Like the rest of the room, it had what could be politely described as a lived in look. The woodwork was scuffed and the varnish in places was flaked and peeling. The keyboard stood open as if it had just been used, and there were sheets of manuscript paper, some on the lectern, others scattered on the top of the instrument or on the floor around the stool.

Kenny picked up a sheet of paper and considered it carefully. It was Luke's work all right. He recognised the hand from the music that Vic had shown him all those days ago. He tried to pick out the tune, humming lightly to himself. Eventually he sat down at the piano and started to play. After a few bars he grew familiar with the melody and quickly picked up on the chord patterns. He started to play with more confidence and was pleased with the result.

"Not bad." Kenny stopped in mid bar and turned to see Erica standing at the door.

"Sorry," he said. "I didn't mean to disturb you."

"Don't mention it. For a split second I thought it was Luke, but your playing is quite different."

"In what way?"

Erica thought for a moment. "I'm no musician," she said, settling on the arm of the sofa, "but I've lived in a house with a musician all my life. I suppose I've learnt to recognise different styles."

"Go on." Kenny turned on the stool, his back to the keyboard.

"Luke is an instinctive, intuitive musician. His weapon of choice has always been the piano. I guess it's something to do with polyphony, but he can pick up just about any instrument and within a few minutes play it proficiently. It's as if he's understood music from the cradle; it's something that he was born to. When he plays, he does so with an abandon borne of confidence, an artist at one with his trade. If he hits a wrong note, he simply ignores it, and you could be forgiven for thinking it was just part of the overall piece. You're different."

"Go on."

"Well, for a start you've obviously taken lessons. You're good, don't get me wrong, but you follow the music note for note. When you make a mistake you go back and play it again until you get it right. It's as if you respect the music, as if you have to make sure there are no errors."

"Isn't that what you're supposed to do?"

"I suppose so, unless you're a musician, that is. For Luke, the music is at best a guide as to how a piece should sound, the composers suggestion of how to recreate what he held in his head. Luke has never lacked confidence in his own ability to embellish, or sometimes to simplify, but always to present his interpretation rather than slavishly following instructions."

Kenny nodded slowly, considering the words. "That's the difference between a true musician and a competent amateur, I guess. I can't write music, believe me I've tried; all I can ever hope to do is play."

"I thought you were the lyricist. I'm rather impressed you can play at all."

"It always helps to have a second string to your bow. If I can play the piano, I can work alone more easily, see how my words fit the music."

"Is that how it works then, you get the music and you write the words to fit."

"It depends. Sometimes it works that way round, others it works in reverse. Some composers like to write a tune that they think will sell and all you need are a few lyrics to give the performers something to sing.

Doesn't really matter what you say, just so long as the lines scan and rhyme in the right places. Other times a lyricist comes up with a song, I guess you could call it a poem, and asks a composer to put it to music. I've done both over the years. What I tend to find works best is when you both sit in a room together and discuss what exactly you want to achieve, and then just try out ideas until you come up with something you both like. That way you end up with a piece that is a whole in itself, rather than being two pieces welded together."

"Sounds fascinating," said Erica without a hint of irony. "And you think it would work, you know, you and Luke?"

"I'd like to think so. I was just about to say that your brother is very talented. This stuff is really good." Kenny leafed aimlessly through the manuscript sheets.

"He is," said Erica, "but then I would say that, wouldn't I? But there has to be more to it than talent surely?"

"There is, lots more. As I said he certainly has the ability; strong melodies, interesting harmonies, clever transpositions, the lot. Looks like he can handle the arrangements as well." Kenny peered meaningfully around at the papers scattered at his feet. "It's a little rough around the edges, but that's nothing a bit of time and experience won't improve. Given the right sort of support, I reckon he could make a go of it."

"You didn't exactly answer my question," Erica said with the suspicion of one who has been let down by life once too often. "I asked if he could work with you."

"That's rather harder to say." Kenny chose his words carefully. "Collaboration is a very special relationship, like a marriage, no, more like a close friendship. There has to be a chemistry there, a meeting of minds. You may both have the necessary technical expertise, but if you don't complement each other, if your styles are different or you just don't get on, then it won't work. Am I making sense?"

"I think so. What you're saying is that you and Luke have to see eye to eye, if the combination of your skills is going to be worth anything."

"It's a personality thing. To answer your question, I can't say for sure how well we could work together, not until I've met him, and even then we'd need to give it a try, see how things go. What I can say is that he has all the necessary skills, and if we don't get on, there's no reason why he shouldn't work with someone else. If I can't work with him, I can certainly introduce him to someone who can. Put it this way, your brother wasting his time in an office is, in my view, a criminal misuse of a rare gift. He should be writing music for a living."

Erica drew a deep breath. "You're not just saying that?"

"To be nice? No, I mean it, and what's more I can tell you that if he has half as much gumption as his little sister, I would consider it a privilege to call him my partner."

Erica swallowed, embarrassed, not knowing what to say.

"So what next?" Kenny asked, diplomatically changing the subject.

"Food," Erica replied. "I'm hungry. It must be neaerly seven and we haven't eaten since breakfast."

Kenny checked his watch. "You're right. What do you recommend?"

"Well, there's nothing in the fridge, so we need to go out. They do midday meals at . It's a bit late for lunch, but we could pop in there and see if they've got any left."

"You're talking my kind of language," said Kenny, as he went to the kitchen to get his coat. "I don't know about you, but I could use a drink as well."

"My thoughts entirely," said Erica, as they left the house and headed for the pub.

Luke shuffled up and down between the rows of safety deposit boxes, his head low, swaying from side to side. He plucked at the shoulder of his shirt, freeing the wet cloth from his skin. Once or twice he overbalanced, his arm making contact with one of the metal cabinets, and he bounced back into the narrow aisle. He stopped for a moment, frowning as if unsure as to why he was there, as if seeing the room for the first time. He stood motionless for several seconds, before resuming his meanderings, dragging one foot and then the other in an effort to keep going.

Simon's voice came from the office, and Luke stopped again, cocking his head to one side, to catch what was being said.

"Luke, Luke, are you there?" Simon sounded concerned, but Luke made no effort at haste, simply wandering back to his desk. When he touched the mouse, the computer terminal sprang to life, and he was faced with the image of Simon filling the video window, as though trying to look through his own web cam, to see what was on the other side.

"Hi, I'm here," Luke drawled.

"Thank Christ for that." Simon ignored Luke's tone, in his relief. "I was starting to worry."

Luke shook his head, beads of sweat peppering the desk. He gave himself a kind of controlled shiver and sat up straight, concentrating.

"Thought I might have popped out?" he said, his voice recovering its customary timbre.

Simon smirked and sat back in his chair. "Yeah, something like that. Can't trust you for a minute these days. It's like one accident after another."

"What time is it?"

"It's just past seven on Monday night. Less than twelve hours to go. Come to think of it, it's as well they're not having the audit until tomorrow afternoon; you'd have made them jump all right!"

Luke came suddenly awake. "Shit, I'd forgotten about that. All the top brass'll be down here, won't they? Best I tidy up before they let me out."

"Don't worry about that, there'll be plenty of time. Anyway, I can't see the auditors being overly concerned about a bit of mess. All they're interested in is making sure the Winsloe diamonds are safe."

Luke relaxed again and as he did so his head lolled onto one shoulder. "Suppose you're right. Are they in the inner vault?"

"The Winsloe's? Too right they are. Metal Mickey had them moved a couple of weeks ago, just after they finished building the inner vault. Made a right song and dance about it, if you recall. New line of business, great white hope."

Luke's eyes closed for a moment, and his head slumped forward. He blinked a couple of times, coming round. When he spoke, it was obviously an effort.

"What were we talking about?"

"The Winsloe diamonds. Are you paying attention?"

"Sorry, can't concentrate. I remember now."

There was a pause as Simon waited for Luke to continue. In the end he became concerned. "Luke, are you still awake?"

Luke sat up straight and took a deep breath. "Sure, I'm fine, just a bit dopey. Talk to me about something or I'll doze off again."

Simon racked his brains. "Were you there when George finally got the push?"

"I remember him emptying his desk. Don't think I'll ever forget it. He was muttering to himself like a maniac, cursing Dalton, promising revenge. He took everything he could carry, stuffed it all in a black sack. Even took that laptop he used to have on his desk."

"Did he really? What a nerve. That was the company's property. Mind you, there's a certain irony there. I think that's why he got the push."

"How come." Luke yawned, but managed to keep his eyes open.

"George had this idea that we should all have laptops instead of the computers on our desks. He thought it would be more efficient."

"Can't see how."

"His plan was that instead of each of us having our own desks, we should all be mobile, so we could move round the bank and work from anywhere. Hot-desking, he called it."

"Sounds logical, I suppose, but I can't see it working in practice."

"Yeah, well when you consider how much time we are away from our desks, I guess he might've had a point. George thought it would look good to the customers as well. You know, when we have to meet them in the courtesy rooms, we could turn up with a laptop and give them the low down on the state of their account, there and then."

Luke shook himself and tried to follow. "But we'd have to plug them into the network wouldn't we? That might not look so professional, wires trailing everywhere."

"Ah, but George had thought of that. He reckoned you could link up by wireless. No need to plug in."

"Sounds fancy."

"It's not that special really. Instead of connecting one desktop computer to a port like we do now, you stick in a wireless transmitter, and then all the laptops have a wireless receiver, and we can all see the network from anywhere in the building."

"Which is why George had a laptop?"

"Exactly. He was experimenting with different transmitters and that. Only problem is, he didn't clear the expense with Dalton. Must have thought he'd present it as a fait accompli, to get in with the boss. You can imagine how that looked when Metal Mickey found out."

"So he gave George the push and threw all the kit away, I suppose. Probably didn't worry about the odd laptop going walkies."

"Guess so. Mind you, if he had a purge on the transmitters, he missed one."

"Really?"

"Yeah. It's in the courtesy room on the ground floor, you know at the back of the building. I had a meeting in there last Wednesday, and I happened to notice it."

"Is it still working?"

"The little green light was flashing, so I assume the answer to that one is yes."

Luke snorted. "Bloody typical. They spend all that money and all they get is one little transmitter sending out its signal to nobody. If I didn't feel so knackered, I'd laugh out loud."

Simon grinned at the camera. "Anyway, I can't spend all day chatting. I've got to get back to the hospital and pick up my family. Emily's over whatever it was that was bothering her, and they can come home tonight. I'll check in later if I get a chance."

Luke ran his hand through his hair and wiped sweat from his brow. "Don't you worry about me. You just make sure your loved ones are safe. I'll see you tomorrow."

The window in the middle of the monitor screen went blank as Simon logged off, and Luke sat for a few moments, in silent meditation. Then slowly his eyelids closed, his head fell forward, and he began to snore quietly.

Chapter 17

He sat in the car until it was quite dark, watching the house. Nobody came to draw the curtains. No movement was apparent from inside. Carefully, he closed the car door behind him, looking warily up and down the deserted pavement before crossing the road.

Glancing at the house next door, he hurried up the drive and through the gate into the back garden. The moon was nearly full, but was obscured by thin clouds, as he edged along the back of the garage to the house. He looked up at the window next to the back door, the half-light wedged open. Peering around the garden he saw what he wanted, a plastic chair. It wobbled a little as he stood on it, but it was steady enough for him to reach through the open window and unlatch the larger one below. In a matter of moments he was through and standing on a stainless steel draining board. Huffing slightly he jumped to the floor.

The Dalton household was a picture of order and tidiness. In the back room he found a desk, on which stood a flat screen monitor. He caressed the wood of the desktop for a moment, as if concerned that he might damage it, and then nudged the mouse. The screen gradually cleared, demanding the inevitable. Sighing, he sat down and took the grubby sheet of paper from his pocket, the list of permutations of Dalton's name and those of his wife and children, the personal details that in one way or another will provide the key to any user's password.

This time there was to be no lock out, and he gradually worked his way through the list, failing and trying again in an almost mindless exercise. It was over an hour later, when he sat back, staring at the still impassive screen, his options exhausted. Idly he toyed with the top drawer of the desk, opening and closing it with his index finger, as his mind tried to come up with new alternatives. At length, he looked inside. The drawer was almost empty, except for a neat stack of credit card and bank statements, along with utility bills. He picked one up and scanned it idly, trying to find something of interest. He was just about to return it when the name at the top caught his eye, J Michael Dalton. Suddenly he was alert, reading the name again to make sure there was no mistake, taking in this unforeseen personal detail. He took the stack of papers from the drawer and leafed through them. They were all similar; Mr J M Dalton, J M Dalton Esq., even a Michael J Dalton. It was the letter from the building society that solved the mystery: addressed to Mr Julian M Dalton.

He looked back to the computer screen, and then down again at the letter. Carefully, he typed in the name, and as the desktop sprang to life he punched the air, strangling the scream of victory into nothing more than a feral hiss. It took him a few seconds to compose himself, and as he did so, he looked around guiltily, as if concerned that someone may have heard. He carefully returned the papers to the drawer and stood, pushing the chair neatly back the way he had found it. He left the house the same way he had entered, closing the window behind him.

Chapter 18

The Billy was warm and snug, after the dank evening closing in outside. Kenny held the door open, and then followed Erica to the bar. The pub was doing a brisk evening trade, locals relaxing at the end of a bank holiday, but Erica and Kenny waited patiently to be served.

When it was their turn, Erica ordered her usual lager and lime, while Kenny asked for a pint of lager.

"I don't suppose there's any food available," Kenny asked.

The barmaid looked at them sternly, half turning to a sign that stated no meals would be served after two thirty, but a quick glance at Erica seemed to soften her attitude.

"I'll see if there's anything left over from lunch," she said kindly, and disappeared towards the back of the pub. She returned in a matter of seconds.

"There's a couple of roast dinners," she said. "They might be a bit soggy but they'll fill a gap."

Kenny looked at Erica, who nodded. "Sounds perfect to us," he said.

"Take a seat, and I'll bring them over when they're ready."

As Kenny sat down, he took a mouthful of beer and sighed. "I needed that," he said.

Erica followed suit. "Me too. It's been a long day."

"It's been a long few days," said Kenny, "but it's nearly over. This time tomorrow, we'll be able to look back on this and laugh."

"I feel like getting wrecked," said Erica.

"Is this a regular occurrence?" Kenny asked with mock concern.

"You sound like a Victorian father," said Erica, smiling, "but since you ask, no it's not. I'm not very good at drinking, and the last time I had a couple too many it took me two days to recover. But right now, my head feels so full that I reckon the best way to unwind is to get lathered."

Kenny raised an eyebrow and looked at Erica's glass. "You're more likely to drown than get drunk on that stuff," he said. "Believe me, I know what I'm talking about."

"So what do you recommend? Brandy? Vodka?"

"Best lay off the brandy, that will make you feel rough in the morning. Probably better not to bother with spirits at all if you're not used to them. You could try a glass of wine. Something white and light should do the trick without putting you in hospital."

Erica looked thoughtful for a moment, and then appeared to make up her mind.

"White wine it is then." And she drained her glass. Kenny returned to the bar and ordered drinks. As he sat down again, the barmaid appeared carrying two steaming plates.

"It's not your actual haute cuisine," she said, as she laid them carefully on the table, producing two sets of cutlery wrapped in paper napkins, "but it should do the trick. Enjoy." And with a wink, she was gone.

Kenny looked at his plate. Roast beef with all the trimmings. He suddenly realised how hungry he was and tucked in with gusto. Erica did likewise. The roast beef was overcooked but still tender. The roast potatoes may once have been crisp but were now soft, not unlike the vegetables which could have been cooking since last weekend. The Yorkshire had clearly come out of a packet, as had the gravy, which was congealing around the edge of the plate. Kenny sighed with pleasure.

"She's not wrong," he said to Erica, who had barely looked up from her plate since it arrived. "Cordon bleu this isn't, but I tell you what, it's the best meal out I've had in a long time." Erica nodded and continued eating, gravy running down her chin.

Neither spoke again until the plates were empty. Erica sat back and swigged half her glass of wine. She winced slightly at the unfamiliar flavour, but then swigged once more and put the glass back on the table. "Now I'm starting to feel human again," she said.

"You'll start feeling legless, if you carry on like that." Kenny's admonishing tone seemed at least partly serious.

"You're doing the Victorian father again. I told you, I intend to get plastered. Watch out, you may have to carry me home."

"I'm the last person to criticise someone for getting drunk, and if you need carrying home, then I will be pleased to help you out. All I'm saying is that the night is still young, and you don't want to be swinging from the chandeliers just yet a while. A couple more of those will do the trick fine."

"Yes, papa," Erica said demurely, and sipped politely at the remaining drops in her glass. Kenny laughed. As he did so he looked up to see Vic walk into the bar, scanning the tables. He caught Kenny's eye and wandered over. Pulling up a spare stool he sat down between them.

"I thought I might find you two in here. How's it going? Have you got to Luke yet?"

Kenny shook his head. "We've managed to track down Mike Dalton, he only lives down the road. But he's gone away for the weekend, so I'm afraid we're a bit stuck. Any ideas?"

Vic looked blank. "Can't think of anything offhand. Don't suppose the police have been much help, have they?"

"Not in the usual sense, no." Kenny decided to spare Vic the details of their conversations with Frank Blaney. "We managed to get the address from them, but they made it clear that was all they could do."

Erica stood up, already a little unsteady. "Well, if you two masterminds don't object, this little lady's going to powder her nose." She wandered off in the direction of the toilets.

Vic looked at her by now empty wine glass, as if seeing it for the first time.

"Hang around a minute, she's half cut. I've never seen her drinking anything but lager and lime. What have you been feeding her Kenny? What are you up to?"

"I'm not up to anything," said Kenny, genuinely affronted. "She said she wanted to get drunk, and so I bought her a glass of wine. Where's the harm in that?"

"Where's the harm?" Vic was starting to get excited. "You're trying to get into her knickers, you dirty old man. I know your sort."

"Leave it out, Vic."

"I won't leave it out. You're old enough to be her grandfather. Should be ashamed."

"I can assure you that my intentions are entirely honourable."

"Like I believe that. Remember, Kenny, I know you of old."

"Maybe I'm a reformed character."

"A leopard doesn't change its spots. You always were a randy old bastard, and by the look of things you haven't changed a bit."

"Climb down off your high horse and have a drink, Vic. You weren't always so lily white either."

"That was all a long time ago. These days, I'm a happily married man, and no thank you, I don't want a drink. I just came over here to see if there was any news. What do I find? Middle age lothario, plying innocent young lady with strong liquor."

"With all due respect, Vic, she is not an innocent. She's twenty-one and quite capable of making her own decisions. I have no immoral designs on her at all." Kenny held out his left hand, palm up fingers splayed and started counting off the evidence. "Firstly, I have never been into younger women, well not that young anyway. Secondly, I have learned to respect this particular young lady over the last couple of days. Thirdly, I still intend to work with her brother as and when he is back in the land of the free, and I won't be able to do that if there is the ghost of a prior relationship with his nearest and dearest, and last but not least, I happen to be in love with someone else. So you can stick that in your pipe and choke on it."

Kenny took a long mouthful of lager and stared at Vic. Vic stared back, clearly unconvinced. Finally, he spoke. "If I hear so much as a whisper that you have been taking advantage of her I shall come find you, depend on it," he snarled as he got up to leave.

"I'm quaking," Kenny said to his back as it disappeared through the crowd.

"Vic not staying then?" Erica returned and plopped down in her chair. She picked up her wine glass and went to drink, before realising that it was empty. She fished in her handbag and pulled out a purse. "What's his problem then?"

"He's got the hump."

"And why would that be?" Erica seemed only half interested in the conversation as she leafed through the compartments of the purse, before finding a tenner.

"He thinks I'm trying to get you drunk so that I can have my wicked way with you."

Erica bore a look of pure innocence. "And are you?" she asked.

"No, of course I'm not."

"Why not?" still the innocent intensity. Kenny was flustered and struggled unsuccessfully for a reply.

"I see," she stood up. "Well I'll leave you to mull that one over while I go to get us both a drink. Same again?" And without waiting for a response, she flounced to the bar.

Kenny sat in confusion. Expressions like a rock and a hard place, the devil and the deep blue sea, damned if you do damned if you don't all flashed through his mind. Erica returned, slopping beer as she handed him his glass, and dropping her change carelessly on the table. She sat down.

"Where were we? Oh yeah, why don't you want to sleep with me?"

"It's not that I don't want to," Kenny began lamely, hesitating as Erica eyed him quizzically. "I'm sure it would be a very pleasant experience."

"Very pleasant," she repeated, weighing the words.

"I'm sure we could have a lot of fun together," Kenny struggled to find the right words.

"You think."

"Yes, all right, I'd have a lot of fun. It might not be so enjoyable for you."

"I don't know. You're not that bad looking. And they tell me that older men try harder. Might be worth giving it a whirl."

Kenny stopped and looked at her. She grinned broadly.

"You're winding me up, aren't you?" he said, with relief.

"I never thought it would be so easy," she said, and took another sip.

"Truth is, at another time and under other circumstances, I probably would have tried it on. But until Vic mentioned it, the thought hadn't entered my head."

"There's a compliment in there somewhere, desperately trying to get out."

Kenny took a drink and paused for thought. This matter still needed treating with diplomacy.

"Once upon a time, I would have said you were not my type. These days, I'm not sure what my type is. What I do know is that I have come to like you a lot over the last few days, and I wouldn't do anything that might jeopardise our friendship. I've said more to you in a matter of a few hours than I said to all three wives in all the years I was married put together. To put it bluntly, I like being with you, and I like talking to you. When this is all over, I would like to think that we could still be friends, and if my experience is anything to go by, that doesn't tend to happen after a one-night stand. So if you want a bit of rumpy pumpy, then I'll do my best, but don't expect too much."

Erica smiled indulgently at Kenny's clumsy candour. "Who says Englishmen can't handle emotions," she said brightly. "And no, that won't be necessary. I can cope with not knowing if it's true about older men for a while longer. And don't bother about what Vic thinks. He always was a miserable old sod, and now it seems he's got a dirty mind to go with it. I could never understand what Luke saw in him and his two bit little band anyway." Erica paused for a sip.

"Vic's OK in his own way." Kenny thought it time to defend someone, who was, after all, one of his oldest friends. "He just lacks imagination, that's all. I suppose it all comes down to having a bad experience when he was young. Vic nearly died, you know, back in the seventies."

"What from, boredom?"

"No, quite the opposite, actually. Sex and drugs and rock and roll. He wasn't the first and he certainly won't be the last. I suppose that sort of thing changes you. Some people think they're immortal, the Freddie Mercury's of this world. They tend to be the ones that die. Others become over cautious, see it as a warning and over compensate. They tend to become boring. "

"So what you're saying is that Vic has got rid of all the dangers in his life and ended up a grumpy old tosser."

"In a nutshell. I've always thought that you have to take some risks to get anywhere in life. We all need a bit of escapism, whether it's drink, drugs or fast cars, otherwise we become moribund, boring."

"What's the point of life if you can't let your hair down once in a while? Is that what you mean?"

"Exactly."

"Good, go and get me another glass of wine." Erica smiled in triumph. As if aware that he was being manipulated, and in no way resenting it, Kenny nodded ruefully and headed for the bar.

He was back in a matter of minutes with the drinks. "Before we leave the subject of Vic," he said, settling back in his chair, "I guess I do have one reason to thank him."

"Which is?"

"Well, if it wasn't for Vic, I wouldn't be here now."

"You mean you wouldn't have wasted an entire weekend."

"I don't think my weekend has been wasted. I've learned a lot over the last few days."

"Such as?"

"Such as, I feel more comfortable sitting in a South London pub than in a West End restaurant; I can sit and talk to an attractive young lady without feeling obliged to seduce her; I prefer lager to champagne; I feel more at home in your house than I do in my own. To be honest, I think I would be a lot happier if I sold up and moved back south of the river. I think I would have more fun working with the likes of Vic and his band than hobnobbing with the rich and famous. I wasn't cut out to be a celebrity, and I've spent the last thirty years or so trying to convince myself that I was. That's probably why my private life is such a dog's breakfast; I've been looking for something that just isn't there."

"What about your mother? If you sell up, what are you going to do with her?"

"I've been thinking about that. You know, she probably would be better off in a home, or a hospital. I've been asking myself who benefits from the arrangement that we have at the moment. Am I doing it for her or for me?"

"I don't think I follow."

"Look at it this way. If you give money to charity, do you do it for the charity or for yourself?"

"For the charity I'd have thought."

"You don't do it because you get a little inner glow, get the feeling that you have done some good, made up for one or two little moral lapses maybe?"

"I see what you mean, the charity gets the money, but the giver gets the pleasure of giving."

"Correct. Surely in any altruistic relationship, both benefit. I think you have to ask yourself though whether you are doing it for the good of the recipient or for purely selfish reasons. Is philanthropy driven by ego? My mum doesn't know what day of the week it is; you've seen that. She isn't even sure if it's night or day. If she were in a home, a good one mind you, would she really be any worse off than she is now? Do I keep her where she is because it is good for her or because it is good for me? I've an awful feeling that it's the latter."

"It's not as if you make a song and dance about it."

"That's the only thing that makes me think I might be doing it for the right reasons. But even then I'm not sure. I'll have to think about it carefully, preferably when I'm stone cold sober."

They sat in silence for a few minutes, each lost in thought. Erica broke the spell.

"So you reckon you should move back across the river and become a miserable old git like Vic? Have I understood you correctly?"

"Not exactly, I was rather hoping that I would be a happy and therefore more complete human being. I'll leave the old gittishness to Vic, if it's all the same to you."

"But it's a risk."

"And like I said, life is about taking risks. It may no longer be life on the edge, life in the fast lane, but I think I can make it work. I'll still want to write songs. I'm not talking about retiring. Maybe it's time to start a family. All I need is the right woman."

"Monica."

"Monica. Kind of all depends on what she wants out of life, and if that life might include me in any way."

"I thought you said that she wouldn't leave Frank, for the sake of the children and all that."

"Well I might have been a little economical with the truth on that one." Kenny averted his gaze and sipped his beer.

"Spill the beans, English. What have you been keeping from me?"

Kenny looked up sheepishly from his glass. "Monica didn't exactly say that she wouldn't leave Frank." He paused, as if searching for the right words.

"Come on, out with it. And no more equivocating. I want the truth, the whole truth and nothing but the truth."

Kenny took a deep breath. "We talked about it on and off for weeks. Monica hasn't been happy with Frank for years now. You've seen them together. There's nothing there anymore, and to be honest, it hardly seems possible there ever was. I guess that's why she fell for me in the first place; we were kindred spirits, both looking for something that was missing in our lives. But Monica is very loyal to her kids, that much is true, and she would never leave Frank unless she was sure that she would keep them. Not that he would be that bothered, from what she's said, he hardly takes any interest in his family. His career is all he's bothered about, and he has no time for anything that might get in the way of it."

"So what's the problem? She walks out on Frank and takes the kids with her, moves in with you, happy ever after. Frank doesn't make a fuss, because it wouldn't improve his career prospects, probably gets visiting rights which after a period of time he forgets about. Give it a year or so and everyone will automatically assume that the kids are yours, game over. Like I said, what's the problem?"

"I suppose I just wasn't ready to be a father."

"You what?" Erica sat up straight in her seat as if preparing to launch a verbal broadside. She was suddenly aware that all other conversations in the pub had stopped and that everyone was staring at her. She relaxed and lowered her voice. Other conversations started again.

"Are you trying to tell me," she continued in a tone no less threatening because it was said in a whisper, "are you trying to tell me that Monica agreed to leave Frank for you, but you refused her because you didn't feel ready to take responsibility for her children? The love of your life offers

181

to make all your dreams come true, but you turn her down because you think you are too young to be a dad?"

"Suppose it does sound a bit odd when you put it like that, but you've got the gist of it."

"It may come as some sort of surprise to you to learn that at your age most men are getting used to the concept of being a grandfather."

"It wasn't an age thing, as such," Kenny groped. "I just couldn't get used to the idea of having kids around. I've never been good with children. I didn't even get on with them when I was a child."

"You just need a bit of practice. If my brother can become a father to me when he was only eighteen it can't be that hard. It's not even as if they're particularly young, they're not babies after all. You could be a really good dad if you tried."

"Do you think so?"

"Stop fishing for compliments. I don't know what kind of a dad you would make. All I'm saying is that if Luke was up to the mark it can't be rocket science. From what I've seen you have the basic requirements. That's as far as I'm prepared to commit."

"Like I said, this weekend has changed the way I look at life. Now I feel that maybe Monica and I could make a go of things. Trouble is, it may already be too late. I'm not sure that she would take me seriously now."

"I can't say I'd blame her if she told you to bugger off and not come back. After all, she offered to make the ultimate sacrifice, and you threw it in her face." Erica's words were lost as the landlord rang the bell for last orders. Wordlessly, Kenny raised an eyebrow and looked at her glass. She nodded and he wandered off towards the bar. By the time he returned, Erica had calmed down and appeared prepared to be placatory.

"If you want my opinion, I think your Monica would be happy to give you a second chance. I saw the way she looked at you this morning. Take it from a woman; she's smitten. Give her the benefit of the doubt, Kenny. Tell her you'll take her on her terms."

"I don't know. She might think I'm harassing her."

"Oh, grow up, Kenny. What have you got to lose? Give her a call and put your cards on the table. Tell her you love her and that you made a mistake. Ask her to leave Frank and bring the kids with her. Tell her she can live wherever she wants. Promise her the world, for god's sake, and with any luck, she'll come across and the two of you will live happily ever after. What's the alternative? You're the one who's into risk taking. If you don't ask, you won't get, and then you'll forever be wondering what might have been. The worst that can happen is she sends you off with a flea in your ear. What sort of man are you?"

"It sounds so easy when you put it that way. I just can't help thinking that it will be a bit more complicated when it happens."

"Whatever, you've got to try. Promise me, Kenny, when this is all over, the first thing you do is give her a ring and try to sort things out."

"Do I have to?"

"Yes."

"Then I promise."

They drank in silence, as around them people started to leave, pushing stools under tables, gathering coats and bags.

"I've just had a thought," said Erica, moving to one side, to allow a rather overweight man to pass.

"Go on."

"If you find a home for your mother, you won't need all those people to look after her, will you?"

"Hadn't thought of that, but no, you're right."

"So how much do they cost?"

"Dunno, never asked."

Erica looked shocked. "You never asked? Blimey you really have lost the plot, haven't you? How many are there?"

Kenny frowned, thinking hard. "Must be ten, or a dozen, I suppose. They work in shifts. Andrew, my accountant, handles all the details."

Erica started drawing in the pools of water that had formed on the table top. "Say ten people then." She wrote ten on the table. "How much do you pay them each? Twenty? Twenty five?"

"Must be something like that." Kenny sat forward, transfixed by the numbers.

"Ten times twenty five is two fifty, plus say twenty percent for national insurance and other expenses. Comes to, let's see, three hundred grand a year."

"Guess you're right. And?"

"And three hundred grand is exactly one year's interest on six million at five percent."

Kenny stared at her in disbelief. "Oh my God, you're right. Erica Marshall, you're a fucking financial genius."

Erica preened. "Looks like I must be," she said.

Kenny ran a hand through his hair. "When I think of what I pay that bloody accountant. He's the one who's supposed to give me this sort of information. Maybe I should employ you instead."

Erica giggled. "Hold your horses, sonny," her voice slightly slurred, "I'm not an accountant, not yet a while anyway. Even if I wanted to be one, I'd have at least three years' more training to do."

"And you don't want to be one?"

Erica tilted her head to one side, thinking. "No, not really. I've had enough of study for now. I want to start earning money; time I got a job."

"You mean something like your mate, what's her name, Joanne?"

"Yeah, why not? Maybe a little less attitude than her pals, but something up in town with a fancy salary and expenses. That should suit me."

"Please yourself, but if you change your mind, give me a call."

"I will, and now it's time you took me home."

They both drained their glasses, got up from the table and headed out of the pub. Erica walked into the night as Kenny held the door open, clumsily half turning, to wave goodnight to the barmaid. He stepped onto the pavement, just in time to catch Erica's arm as she wobbled in front of him.

"Gordon Bennet," she said, "it must be the cold air. I suddenly feel rather woozy."

Kenny manipulated her so that she stood on the inside of the pavement, her right arm held firmly in the crook of his left. Slowly and gently he manoeuvred her towards the house. On the doorstep, Kenny held her bag as she fished for her keys, unable to cope with the dexterity required to manage the job on her own. Taking a deep breath she concentrated hard to put the key in the keyhole and turned. As the door opened, she tripped over the threshold and would have landed on her face in the hall if Kenny hadn't held onto her arm. She staggered upright and allowed Kenny to lead her into the kitchen, where he deposited her as elegantly as possible into a chair. Making sure that she was sufficiently in balance not to fall on the floor he went to the sink and ran a glass of water.

"Come on, young lady," he said, lifting her from the chair, "it's bedtime for you. You're drunk."

Erica didn't complain as he helped her up the stairs, carrying the glass in his free hand. At the top of the stairs Kenny allowed her to lead the way to her own bedroom, putting the glass down on her bedside table before laying her gently on the bed. As he pulled the duvet over her body she opened an eye and smiled at him wickedly.

"Aren't you going to join me big boy? Let me show you a good time?"

Kenny smiled at her in the darkness and ignored the invitation. "You get some rest. I'll see you in the morning." And with that he left the room.

As he walked across the landing, Kenny passed the door to what had to be Luke's bedroom. The door was slightly ajar, and he peered inside at the bed. Suddenly Kenny felt unbelievably tired. The effects of a surfeit of alcohol and a withdrawal of adrenalin combined to bring on an insurmountable torpor. Come to me, the bed seemed to say, come to me and rest your weary limbs. Kenny was powerless to resist and drifted into the room. Slowly he unwound on top of the duvet. Within seconds, he was fast asleep.

Chapter 19

Luke pulled himself into a sitting position at the end of the sofa. He put his head between his knees and retched. Slowly, he managed to lift himself upright and, like a blind man groping the walls for support, he gradually negotiated his way to the bathroom. At the sink he retched again, his whole body heaving but producing nothing more than a thin trickle of green bile. He groaned, holding himself up by the sink, as his muscles contracted and relaxed, time and again. Finally, the fit subsided.

He looked up at the mirror above the sink, taking in the sunken bloodshot eyes, the florid complexion. He groaned. Pushing down on the sink he managed to raise himself onto tiptoes, stretching in an effort to relieve his aching muscles. He leant his head back, raising his nostrils high and inhaling. The action seemed to make him feel better, and he repeated it twice more, before the effort became too much. He lowered himself back to a standing position and looked again in the mirror. This time there was a semblance of life to his features, at least a recognition of his own reflection.

Summoning up his strength he stretched again, this time taking in five or six lungfuls of air. When he returned to standing, he found he could do so unsupported, and that he could walk back to the office unaided.

Back at the desk he moved the mouse and the screen sprang to life. He looked for Simon, but the window was empty. He thought for a moment and then came to a decision. Opening the message screen, he typed tentatively.

Simon, I know you're not at home, but I need to say this now. Something's wrong, I don't know what but I get the feeling I'm not going to make it. Can't be more than a few hours now I know but I'm fading fast, mate, so I have to make the most of this moment of clarity because

```
it may be my last. I can't seem to stay awake
for more than a few minutes at time; it's like
my whole body is shutting down bit by bit.
```

He stopped and read what he had written. As he did so his head lolled forwards and he had to shake himself awake again. He held both hands together in an effort to concentrate, then released his grip and carried on typing, this time with more determination.

```
If I am going to die, then there's something
I have to tell you, something important. All
that stuff we talked about, you know living your
dream and that, being famous, all that stuff I
said was rubbish. Going on about not wanting
to be a success, that was bollocks, complete
bollocks. To tell the truth I was frightened
of it, all of it; working with a well known
lyricist, seeing my name in lights, being rich
and famous. Scared the shit out me, if you must
know.
But deep down, that's all I really want; to
write music, and perhaps one day to have someone
say they like it. Give me half a chance now, and
I'd grab it with both hands, take your arm off
at the elbow. If I ever get my sorry arse out
of here, there's only one thing I'm going to do;
find Kenny English.
He'll have forgotten about me by now, but that
doesn't matter. I'll camp out on his doorstep
if I have to, because what's the use of a dream
if you haven't the courage to go for it. Sure,
I may not come up to the mark, but at least you
won't be able to say I bottled it, least I can
do is give it a shot.
```

Luke sat back from the screen, his head rolling uncontrollably on his shoulders. Somehow he found the strength of body and mind to continue.

```
I might never see you again, Simon, I know
that, and if I don't, all I hope is that you
have a dream you have the courage to go for it,
to take the chance when it's offered, to give
yourself the opportunity. For fuck's sake don't
blow it like I did.
```

Luke paused once more before adding.

```
Tell Erica I love her.
```

He pressed the *Send* button, but by the time *Message Sent* appeared he had slid from the chair and was lying on the floor, crumpled among the sheets of manuscript paper.

It was after eleven when Simon and Jeanette returned home. Simon carried Emily proudly in a Moses basket, careful not to wake her.

"That was a result, her dozing off like that," said Jeanette as they tiptoed upstairs.

"Right, we'll have to remember that for later, in case she has trouble sleeping," said Simon, as he watched his wife settle their daughter in the new cot.

"She won't be any problem, will you darling," Jeanette cooed at the sleeping form. "You're going to be a good little girl."

Simon grinned. "Did you want anything, love?"

Jeanette shook her head. "All I want to do is unwind in my own bed thank you. What about you?"

Simon thought for a moment. "I suppose I should pop downstairs and check that Luke's all right. I haven't spoken to him since this evening, and he was a bit fuzzy then. Maybe I should just log on and see that he's OK."

Jeanette rolled her eyes. "You've done more than enough for Luke already. Look at yourself Simon, you're all in. Come to bed and have a good sleep. You'll see Luke first thing in the morning."

"I guess you're right," Simon said, with a sigh. He wandered downstairs and locked the front door. As he put the lights out he passed the door to the back room, the computer sitting inert in the corner. For a second he dithered on the threshold, as if about to walk into the room, but then he had second thoughts and turned away.

"See you tomorrow, mate," he said over his shoulder, as he went back upstairs.

Kenny's phone chirruped, quietly at first but like a petulant child, with ever increasing urgency as it was ignored. Groggily he took it from his pocket, at the same time checking his watch. Frowning at the time, taking in the still dark room he pressed the green button.

"Kenny English."

"Mr. English." The voice at the other end was unfamiliar, the manner precise, clipped almost, without a discernable accent. "My name is Mike Dalton. I understand that you have been trying to reach me." Kenny sat up straight, suddenly wide-awake and sober.

"Mr Dalton," he said, "thanks for calling. I thought you had gone away."

"Got home about an hour ago." That terse tone again, military, air force. "Fellow next door came round just now and told me you had dropped by, seemed to think it was important. What can I do for you?" Kenny blinked a few times, trying to concentrate on the conversation.

"Probably something and nothing," he said at length. "One of your employees seems to be trapped in the vault in your offices."

"Who?" the tone was still perfunctory, but now there was just the hint of concern.

"Luke Marshall."

"Since when?" Concern definitely, maybe a touch of alarm.

"Friday night."

The change of attitude was now complete, alarm moving towards panic.

"Holy shit!" A pause. "Look, where are you?"

"Penge."

"Where exactly?" Dalton snapped at Kenny down the phone. Kenny gave him Erica's address, repeating it slowly as Dalton wrote it down. "I know where that is. I'll be with you in twenty minutes." And the line went dead.

Kenny looked blankly at the phone as if expecting it somehow to reconnect. He stared into space and tried to collect his thoughts. No doubt about it, Dalton was concerned. No choice but to wake Erica.

He stepped quietly across the landing and back into Erica's room. She lay cocooned under a quilt, apparently still fully dressed. Tentatively he shook her by the shoulder. No reaction. He shook harder, she muttered something and turned away. Kenny thought for a moment.

189

"No time for subtlety," he muttered to himself. "Extreme situations call for extreme measures." He shook her firmly by both shoulders, lifted her into a sitting position and turned her to face him.

"Erica, it's Kenny. You have to wake up," he said, decisively, trying to impart gravity without shouting.

Erica mumbled a couple of words, the second of which was *off*, but her eyes remained closed and her head slumped sideways onto her shoulder. Bracing himself, Kenny shook harder. This time Erica's head whiplashed back and hit the wall with a hollow bump. Erica's eyes snapped open.

"What the fuck?" she managed, as Kenny let her go "Piss off!" No doubt about the expletives this time, but at least she was awake. She rubbed her head and glared hard at Kenny.

"Erica, I'm sorry," Kenny said, holding up both hands as if fending off a blow, "but you have to wake up."

"Why? What time is it?" Kenny ignored the second question.

"Mike Dalton just rang. He's on his way here. He seems to think it's urgent."

Now it was Erica's turn to wake up in a hurry.

"What did he say?"

"Nothing tangible, just that he would be here in twenty minutes." Kenny looked at the bedside clock. "Make that fifteen. I think we'd better be ready for him."

Erica needed no further bidding. In one move, she was out of bed and heading for the bathroom. While she tried to make herself look presentable, Kenny went to the kitchen to make tea. As he poured milk into the mugs, Erica joined him. They drank in silence, neither willing to instigate a discussion over what might have caused Mike Dalton's reaction. When the doorbell rang, Kenny went to open it.

The man on the doorstep bore no resemblance to his imagined stereotype of an air force officer. He was about Erica's height and slightly built. His sandy hair was cut short and parted on the left with laser guided precision. He was dressed in a style that Kenny recognised as business casual, chinos and open necked button down, brown brogues freshly polished.

"Hi, I'm Mike Dalton," he said, not offering a handshake. "We'd better get going." And he made towards a blue people carrier parked at the kerb. Kenny called to Erica, and within seconds, they were all bundling into the car. Kenny made the introductions, as Erica found space on the back seat between children's books and stuffed toys.

"Sorry about the mess," Dalton said, as he pulled away. "Haven't had a chance to clean up since we got back."

As they drove north towards Central London, Kenny finally broached the question that they had been avoiding.

"You seem to be rather worried about Luke's predicament. We sort of worked out that he shouldn't be in too much danger. What did we forget?" Dalton paused for a moment, as if choosing his words carefully.

"You say he has been there since Friday evening. I assume you mean he was in the vault when the automatic timer closed the door at six o'clock."

"That's what we think happened," said Kenny carefully, looking at Erica who was watching, in wrapt attention.

"That means he's been in there for what, eighty hours or so."

"Seventy eight," Erica interrupted, hopefully.

"It's not an exact science, depends on too many imponderables. An hour or two either way won't make that much difference. The bottom line is that if we don't get to him within the next three or four hours he will almost certainly die. It may be too late already. Depends on how active he's been, his metabolism, that sort of thing. If he's fit and hasn't been exerting himself, you know trying to escape or whatever, he should be OK for now, but there's no way he can last out until the morning. He'll suffocate long before then."

"But we worked out that he had enough air for days." Erica tried to keep the note of accusation out of her voice, but she looked at Kenny and he looked at Dalton.

"There's plenty of air. That's not the problem," said Dalton, and Kenny breathed again. "When I said suffocate what I meant was that he will die of hypoxia if we don't get him out."

"What's hypoxia?" Kenny asked before Erica could.

Dalton accelerated as they passed through West Dulwich, ignoring the speed limit. "Lack of oxygen in the blood system." Kenny still looked confused.

"Isn't that the same thing as suffocation?"

"Not exactly. Suffocation means depriving someone of air to breathe, with hypoxia there is air, it just doesn't get into the system in sufficient quantities." Both Kenny and Erica were still looking confused. Dalton sighed.

"We breathe air so that oxygen can get into our blood stream and be used by our bodies, correct?" he began, and looked across for acknowledgement.

"Understood," said Kenny, and Erica nodded.

"Air goes into our lungs, and haemoglobin in the blood attaches itself to the oxygen."

"Right," from Kenny, and another nod from Erica.

"At the same time, carbon dioxide in the blood, which is the waste product of respiration is let go by the haemoglobin and breathed out." This time both Kenny and Erica made do with a nod, willing Dalton to hurry up and get to the point. Instinctively, he got the message.

"The problem is that the oxygen haemoglobin relationship is rather unstable. To put it simply, haemoglobin would rather attach to any number of gases other than oxygen. Carbon monoxide is one, carbon dioxide is another. What makes it pick up oxygen is the fact that there is so much of it in the atmosphere we breathe. Give haemoglobin a decent concentration of one of its preferred alternatives, and it will ignore the oxygen. If the level of carbon dioxide in the air reaches three percent, the level of oxygen that makes it into the blood is too low to sustain life. The air effectively becomes poisonous, and the more you breathe the more poisonous it gets. Remember, we exhale carbon dioxide. In an enclosed space, each breath raises the level of carbon dioxide. The air becomes unbreatheable long before it runs out."

"When you're scuba diving, you expel the air that you have breathed and take fresh air from the cylinders." Kenny was starting to understand.

"Exactly, whereas in a closed and sealed room, you simply make it more and more poisonous the longer you are there."

"How do you know all this?" Erica had heard enough. She didn't need to understand the details. To her all it meant was that her brother was in trouble.

"It happened once before, when I was in Singapore. One of the cleaners brought her young grandson to work one Saturday. Totally against the rules of course, but the child wandered into a storage area and got trapped. We didn't realise the severity of the problem until it was too late."

"What happened?" asked Erica quietly, as if already knowing the answer.

"The child died. That's when I mugged up on the science. But remember, that was a much smaller room and it was a child. This time there is still hope if we can get the door open tonight."

They drove towards Kennington.

"Luke said that you had come to London from Hong Kong. You just said you were in Singapore." Erica made the statement as much to break the silence as anything.

"I worked for a Hong Kong based company in Singapore. That's where we got the bug for sailing. Nothing much to do in Singapore at the weekend if you're not a member of the Yacht Club, and not much point belonging to a yacht club if you don't own a yacht. Can't say it's the same here though, not the weather for one thing."

"So why did you leave Singapore?" Kenny asked, without any real interest, but it was better than thinking about Luke's predicament. There would be plenty of time for that when they got to Victoria.

"When they handed Hong Kong back to the Chinese, the company moved a lot of their head office functions to Canada. That didn't affect Singapore directly, but it meant that a lot of people who wanted to stay in the Far East were looking around for jobs. Made it tricky to see how a chap's career could develop when there were so many takers for any position going. Friend of a friend introduced me to Seymour Hodgson. He was having a holiday on his way back to London, and when he told me he was going to take over his old man's bank, it seemed like an opportunity to move home. I'm beginning to wish I'd stayed on to take my chances."

"Because of Luke?"

"Not just that. I've been having second thoughts for some time now. It's not the job it was cracked up to be, that's for sure."

"You mean the cuts?" Erica sounded damning.

"Look, my role is purely administrative." Dalton was immediately on the defensive, as if used to the accusation and ready with his alibis. "Seymour brought me in to sort the place out. He would be in charge of finding customers; all I had to do was to keep costs down. That was no problem at all. I've never worked in a place that had so much spare fat. The business was haemorrhaging money. Cutting back on staffing costs was a cinch. Some of the employees hadn't done an honest days work in years. Not that you could blame them exactly. Far as I could see, that was all the fault of George Parker, my predecessor. Talk about a dinosaur, he ran the place like some kind of social club; bring your friends, we'll find them a nice cosy chair and a desk to put their feet on. No thought of the bottom line, no idea about systems, responsibilities, that sort of thing. Once I got shot of him we had the expenses under control in no time flat.

"Trouble was, Seymour never came up with his end of the bargain. Lots of ideas about new sources of income, nothing ever materialised. Problems only started to arise when I had to cut too far."

"You mean like cutting staff who were there to make sure accidents didn't happen?" Kenny's mind went back to the conversation with Simon.

"You got it. Soon as you start cutting back you start taking risks. I remember when I discovered that the air conditioning was on all night. I went ballistic, it was costing thousands. All it took was a new switch to set it on a timer and we could save a fortune. What was the point of air conditioning when no one was supposed to be there anyway? I asked about the danger of being trapped in the vault, remembering the child in Singapore, but the engineers did the sums and said it was OK for about seventy five hours. That's enough for a weekend, just means running a bit of a risk on a bank holiday. I decided that considering the amounts of money involved it was a risk worth taking.

"And so it went on, another day, another cut, another calculated risk. It had to be done to prevent the bank from going under. I really had no alternative until Seymour came up with an income stream."

They crossed the river at Vauxhall Bridge making quick progress through negligible traffic. Dalton parked the car on a meter in Grosvenor Gardens, and they all clambered out.

Chapter 20

In Eaton Row he booted the laptop with renewed enthusiasm, checking the wireless card and fidgeting impatiently as it found the network.

He entered Dalton's user name and then tried JULIAN as a password.

Please enter password..............

Now his face creased in frustration, and he clenched both fists to subdue the curses building up inside his mind.

He went through his deep breathing routine and tried to focus. He typed the password again, this time in lower case, but again without success.

He held both hands to his temples, scrunching his eyes shut, maintaining the pose until he gradually relaxed, which is why he failed to notice the Mercedes until it stopped a few feet away on the other side of the narrow street. A low slung coupe, sixties vintage. Even in the pale light from the streetlamps the pink bodywork could only be described as shocking. His first reaction was to duck below the level of the dashboard, but as he did so, he realised that the driver was ignoring him as if oblivious of his existence. Instead, she was squinting at a large A to Z, brushing a peroxide blonde lock of hair from a face that must once have been attractive, probably about the same time as the car was new. Cursing she threw the book into the back, slung her left arm over the passenger seat and reversed in fits and starts towards the main road. It was then that his attention locked onto the number plate: BAR 81E. BARBIE. His lips formed the word, but no sound emerged.

He closed his eyes, concentrating, before looking down again at the keyboard. He typed JUL14N, and then paused for several seconds, staring at the word, muttering a short prayer. When he stabbed at the Enter key, he did so as if it was red hot.

Please choose from this list of options.

He punched the air with both fists.

Chapter 21

As they approached the front door of the bank Dalton took a bunch of keys from his pocket. He selected a key and inserted it into the lock. It seemed surprisingly small for such an imposing door, but it did the trick and the door swung open. In front of them all was darkness.

"Wait here a moment," Dalton said, as he disappeared into the gloom. Kenny heard the unmistakable sound of a burglar alarm being disarmed, and as if by magic, the lights came on. Dalton reappeared, framed by the splendour of the marble banking hall.

"Come on," he said abruptly, "we haven't got time to hang around." And he led them towards the lifts. Kenny followed, and Erica thoughtfully closed the door behind them. Dalton was pressing the lift button angrily. Nothing seemed to happen.

"Bugger," he said, running his hand through his hair, "of course, the bloody things are switched off. We'll have to use the stairs." Without waiting for comment from the others, he led to a door beside the lift shaft. Kenny and Erica found themselves in a service stairway, not dissimilar to the one in Kenny's house. Dalton was already half a flight below them and running ahead as if they weren't there. Kenny looked at Erica as though waiting for permission. She brushed passed him and in no time was right behind Dalton, her feet moving quickly on the metal stairs. Kenny followed.

After three flights they found themselves in the lobby outside the vault. The imposing metal door stood in front of them like a cliff face, a solid wall that blocked their way. To their left was a desk and on the desk a computer terminal.

"What are we going to do?" asked Erica.

By way of reply, Dalton pulled up a chair and sat at the desk, the computer in front of him. He pressed the on switch and the monitor showed the computer going through the boot sequence.

"Shouldn't be too difficult," said Dalton, as lines of code scrolled in front of him. "All I have to do is log on, get into the security system and override the time settings. The system is set so to remember weekends and bank holidays, so that it will open automatically as soon as the bank is open, but with my permissions I can disarm that function and open the door at any time. I had it built in as a fail safe in case something like this ever happened."

The screen in front of him turned blue and text appeared.

```
Please enter user name...............
```

Dalton typed and pressed enter. Now the text was replaced with:

```
Please enter password.............  .
```

Dalton typed six characters which showed as asterisks. He pressed enter again and then stared at the screen.

"What the fuck!" he said in disbelief. In front of him was the message

```
Cannot access system. Multiple logins are not
permitted.
```

Erica peered over his shoulder. "What's wrong?" she said suspiciously.

"This can't be right at all." Dalton ignored her question, pressed Enter and went through the process again. The result was the same.

"I don't believe it," Dalton said through gritted teeth, and he tried again. This time when he got the error message he said nothing, just stared at the screen in confusion.

"Tell me what's going on," said Erica, her voice quavering. Dalton said nothing. Kenny stepped forward and placed his hand on Dalton's forearm.

"I think you had better answer the lady," he said quietly.

The menace in his tone, coupled with the latent threat of physical action, snapped Dalton back to reality. He turned around, as if he had forgotten that they were there.

"I don't understand," he said lamely. "The system is set up to prevent users from logging on in more than one place at a time. It's a security thing to make sure that machines aren't left connected to the system when the operative goes off somewhere. Stops improper access, that sort of thing." He looked hopefully from Kenny to Erica as if expecting sympathy. All he got were impatient stares. He ploughed on. "According to this message, I'm still logged on to another machine somewhere."

"So all we have to do is find that machine and log you off." Erica came up with what sounded like a logical solution.

"Or I could open the vault from that machine." Dalton seemed to brighten. Then he thought again and his shoulders drooped. "But I can't be logged on somewhere else," he said, sounding defeated.

"Why not?" Erica asked.

"Well, for a start, I'm always very careful about logging off. Remember I have administrative rights. Anyone getting on as me can change the system, could cause all sorts of problems. More to the point, the system automatically logs you off if you are inactive for more than half an hour. Again, it's a security thing. I wasn't in on Friday, so I would have been logged off more than four days ago. I just don't understand it."

Erica looked from side to side. "There must be another computer that you've used around here," she said, her panic rising. "What about upstairs in the offices. What if there's someone up there who knows your password? They might be on the system right now."

Dalton shook his head. "There's no one else here. I took the alarm off before we came in. No one else could be in this building without me knowing about it. I just don't understand."

"It must be a hacker." Kenny said in a flat monotone.

"What do you mean?" Dalton turned to look at him.

"Someone has got into your system remotely. Hacking's not exactly the hardest thing in the world. People do it all the time. Someone has broken into your network and is pretending to be you. From what you've said they must be active right now. God knows what they're up to."

"So where are they? How can we get to them?" Erica's voice started to break.

"They could be anywhere." Kenny spoke slowly, trying to remain calm and objective. "If they've broken in through the Internet they could be next door or the other side of the world. We simply don't know. They might log off in the next five minutes, or they might stick around for hours. For all we know they're rejigging your security settings so that you'll never be able to open the vault. Face it, Dalton. You're stuffed."

There was a moment's silence, and then Erica spoke in a small voice. "Are you saying that we might never get that door open?"

Dalton looked up sheepishly. "I'm afraid we are," he said, trying to look away.

There was another pause as Erica digested this last comment. And then she cracked. After all the waiting and wishing, hopes raised and then cruelly dashed, the worry and the lack of sleep, Erica finally lost it. She wanted to scream, she wanted to rant, to stamp her foot, to beat against the thick metal door that stood between her and her brother. She wanted to call out his name, to let him know that she was there, that she hadn't forgotten him, that she loved him. All the frustrations of the past few days welled up within her like a volcano about to erupt, but when it came to it she couldn't find the strength. She was simply drained, all she could do was cry.

It started as little more than a whimper, a low moan. She sat on the edge of the desk with her head in her hands, and the moan turned to sobs. As she gave way to her grief, the sobs became great wracking howls, the tears flowed uncontrollably as she bawled like a baby. Kenny stepped towards her, close to tears himself. Awkwardly, he put his arm around her shoulder.

"Come on, mate," he started, trying to think of something positive to say. "We're doing all we can. We'll get your brother out. Just you see if we don't."

Strings of snot flew from Erica's nose as she shrugged him off with a savage twist. She turned on him, her eyes red and screwed up in rage.

"You just don't get it, do you? He's not just my brother, he's my mother and father as well. He's all I've got in the world and he's on the other side of that door. He's dying and I can't do a fucking thing about it. Don't fucking patronise me, you bastard!"

The vault door swung open noiselessly. With her back to it, Erica was unaware until she saw the look of amazement in Kenny eyes. For a moment, she thought it was brought about by her outburst, but she could see him watching over her shoulder. She turned. The Plexiglas panel allowed her to see into the room beyond, the light from the office glowing in the background, and then with a small hiss this too opened. A rush of warm stale air hit her in the face as she tried to understand what was happening.

"Luke?" she said in a small voice. "Luke!" she screamed.

Chapter 22

Erica sat in the hospital waiting room, holding Kenny's hand. The tears had stopped long ago, and now she sat quietly, feeling the safety and security of the older man's presence. She watched a nurse pushing a trolley past, the urgency of the action tempered by the need for care.

"You look exhausted," said Kenny, as she stared up into his face.

"I am," she said. "You must be too."

Kenny shrugged. "I'm sort of used to unsocial hours, I suppose," he said dismissively. He stifled a yawn. "Well, maybe I am getting a bit long in the tooth for late nights."

"It doesn't seem possible that I've only known you for a few days," Erica let the words hang in the air.

"I know what you mean. We've been through a lot, haven't we?"

Erica felt warm tears of gratitude press against her eyelashes, and squeezed the hand harder, at the same time swallowing to control her feelings. Kenny looked at her and smiled.

"I guess this means it's over," Erica began, a little croakily. She cleared her throat and continued. "We can all go back to living our lives."

Kenny frowned. "You mean this is goodbye?"

Before Erica could respond, Kenny's phone rang. Erica glared at him and then looked pointedly at a notice on the other side of the room, a picture of a mobile phone crossed through with a red saltire.

Kenny took out the phone and sheltered inside his coat. He grunted a couple of times, waited and then said, "OK, I'll be down in a minute." He emerged, pointedly switching off the phone.

"That was Dalton. He's downstairs."

"What does he want?" There was no hiding the venom in Erica's tone.

"Probably wants to know if Luke's all right. I said I'd pop down and talk with him."

"If he had any principles, he'd be up here finding out for himself."

Kenny gave Erica a long look and at last she relented. "OK, so maybe it's better if he and I don't meet. Why don't you go and see what he wants. I'll wait here."

"I won't be long," said Kenny and disappeared.

Dalton was waiting on the pavement outside the hospital, surrounded by the roar of mid morning traffic, sheltering under an overhang from the persistent drizzle. Kenny joined him.

"Surprised to see you here," he began. "Thought you'd have a lot on your plate at the bank. The way I recall there was some sort of hullabaloo when we left."

Dalton shrugged. He looked dishevelled, in a controlled sort of way. "I've resigned," he said flatly. "After everything else that's happened, this was the last straw. Luke could have died. How is he by the way?"

"They haven't let us in to see him yet, but it looks pretty good, all things considered. He was still breathing when we pulled him out, and the paramedics had him on oxygen as soon as they arrived. The doctors don't think there'll be any brain damage, so he should make a full recovery. But it was touch and go."

Dalton nodded, but said nothing.

"So have you worked out what happened?"

"Eh? How do you mean?" Dalton's manner was less defensive than confused.

"Who opened the vault? We know for a fact it wasn't you."

"Damnedest thing." Dalton shook his head but still refused to comment further.

"So who was it?" Kenny was starting to get impatient and it showed in his voice

"George Parker."

Again, Dalton seemed to think that was enough, but Kenny was not in the mood to be fobbed off. "Listen here, Dalton," he said, turning to face him square on, the pose unarguably aggressive. "I think the least you can do is come clean and tell us what the bloody hell went on last night. George Parker was your predecessor yes? So what in God's name was he doing in the bank?"

At last, Dalton seemed to recognise the impatience in Kenny's tone, and he frowned for a moment, as if gathering his thoughts. "After you left in the ambulance, I was talking to the police."

"Yes, I remember that. Go on." Kenny's tone suggested that his patience was paper thin.

"Well, he just appeared, you know like from nowhere."

"Who? George Parker?"

"Yes, old George. I don't know who was more surprised, him or me. He came down the back stairs, same way as we did, and just sort of wandered in as if he owned the place."

"So he was there all the time?"

"No. I thought so at the time, but now I think I've figured it out."

"Well go on then."

"It must have been George who hacked into the system. That's why I couldn't log on. He must have used a laptop and wireless connection and guessed my password, don't ask me how. Anyway, it was him who opened the vault."

"So how did he get in?"

"There's a door at the back of the building, used to be the tradesmen's entrance, I suppose. Some of the staff were in the habit of using it to skive off, skip out without anyone knowing, so I had it locked. The only way to release it is through the computer system. Once he was logged on, he could open the vault, switch off the alarms and open the back door. After that, it was easy."

"So what was he up to? Was he robbing the bank?"

"Well, that's the thing, we can't tell. When he saw me and all those police officers he flipped. Started jabbering away, making no sense at all. They've taken him off to the station, but if you ask me by rights he should be here. The bloke's completely gaga."

Kenny thought for a moment. "So if it wasn't a robbery, what did he want?"

"That's what I've been trying to work out, and I think I've got it. He wanted to embarrass me."

"Go on."

"Have you heard of the Winsloe diamonds?"

"As it happens, I have. They belong to my neighbour. What have they got to do with all this?"

"Like I told you last night, Seymour Hodgson has been trying to drum up business, trying to make money. His latest scheme was to use the vault as a safety deposit for all his wealthy friends to leave their valuables. Way it is at the moment, most of what they look after is legal documents and such. Seymour reckoned there was a market for protecting more tangible forms of wealth."

"So that's where Lenny Hodgson keeps his famous diamond collection."

Dalton nodded. "Has been for the past three months. Seymour convinced his dad to use the bank on the basis that if he couldn't be trusted to look after the family jewels why should anyone else give him the time of day. But his old man wasn't what you might call too happy about it."

"Why was that?"

Dalton sighed. "Lord Winsloe is a very successful businessman; he checks the details, doesn't take risks. He knows full well that his son is a maverick, a wild card, loose cannon, whatever. The diamonds are worth a fortune, and he didn't want to risk losing them. But like they say, blood is thicker than water, and he couldn't refuse his only child the opportunity to make a success of things."

"So Parker knew where the diamonds were and was trying to steal them." Kenny said it as a statement, with an air of finality, as if it was too obvious to be a point of discussion.

"No, I don't think so. I reckon his plan was to open the vault, move some of the diamonds around so that the auditors would see they had been disturbed, and then close things up again."

"Auditors, what auditors?"

"One of Lord Winsloe's conditions was that the diamonds should be checked by his representatives every three months to make sure they hadn't been tampered with and confirm they were safe. The first audit is scheduled for this afternoon."

"So Parker didn't have to steal anything, all he had to do was show that it was possible?"

"Precisely. Sort of phantom burglary, to demonstrate how easy it would be."

"And then this afternoon the auditors would have told his lordship that the diamonds weren't safe, and he'd have moved them somewhere else. End of new product line."

"And curtains for yours truly, which is exactly the retribution that George was looking for."

"And if it hadn't been for Luke, you'd have been none the wiser." Again, it was a statement of fact.

"No, not really. You see George could get into the vault, he could even get into the boxes, but he couldn't get at the diamonds."

"Why not?"

"Because Lord Winsloe's other condition was that we build another vault especially for them. George knew all about the diamonds, and the audits, but the inner vault came after he left. We shifted the diamonds a couple of weeks ago. He could have opened all the boxes he liked and never found a thing."

Kenny let out a low whistle. "So what are you going to do now?"

"Going home to get some sleep, I suppose, then try and work out what to do with what's left of my career. Worst comes to the worst, I can always go back to accountancy, set up in private practice. To tell the truth, I've had it with banking. You say Luke's in the clear?"

"That's what they reckon."

"Well give him my best when you see him. Can't imagine he'd take too kindly to a personal visit, if you know what I mean."

Dalton turned on his heel to go, but on impulse Kenny held him by the shoulder, turning him back.

"What did you say about accountancy?" he asked carefully.

"I could go back to private practice. It's what I did before I went to Singapore. It's what I was trained to do."

Kenny thought for a moment. He took a wallet from his coat and extracted an embossed business card. "Here, when you get yourself sorted out, give me a ring."

Dalton stood looking at Kenny, ignoring the card. "Why?" he asked.

Kenny shrugged. "Because I'm seriously thinking of changing my accountant, that's why. You seem to me a pretty straight up and down character, reliable. Let's just say you're a bit different to what I've been used to. No promises, but maybe we should talk."

Dalton took the card and looked at it for a second or two, before slipping it into his breast pocket. "Thanks," he said. "See you about." And he melted into the crowd.

Erica was still waiting patiently when Kenny returned.

"No news?" he said, sitting down.

"Nothing," she said glumly. Then she looked up at him, and her mood brightened. "Where were we, oh yes, I remember, getting on with our lives."

"Yes, you were giving me the brush off, as I recall. Listen, I'm not going anywhere, not until I am sure that you and Luke are all right."

Erica smiled at him, warmly and sincerely, as she sensed the tears coming again.

"I'm not trying to get rid of you," she said, and she squeezed the hand again. "But we know that Luke is fine, just needs a bit of rest. That's what the doctor said, no long term harm, no suggestion of brain damage, just a bit tired and very hungry. They'll let me see him soon, and it's all thanks to you."

Kenny shrugged. "I'm not sure what I did in the end. According to what Dalton told me, it was all down to George Parker."

"Whatever happened, I know I'd never have got through it without you by my side. You've taught me a lot, about trusting people, about trusting myself to trust people. I won't ever forget it, Kenny. Thank you." She rested her head against his shoulder.

"But now you've got something to do, something you promised." Kenny looked perplexed for a moment and then he remembered.

"You mean phone Monica. I'll do that as soon as I get home."

"Do it now. You promised you would as soon as this was over. Well, now it's over, so get on and do it."

Kenny pointed to the notice on the wall opposite. "Not allowed to," he said in a little boy voice.

Erica gave him a look that said she was not to be messed with. "If you go down the corridor," Kenny followed the line that she pointed, "you will find a public phone, you know, the old sort with nice big buttons for your clumsy fingers. Go and make the call."

Kenny rose, and then stopped and looked down at her. "You're not going to run off or anything, are you?"

"You won't get rid of me that easily. The only place I'm going is into that room," and she looked straight ahead, "to see my brother, when they think he's up to it. If we do miss each other, you know where to find me." Kenny took a couple of steps and then stopped and turned, as if he had just remembered something.

"Make sure he's well," he said, "and make sure he gets fit soon. That boy's got a lot of work to do."

"Go on, make the call," Erica scolded him, but with a smile that could have illuminated the whole hospital.

Erica watched Kenny's back as he shambled towards the phone. The door in front of her opened and a young doctor with unruly red hair appeared.

"Miss Marshall?" he said, looking at a clipboard. Erica nodded. "You can come in and see your brother now."

The room was not much larger than the bed, just enough space for a small table and a visitor's chair. Through the window on the opposite wall Erica could see the Thames and on the other bank the Houses of Parliament, the sun suddenly breaking through the cloud and glinting off gold leaf. She looked at Luke, who looked pale but otherwise unharmed. He sat up in bed and grinned at her. "Hello, sis," he said, his voice a little shaky, but amazingly controlled.

"Oh, Luke," she said as she sat on the bed and took his hand. The tears were threatening again, but maybe she was all cried out because despite the occasional heave nothing came. "Oh, Luke," she repeated, "you gave me such a fright. I thought I was going to lose you."

"It was a bit of a worry for me," Luke said almost nonchalantly, as if trying to keep the mood light. "I thought I was a goner for a while there. But the doctor says I should be back on my feet by tomorrow and right as rain in a week."

"You've had a very lucky escape," was all that Erica could manage.

"Not just one lucky escape, I've had two."

"What do you mean?" Erica was holding Luke's hand tightly, as if frightened that he might be taken away from her.

"Remember what I told you on Thursday night about the meeting I was supposed to have on Friday?"

"At The Ivy with Kenny English. Yes, I remember What about it?"

"Well, as you can imagine, I've had rather a lot of time to think over the last couple of days, and by my reckoning missing that meeting has saved me a lot of trouble."

"How do you figure that out? I thought he was going to make your dreams come true, give you a chance to show that you could handle it as a composer. How can missing the meeting be a good thing?"

"Like I said, I've had time to think," Luke paused, organising his thoughts. "I know that I've always wanted to write music, you're right, that was my dream. But it was only ever a dream, wasn't it? The only person who ever said I was any good was Vic, and what does he know about it? He's barely even a has-been. *The Souls* are his life. He'd say anything to keep them together. The only place that my music was any good was in Vic's rather biased imagination. Sure, I want to live the dream, but what chance have I got? I've had no training for one thing, I sort of made it up as I went along. If I started even talking to the likes of Kenny English, he'd soon see what an amateur I am and head for the hills. Probably dine out on the story for weeks with his show biz mates. I'd be a laughing stock." Luke paused. His face showed no sign of self pity, rather he seemed to working hard to be pragmatic.

Erica stared at her brother, but stayed quiet as though waiting for him to make a fool of himself. Luke carried on.

"I thought about trying to write music for a living, believe me I did, and for a while I even managed to convince myself that I could make a go of it. Give up the job, write full time and then blag my way around town until I get a fair hearing, you know, the whole starving artist in the garret routine. But sitting here this morning, I can see that was just another dream; it would never work. What would happen to you for one thing? It's all very well having big ideas but dreams don't put food on the table. What would we live on? Who would pay the bills? If we ran out of money, we would have to sell the house."

Erica decided that this had gone on quite long enough. She pulled her hand away and sat up straight. Luke stopped talking, suddenly aware that his sister wanted to speak.

"So what?" she said, aware as she did so that her tone might be just a little harsh for someone in her brother's questionable physical condition. "It's only a bloody house."

"It was our parent's home," Luke said feebly. The words made Erica forget about physical considerations. She let him have it with both barrels.

"I know whose house it is! Don't you think your parents loved you?"

"Of course they did." Luke looked alarmed at the vehemence of the onslaught.

"Then surely they wanted you to be happy." Erica lowered her tone, moving closer to look into her brother's eyes. "Do you really think that they would want bricks and mortar to get in the way of your achieving your dream? I don't think so, mister. If there is a heaven somewhere and they're watching us now, I bet they'd be willing you to sell the bloody house if that's what it takes, if that will make you happy." Erica paused, but not long enough to allow Luke to say anything.

"It's not even as if you have to provide the living any more. I can go out to work in a few months, that's if you stay out of trouble for long enough to let me finish my dissertation. I can put food on the table; it's not even as if we need that much to live on."

"I wouldn't want to be a burden. You've got your own life to lead."

"Oh, I could slap you, Luke Marshall," and Erica took her hand half way back as if she really meant it. "Look what you've done for me for the past seventeen years; don't you think you deserve something in return? And as for my own life, you are my life, can't you see that? If I've learnt anything in the last couple of days, it's that you've given me everything I possess, that I love you more than I can say and that my life means nothing without you. The least I can do is make sure that you have every chance at happiness." Erica paused to let the full implications sink in. Rather nervously Luke spoke.

"You mean that you would support me, that you would pay for me to stay at home all day bashing out songs on the piano?"

"If that's what it takes, yes."

"But what if it all turned out to be rubbish, what if Vic really has been having me on?"

Erica thought for a moment. "What you write, the quality or whatever, is irrelevant. Writing is what matters. If you can sell it, so much the better. If you can make a living out of selling it, brilliant. But at the end of the day, the only thing that you have to think about is writing music. That's the dream, that's the life you want, am I right?"

Luke nodded. "I suppose so."

"The only question you have to answer is do you want to write music."

"Yes, I do." Luke looked at Erica whose expression suggested that she was less than convinced. "I really do," he said. "It's all I've ever wanted."

"Then that's what you shall have."

Luke looked at his hands as if imagining them on the keyboard, and then a thought struck him and he looked up at his sister.

"Shame about missing out on Kenny English after all. Guess he could've been a real help, if he'd wanted to."

Erica laughed. She threw back her head and roared. She looked at the ceiling as the air rushed out of her lungs, a final release of tension. When she recovered herself she looked Luke in the eye, and this time the tears had returned.

"You just write music, brother dear," she said quietly, choking back the emotion. "Leave Mr English to me."

THE END

Printed in the United Kingdom
by Lightning Source UK Ltd.
133852UK00001B/118/P